# STAY UPDATED!

If you haven't heard anything from us in a while, it means you're no longer on our list.

So if you'd like to get updates on our new releases (And we have a lot of them!) please consider signing up here!

Newsletters not your thing? Consider joining our exclusive Facebook Group!

Printed in the United States of America

Rebellious Valkyrie Press, 2016

ISBN 978-1-943773-26-8 (eBook, 2nd edition)

ISBN 978-1-943773-28-2 (paperback, 2nd US edition)

ISBN 978-1-943773-45-9 (paperback, 2nd INTL edition)

Cover Design by Untold Designs Romance and Fantasy Covers

https://www.facebook.com/untolddesignscovers/

Copyediting by R.A. Weston

http://www.rawestoneditorial.com

We want to hear from you!
Write us at guinevere.libertad@gltomaswrites.com to discuss
your fave stories by us! Comments, Suggestions, even requests
what you'd like to see in our next publications!

Also, if you loved this book, please consider leaving a review. It
really makes an authors day to read them and they're so, so
helpful in determining if this is the sort of read for the next
reader who may stumble across it. You can do so by clicking
here. And remember no review is too short!

SUMMARY:

Teddy's back in Miami with her mind made up. Live like it's your last day. Love like it's your last day.

The moment those steel-blue eyes gazed back into hers, there was no question. Asher wasn't just the only one she wanted, but the only one she needed. This time around there would be no more room for regrets, but would they ever be more than friends that still...?

*Friends That Still is Book Two that is a continuance of F*THS.*

CHAPTER ONE

**Teddy**

I wanted to feel good *so* bad. The past few weeks were torture. My body was living proof. It'd only been a little over three months since I'd left Miami. My main oncologist, along with my mother and father, advised me to participate in a clinical trial in the North Star State, and I didn't have many other options. My refractory status made it almost impossible to qualify for anything else conducted in North America, so he said I should consider myself lucky.

Yeah. I was real grateful for three months of blood in my stool, dizziness and fainting, mood swings, and unexplained weight loss.

I was scared, but I was a little desperate, too. What were you supposed to do when you didn't respond to chemotherapy? If it wasn't my answer, what other hope did I have? It was hard not to have some mistrust of doctors at this point. Sometimes it felt like they cared more about results than patients. But apparently all I did was complain. My father pulled a lot of strings and connections to get me here, but I'd hated every minute since I'd stepped foot in Minnesota.

The first month was mostly testing periods. To see if I'd react to the monoclonal antibodies I'd be taking, none of which had comfortable side effects. One of the drugs was administered through an IV but made every single part of me suffer, no matter what I did. I hated eating, using the bathroom, moving, existing...

By the time I stopped reacting to the drugs, I'd felt feeble and weighed significantly less than when I came. I wasn't perfect, but I'd liked my old body. I'd always been thin up until five years ago. The first time I went into remission felt like it'd be the last, so when I reached my weight's height at 165, I thought I'd never look back from it. I'd been 90 lbs at my worst, so it didn't bother me. Weight gain made me look less—of what I was. So to look down at what was left of me? I nearly cried every night. At this point, I wanted about to give up. I wasn't sure how much more of this shit I could take. I was in more pain than when I'd gotten here, and so far from home, I wasn't happy.

I didn't want to spend my youth like this. If I was going to die anyway, I wasn't about to spend it this miserable. In three months, I'd seen a combination of three investigators—or supposedly qualified oncologists—go back and forth with patients. I had a little less than three months left according to my contract, but I'd be willing to empty out bank accounts to get the hell out of here.

"Quick question. Who do I talk to when I'm done? I just want to go home." I hadn't bothered getting to know the investigators, so I wasn't sure if her "That's fine" response was normal for her.

"That's it?" I asked, expecting more of a fight.

"Theodora King, I'd rather you stay. There's no way of knowing what three more months could bring, but you've responded well. I wouldn't keep you against your wishes."

Responded well? I was going to need some clarity on that.

"What does that mean?" She was not about to go without telling me something.

"Well, I've only seen it happen in a few cases so soon. Everyone responds differently to monoclonal antibodies, as unpleasant as they may be. You are one of its success stories."

Now this woman was talking in circles. She must've read the confusion on my face. I was about two seconds from ripping the IV out of my arm and splashing her in the face with it. I definitely would've felt bad later *if* I had, but not long after her "success story" comment, she spoke the most beautiful words a cancer patient could ever hear.

I was in remission.

* * *

That was the best news I'd heard since the New Year. There was some paperwork to follow up on, and I had to agree to receive similar treatments for a few months after I got back, but I'd never felt so good about going home. I'd locked myself in the airplane bathroom three times to hide my hysterics. I couldn't stop crying and laughing.

Zinc already wanted to follow up, so it meant I wouldn't be home for three more days. But I managed to stop by my untouched place to grab a change of clothes and the cell phone I was bringing out of hibernation. I'd been so far from home, it hadn't made sense to bring it. I expected a few texts here and there, but not the explosion of messages and notifications. Emails, texts, voicemails. Three months was a long time for things to pile up.

I threaded through the texts. Hostility in some, worry in others. Burned bridges in the rest...

Racer: *Hope you're okay* :(

Marta: *Tell us how it goes*

Monica: *What, you don't know how to text nobody???*

Noe: *How come you don't call me anymore?* (As if I ever had.)

There were too many to fish through. It was probably best to just go to the ones I was most anxious about. It wasn't worth it to read *every* message. I challenged myself to delete entire threads save for the last one message they sent. That would tell me everything I wanted to know about where we were with one another.

With Reggie, his were harder. There were twenty-three newbies, and even though I fought the urge to read, it was hard not to notice the hostility in a few. Asher's was easy. Seven times in three months. He'd had a heads up, though. I took deep breaths as I entered each thread, selecting all but the last message for both.

I felt bad for Reggie, but I didn't owe him anything. The same way he didn't owe me his time. What I hadn't expected was for his last message to read:

*You must not have been serious. Real talk, you just wanted me to want it*

So what if I had? I'd never asked him to change, but I was tired of doing the chasing. With Asher, it was so much easier. He liked the chasing, along with what came with it. I didn't know how I felt with Asher, but I liked that he was always sure. Sure that he wanted me, sure that he wanted something between us, sure that he wouldn't change his mind if it happened. It was never like that with Reggie. I was so confused—sometimes it made me wish I hadn't messed with either of them.

Asher: *I hope you're ok. Miss you :)*

Dramatic difference from Reggie's. I was so all up in my feelings that I texted replies to both. "*Sup*" was all I could manage.

It'd been so long since I'd spoken to or seen either of them, so I didn't expect or receive immediate replies. Asher and I exchanged the occasional letter or two, but other than that, I hadn't written him in weeks. Can't say he'll be happy to see me—

let alone be available. For now, it was best not to consider anything.

After packing a few things, I called a cab and was on my way. I didn't do much but wait my first night there. I was used to it by now, but bored.

When I finally did see Zinc, I wasn't too happy with the news. Even though I was in remission, he felt my case of Hodgkin's was unique and hard to predict. He suggested maintenance therapy, something he claimed would prevent my cancer from coming back, but at the cost of having to go through chemo for months, possibly even years. It might even mean I was never going to not feel sick.

I wanted to be done with this. My body wasn't letting me. He gave me something to prevent some of the side effects of *one* of the drugs, but my body still reacted. Horribly. The first day sucked the most, and then I'd be down a long road of more chemo. I guess it was better than the alternative.

I hadn't eaten in eighteen hours, but I was pretty sure what they were feeding me was through whatever was in that IV they replaced every four hours. I saw a big, fat, juicy burger in my future. I needed to gain weight, work out or something. I was so skinny-fat. I'd never had a rock-hard stomach, but at least I owned it. I hated how my stomach caved in now. Months-old scratched nail polish adorned my toes. I really did have big feet. Or they looked bigger now that my legs weren't as full.

*Knock-knock.*

I grabbed my phone from under my pillow. I'd hid it and almost forgotten it was there.

Asher: *You okay up there in Minnesota?*

It surprised me he replied so soon. I plopped down on the bed, as comfortable as I could get here.

Me: *Not in Minnesota.*

Asher: *Miami then?*

Me: *North Miami*

Asher: *Hospital?*

Me: *Hodgkin's Disease Center*

It was both awkward and easy to text Asher things like that. I wasn't always comfortable, but at least he didn't freak out.

Asher: *Can you have visitors?*

Me: *Ugh. Look like shit. No.*

Asher: *That must mean you can.*

Me: *Why do you want to come here anyway?*

Asher: *Cuz I miss you dummy :-)*

I laughed out loud. I swear, he was the only person at this point I'd let call me that.

Me: *You're gonna get your ass kicked for real.*

Asher: >:D

I bit my lip, rustling to find comfort on the bed, and spent three hours texting about nothing.

* * *

I woke up weaker than usual, but motivated by the thought of leaving in six hours. My butt hurt sitting in one position for too long, and I was sick of the glare from the window. A dozen, pale-pink frilly flowers stood in a water-filled vase on the table across from me. I had a strong inkling who they might be from, but I suspended belief to feel surprised.

Didn't know         Hope
roses cost so       carnations
much. :p            are okay.

I was a little pissed off. I picked up my phone to send a puppy dog face selfie.

Me: *You came to see me.*

Asher took his time replying, which I gave him a pass for after he admitted he was at work.

Asher: *You weren't awake.*

Me: *You didn't wake me.*

Asher: *You looked peaceful.*

So I asked him *not* to come, and he does anyway. He does, and then he doesn't say anything. Not that I wanted to see him. Or at least…not like this. I got up and looked in my room's bathroom mirror. I smiled but didn't really mean it. Maybe…maybe he just wasn't attracted to me. I'd lost a lot of weight. I only *kind of* looked the same. I wasn't sure Asher was that shallow, but he didn't seem particularly interested in conversation as much as last night.

I looked at the shadow of me—which was looking less and less like regular me every passing day. I was probably being too strong, but it felt time to put my bitchface on and power through.

No one was going to hold my hand and make me feel better about myself, so I had to.

# CHAPTER TWO

**Teddy**

My eardrums should've been bleeding by now. I'd raised the volume to my car radio so loud, I'd probably be deaf by the time I reached my destination. I knew it was dangerous to listen to music this loud, but I had little options when it came to guarding my thoughts during the ride to Aventura.

City of Excellence.

That was the of Aventura's motto. Aventura housed some of Miami-Dade's wealthier neighborhoods, so I suppose it lived up to its name. It definitely didn't surprise me that since they'd became permanent Florida residents, my parents had always lived here.

My parents had an interesting journey, or at least by the way they've always told it. They had me much later in life, so we literally felt a generation away. I was only twenty-five and they were already in their sixties. So one can imagine how different life had been to them, especially from their lives in Cuba.

My parents hadn't come to the United States through the means most people assume Cubans came here. They were actually American citizens before they'd ever stepped foot in Miami, having spent much of their teenaged years and beyond in Puerto Rico. My papi's family came from Cienfuegos, while my mami's family hailed from one of Cuba's poorest areas, Camaguey. Both families had similar ideas when they decided to leave Cuba's confinement to move to Puerto Rico for more opportunities. It sounded like a rough transition, yet there they were.

My father was biracial, but he'd learned much sooner than my mother how he'd be viewed by other people once living in Puerto Rico. Even though he was fair skinned and light eyed, at his height and commanding voice, he knew he was Black, or would be perceived as such. I think that was a good thing, because I don't think he would've made it half as far in the United States if he hadn't realized it so early on.

My mother was a little different. While she embraced her Blackness, if you asked her, she'd always say Cuban first—Black second, on the count that she was born in Cuba. She'd definitely felt the hardships of what being a dark skinned woman in Latinx culture meant, so I was glad I had such Afrocentric parents that thought me to be proud to be both. Black, pero Cubana también.

If I'd been born in Cuba, I would've constantly been in poverty—something Black Cubans weren't likely to get out of. So in a way, it seemed like kismet that my parents—Cubans living in Puerto Rico—found each other. From the moment they attended university in San Juan, they'd been together. Even when they moved to the states (by plane, not by raft) and attended different graduate schools than each other.

After nearly forty-three years of marriage, it was safe to say my parents were perfect for each other. Despite my papa being as old school as men came, he still knew how to treat women—especially my mother.

My parents had no issue adhering to traditional gender roles. But my father cooked for his wife, nursed her when she was sick, cleaned the house when she didn't feel like it and supported her engineering career. They still held hands for god's sake.

From a distance they sound perfect, right?

Around each other, maybe they are. Before I was born, maybe they still were. But up close? The love they had before me, was a different kind of love they displayed after me.

Don't get me wrong. There isn't a question that my parents love me. They support me financially. I obviously wouldn't be here if it wasn't for their efforts to have me, and I'd definitely be a goner had it not been for the precautions they'd taken when it came to my health.

But there was a voice missing from their lives. A void that I'd never be able to fill.

And it's why I needed a distraction. I only had thirty minutes before I was in that house, and once I was there? Everything—and I mean everything, always reminded me of…her.

* * *

I parked my car in my parent's house driveway, but they'd already been waiting for me at the front door before I could even get out the car. You'd never know my parents were in their sixties just by looking at them. Not to say they didn't look it, they just looked really good for their age.

I used to call my papa Day-O, on the count that when I was a kid, he looked just like Harry Belafonte to me. His old black and white photos proved how handsome he was in his youth. I'm sure he still was to my mother. No one ever openly admitted it, but I looked just looked a lot like Mami.

She'd spent a lifetime fighting her hair's natural texture, hiding it or "fixing" it in the number of protective styles I'd seen her grow through, before she finally embraced her teeny weeny afro. I thought it made her look elegant and strong. Often, I told her it made her pass for at least fifty, but she was never good at taking compliments, or giving them for that matter as much as me.

The walk from my car to their front door felt like the longest walk. I tried not to expect the worst, as I bit my tongue and gave both my parents light greetings. "Hola, mami. Hola, papi." I said, kissing both of them on the cheeks that I added with light hugs.

"Hi, m'ija." My mother said, patting me on the back instead of returning the hug. My father wasn't much different. He just preferred to speak only English when he was around me. "Hi, baby. You doing okay?"

I nodded before going through the front door, as they parted to make room. They wanted to know what my experience was like in Minnesota, and what to expect now that I was back.

I could've explained this over the phone, but they didn't like to hear news that important over the phone.

Sitting in the living room should've been more comfortable than it was. I did live here for twenty-one years. Maybe it was, so long as my attention was on them.

But the moment it wasn't, that sinking feeling set in, and it never became more real than when I was forced to examine the house from the inside.

Parents usually had pictures of their children, in different stages, especially as they grew. While my parents did have pictures of children around the house, more than half of them weren't of me.

Maybe if you squinted your eyes and didn't look for the differences, your eyes might fool you. We had the same DNA, but only resembled each other based on that—the rest of the subtle differences obvious. Finer hair, fairer skin. However, unlike me, suspended in time. Like their living room was in a time loop, unable to move forward.

I should've existed more in the house than I did. I'd been around it more than her. But her absence, conscious or not, always brought me pain. So it's a shame we never met.

If you traveled throughout the house, some rooms screamed her existence. Others, whispered.

Yenelisa.

My sister. The daughter my parents had, that I'd never met.

My parents waited to have me, but had their first child a little after graduate school. So when you saw them in pictures, before me, they reminded me of the loving, engaging, endlessly affectionate parents I'd always wanted.

But one thing you noticed in pictures? Yenelisa stopped aging. She should've been forty-two right now, had she not been killed by a drunk driver when she was a child. We were seventeen years apart, and it made me wonder a lot about her. What she was like, or what kind of sister she would've been to me, had I'd known her.

Would we have had anything in common? Would we have bumped heads like most sister do, or would we have gotten along? Would she have showed me how to apply makeup, or shared her old clothes with me, when I didn't have anything in my closet worth wearing. Would she have warned me about boys, or girls for that matter, if I'd been brave enough to tell her I liked both.

Would she have gone to chemotherapy with me, when my parents were often to busy or afraid to attend themselves.

Those were the things I'd never know about her, because I never knew her. All I'd ever known was her absence. And I hated myself, because I hated her for it.

* * *

A sense of relief washed over both my parent's features, then moment I shared my good news. They even surprised me. I didn't expect them to be that happy, or at least show it. Most times I was lucky if I could get them to smile around me.

They'd even invited me to dinner. Technically, I had an open invitation anytime I wanted. But I couldn't bring myself to come down here all the time, as dinner at the King residence had never been my idea of fun, even when I lived here. But I'd be a fool to turn down free food, especially since I didn't cook half as good as they did.

My parents could live on pork, but they decided on a simple sea bass dish, served on grilled eggplant and arroz imperial. It was too much food to eat in one sitting, but the combination of spices, cheese and baked vegetables made my mouth water enough to consider taking a plate home with me. At least the food was good. I couldn't count on the conversation at the table to be.

There weren't restrictions on what we were allowed to discuss at their kitchen table, but I'd known for a long time that there were only three topics that produced optimal conversation.

College, career and cancer. Since I'd spent my first half hour discussing the latter, I didn't plan on bringing it up more than I had to.

"Papi? I was wondering. Is that offer to finish my undergrad still on the table?"

I knew my father's interest peaked, but he wasn't the type to betray his stern mannerism. I just knew him well enough to notice when he ate, he chewed slower, when his attention was caught. Both my parents expressed interest in me finishing my education.

I wanted to go straight after high school, but they claimed it wasn't a good time, and that I should focus on my health. They'd suggested continuing my education in stages, community college first, then university should I be in better health to commit to a two plus year commitment. But after my first refractory period, they brought it up less and less.

"You want to go back to school? That's interesting Theodora. Did you know this, Mireya?"

My mother's small brown eyes grew wider upon being called

on. She shuffled her food from fork to plate, before deciding on a light shrug and saying, "No."

I got more nervous by the second, but I'd only have their attention so long before I lost the nerve. "I just remember you saying you'd help, should I want to go back. Just wondering if the subject was open for debate."

*Here comes the catch...*

"Depends," My father snarled in between chewing the last scoop of his rice. "Where'd you plan on attending?"

"University of Miami." I mumbled under my breath.

"¿Donde?" My father asked.

"University of Miami." This time with more clarity. My father went back to eating at his normal pace. I knew it was coming, but I prepared for an exchange. I inherited my father's temper, after all.

"And what do you plan to do there?"

I shrugged. I knew he was baiting in that passive-aggressive way he was used to when it came to me. But I didn't hold back, and held my ground. "I don't know. Maybe get a degree in anthropology or something?" But I didn't get to go further than that. My father interrupted with a sharp laugh, particularly high pitched considering his deep monotone voice. The only time you could really hear his accent was when he spoke fast, and this was one of those times it was on fire.

"Anthropology? And what pray tell do you plan to do with that?"

"I don't know! But what'd you expect me to say? That I'd take up medicine or engineering blindly, just because you want me to?" I'd made a loose at best, but verbal agreement that should I finish college, I'd take up something practical.

Translation: Something that actually made money.

That agreement was more than seven years ago, though. I'd been off and on during my remission, so I thought it was safe to say anything I'd said as a teenager, should've been as good as void.

"Theodora King. You are not going to be spoiled forever. One of these days, you're going to have to take responsibility for your life, and a degree in anthropology won't do that."

"Look, I'm not going to beg you for the money. You don't have to tell me that I'm a disappointment to the both of you. Sorry I can't follow your every move."

My father but his fork down and pointed, something he only did when he was angry and confrontational. "You put words in my mouth Theodora. Do not put words there, that aren't there."

"Just…Tumba eso. Drop the whole thing."

My mother sat quietly on her side of the table, waiting for things to blow over. Clinked forks and muffled chews filled the room from now, until she chose to break the ambience. "So, are you still considering University of Miami?"

I put my fork down, and leaned my elbow on the table in her direction. "Yes, I'm still considering University of Miami. Want me to take responsibility for my life? I'll just get a job. Because it beats having to ask either of you." As I pushed my seat out, excusing myself from the table.

It felt time. The conversation might only get worse, and I was tired of having it. Normally, I wasn't that disrespectful toward my parents.

I just wasn't their wind up doll. Nor their prodigal child. Or their model daughter. And as much as it pained me to admit this —because I knew they never would, I wasn't Yenelisa. And I was never going to be.

CHAPTER THREE

**Teddy**

I can't believe my parents. What a shitty ultimatum. I wanted to do something with my life while I still had a life to do something with, and it was between getting a job and finishing my undergrad.

My parents were both first-generation college graduates, so it'd been their goal for me to finish college, too. *"Es mas dificíl cuando eres negra,"* my father'd always said. My mother typically sung a different tune. *"Never rely on beauty, because when you're Black, you have to prove it."*

Not the warmest conversation starters. I guess they just wanted me to know how privileged I was to be in the position to have parents who could pay for my tuition without having to take out loan after loan. But there was a catch. They'd only pay for it if I went to universities of *their* choice.

I wanted to finish my undergrad here, in Miami. I'd spent so much time away from home, I didn't want to spend two years in some other place far away, where I'd have to wear winter jackets and plow my car out of the driveway every December through

March. Dad wanted me to go to his alma mater, Howard. It was his "American" dream to get his Doctorate in Medicine there, which he did. It *was* a really good school. But it was all the way in Washington D.C. And I wasn't even considering my mom's first choice, Columbia.

It looked like if I wanted to stay in Miami, I'd have to get a job to pay for it myself. I'd tried my best to be independent, but from the time I'd been diagnosed with Hodgkin's, my parents babied me. I'd never needed a job until now. It was my own fault. It was easier to kick back and enjoy the labor of my parents' wealth.

But I wanted to do some things on my own. Even if it meant the lack of their financial support, I'd have to figure things out.

* * *

Finding a fucking job was hard as hell. I tried to use the few connections I had through my parents. At least *that* was something my papi would help me with. I thought it'd help to know a lot of doctors who had their own private practices, but even being cool with my father wasn't enough. Most administrative positions required associate degrees, which I had, but on top of that, they wanted three to five years of experience. Who graduates with three to five years of experience?

Six rejections later, I started thinking smaller, more accessible. I applied for everything I could online. Retail. Hospitality. Housekeeping. But nobody took cold calls anymore, so I couldn't even follow up. This was bullshit. How was I supposed to gain job experience when no one would hire me?

I'd heard from a few folk since I'd gotten back, and it seemed like that time again. I hadn't been to any support groups in the months I'd been gone, and I hadn't planned on making any new commitments while I was in Minnesota. But it was about time for an *unofficial* meeting, and I managed to get a few people interested to meet.

Racer had school, and Marta needed a babysitter, but Sol, Lucious, and Bridgette were down and good enough company. Bridgette I knew the least. She was a quiet white girl who always hid underneath a baggy hoodie despite Miami's weather. I guess I knew all I needed. She loved weed, and we were almost the same age. She tended to laugh at jokes when she was high, even when they weren't funny, so I guessed her sense of humor was lacking.

Sol was in her thirties and fighting cervical cancer. By the look of things, it seemed painful. Sometimes it was so bad, she preferred to use a wheelchair to get around. She'd been living with it for less time than any of us and never smoked before this. She could've fooled me. At first I'd thought she was a fair-skinned Latina, but she was originally from Turkey or something like that.

I was a little surprised when Lucious showed up. Of the eighteen times we'd held the floor for a session, he'd only been to three. He'd survived prostate cancer. Ouch. Lucious was a sweet, middle-aged Black dude that, despite how shy he was, never missed a moment to tell me how much he was into me. It was my fault. I'd hooked up with him once, and even though we weren't that sexually compatible, he'd worshipped the hell out of my body. Maybe I flirted with him too much. I needed to stop.

He put an offer out there this time, too, and I almost took it seriously. Side note: never get high when you're horny. I wasn't *that* high, but it definitely made me think about things. I was overthinking things. Asher hadn't texted me since the hospital, and it had me considering the worst. I was afraid I hadn't heard from him because he wasn't as attracted to me. I looked the same, but I couldn't help the weight loss. I had to assure myself it wasn't worth it if he was going to play the same games people played with me before.

Reggie: *Who dis?*

I picked up my phone to view the message. Classic move. Deleting my number or pretending to. This dude learned too much from me. It'd been days since I'd heard from anyone, but I hadn't expected to hear from Reggie.

Reggie: *Number look familiar doh*

I was losing my edge, but it was the first time I'd ever written an immediate reply to Reggie since I'd know him.

Me: *Of course it's familiar doofus. It's Teddy.*

Reggie: *I only know one Teddy. She bounced.*

This dude was aggy as hell. It took everything not to ignore the messages.

Me: *Well, she bounced back.*

Reggie: *I just don't believe this is Teddy.*

We called our session quits, but I tried to get one last puff before it came down to the roach. I managed a selfie only a stoner would appreciate.

Reggie: *Where you been at doh*

He was about to find out.

* * *

We were set to meet up downtown. When I finally did catch up to him, he pretended not to recognize me.

"Damn, girl, what'd you go to a weight loss spa or something?"

It was Miami. I guess you can't put it past anyone. An uncomfortable shift of mood stained the air. I rolled my eyes, placing my hands in my pockets. "Nice to see you too, Reggie," I said with a distinct sharpness.

"Damn, did I say something wrong?"

I rubbed my forehead and continued on in a defeated tone. "I'm just going through stuff. Chill on the funny stuff."

"So where have you been?"

I watched the rollerbladers zoom past, diverting my attention to avoid looking Reggie in the eye. "Around."

"Where's around?"

"Damn, Reggie. Around."

"Don't tell me you was with homeboy."

I shook my head in a fit of laughter. "That's all you care about? I'm gone for a few months, and you think all I care about is some fling you got butthurt over."

"I was not butthurt over no buster."

"Well, obviously you were, because you're bringing up old shit."

"Because you're bringing up old behavior." I threw my hands in the air, and went off like a canon.

"Believe it or not, I have *real* problems. Problems you don't bother to ask about if the conversation doesn't pertain to you. If you must know, I was at a Hodgkin's disease center, because I happen to have Hodgkin's lymphoma. So while you're worried about a mistake in your check, someone not texting you, or whether or not I was with 'homeboy' this entire time, I'm usually spending my time trying *not* to die."

Should I have been offended when Reggie burst out laughing? There were times when I was petty for next to no reason at all. But this time wasn't one of them, and I reached my boiling point. "What the hell is so funny?"

"Teddy, why are you doing this to yourself? You're just making yourself look bad. That is by far the most elaborate thing you've ever said for attention, and I've known you to be a lot of things. But that's a story you can't pretend your way into."

This is what I wanted to deal with. I chose to do this. *Willingly*. I can't blame any outside source. I was just stupid. Stupid for thinking Reggie was ever the guy for me.

"Reggie, do me a favor. Lose my number!" I said, marching off. We were full of so much drama. I'd be a fool to walk into it again. I'm glad he didn't stop me because I was done. Done with him. Done with us. Done with everything.

***

*Asher*

I was going to feel this shit in the morning. It started out for fun—just a few kids from the neighborhood, passing a ball around. I wasn't even supposed to be there. Reggie asked me to meet up around his way, and I got caught up with someone I knew. The Alice Wainwright Park was lit up. A friendly sporting event turned into a neighborhood game, a bunch of trash talk letting things get heated.

Dudes didn't know I was nice like that, and it could've lasted longer if the sun hadn't gone down. Reggie still wasn't on good terms with Lala, and I told him to meet me there since it was close to Coconut Grove. When he finally did show, we switched seats, going with the usual plan.

"Wainwright was live as fuck tonight."

"I'm not worried about this damn game. I'm just trying to get this kush. I am stressed out." Here it came. Another Drake verse dressed in conversation. "Guess who I saw the other day?"

In the pit of my stomach, I knew. It wasn't likely Reg wouldn't hear from Teddy. She'd known him longer. But I waited it out, using a smile to betray how I felt.

"Teddy. That girl you met? The one I used to mess with?"

I nodded, trying to convey a sense of familiarity. "Yeah. I saw her around a few times a while back. Got high once or twice." Which wasn't a lie. Reggie sent me a suspicious look that I countered with a clearer explanation. "At a party or some shit. It's a small world."

Reggie went on the animate, painting his story the same way I'd heard every time. That Teddy was playing him or she was making up shit for attention. I knew Teddy about as much as he did. She did a lot of things, but she didn't *make up* shit. And not for something as small as attention either. I shouldn't have even asked for a follow-up because it just made me tight.

"She goes into this rant about having cancer and shit. Like

that was the reason she was gone for months. Girl never looked healthier in her life."

I couldn't believe I felt the need to defend her—she wasn't my girlfriend—but that was just going further than I was willing to let Reg go. He didn't know her situation. It wasn't my right to, but she'd already told him and I wasn't cool with him making her out that way.

"Reg, seriously. You're fucked up. Maybe I don't know her like you do, but I know Teddy wasn't lying."

Reggie squinted, wearing an expression of confusion and a hint of suspicion. "What are you talking about?"

I laughed him off like he was seeing things that weren't there. To prevent any further speculation, I decided it best to feed him something *without* giving our past situation away. "So I get up with her at this party, right? We're both high as fuck. We get to talking. She goes 'I have Hodgkin's lymphoma' or some shit like that. And I don't know her, so she really didn't have a reason to lie to me." Which was only a little true, but by now it got the reaction I was hoping for. Reggie went a while not saying shit, even though his jaw was basically on the dashboard.

"Well, why the fuck didn't anyone tell me?" he asked, his voice swinging to a high-pitched tone.

"Kid, she just did."

"I was talking *mad* shit. I didn't think she was serious."

"Better call that girl up," I joked, dropping him off at the corner before hitting up Lala. All this time, I'd thought Ted was just avoiding me. At least now I had my answer.

# CHAPTER FOUR


**Teddy**

Reggie: *Damn, can we talk?*

For what? You said enough. I was getting tired of deleting every message Reggie sent me. I wasn't in the mood. I'd get back to Reggie…eventually. But he wasn't a priority right now. I'd been back almost a month, and I needed a break. From everything. Not that there was much to break from. When you went four months with little communication, people moved on.

But I was bored. There wasn't much to do but to see what everyone else was doing. Instagram always bugged me with all the rush-to-get-likes crap, but it was the only social media I got into. I scrolled through my IG's timeline. Fake. Fake. That dude know that isn't his real car. My phone was on five percent, scrolling on nothing. I didn't even know what I was looking for.

Ashman 420: *Follow me mother*!%@$

A picture of a Snapchat icon accompanied it. I hadn't heard from Ash in three weeks, so I didn't know if he'd been avoiding me or waiting on me to text, but I wasn't the type to be up someone's ass. I wasn't very good to him, but I felt a little jilted over the hospital visit without saying anything. Maybe it was shallow and pessimistic, but I couldn't help thinking… Never mind. I wanted to see him, but would he want to see me?

I used the last of my phone's battery and caved.

Me: *Working today?*

My phone chimed to life and gave me one more message before shutting off.

Reggie: *Nah. Can we talk?*

Reggie wouldn't be at PriceSlash. If I was going to choose the best time as any, now would be the time to go.

* * *

I sat in my car for the longest time. I listened to the radio, peering out my car window like I was waiting for the world to end. For some reason, it seemed like a good idea this morning. But now that I was here, I wasn't as sure. Maybe coming was a bad idea in general. I had the potential to get my feelings hurt. I wasn't even sure I was strong enough for that at this point. Everything seemed to be closing in on me, and I needed air.

I'd take it as a sign to leave things alone if he wasn't here. Just because Reggie wasn't, didn't mean he was. As soon as I walked through the moving doors, I paced around the store. I expected Asher to be in the front, but when I didn't see him, I walked around. I ate out more than I cooked, so I didn't know if the prices for anything in the aisles were cheaper than a huge chain store, but the signs pointing out everything was at an "everyday low price" seemed legit.

It wasn't until I was near the bread aisle that some thirtyish old dude tried to talk to me. I guess he wasn't bad looking, but he was a bit eccentric for my taste.

"I'm flattered, but I'm kinda working on me right now."

"You probably only playing me because you ain't trying to

fuck with a dude who works at a grocery store," he said in a joking manner, like he was trying to add light to the situation.

"I already told you. It doesn't have to do with you. I'm just not interested. Besides, at least you have a job. I can't even find one."

"Why don't you just apply here?"

I scratched the back of my neck. Not that I wanted to apply here, but it caught my attention. "Are they hiring?"

"Oh, please. They're always hiring," he said, before mumbling something inappropriate about me working here and how he'd be around me all the time if I did. Dude was a little shady, but if they were always hiring, I was looking. He even took it upon himself to walk me to the kiosk, like I wouldn't be able to find it myself. Thirsty ass.

It was one of those digital kiosks that was dated, but seemed just as accessible online. I hadn't seen Asher at all, so I was convinced I'd missed my chance. But it didn't mean I couldn't fill out an application. It asked me all these dumb-ass questions, sometimes more than once, but in a different way, before it even let me put in my basic information. What was I applying for—the government?

Something I didn't expect to take more than fifteen minutes took nearly forty-five. I probably wasn't going to get it, and I wasn't even sure I wanted it, but you never know. I was done here. What I came for hadn't happened, so I wasn't going to waste the rest of my afternoon here. I rushed for the exit door and bumped into an employee.

"Teddy?"

Asher... I didn't notice him until it was too late. I would've avoided him, but I hadn't put him on the radar. I'd been passing by him the whole time. I was looking for him to look the exact same. Even though his hair had always been between colors, there was no mistake his hair was platinum blond now.

He didn't look too happy to see me, but concern was in his

eyes all the same. "Hey." We didn't say anything for a few seconds. "Can I get a hug?" Asher asked, breaking the silence.

I opened my arms, and he bent down, picking me up by the waist, my feet dangling to the floor.

"Damn, girl, you're light as shit," he said in a jovial manner before putting me down.

I didn't know what response wouldn't sound weird, so I gave a fake laugh with a standard, "Ya know?"

"You okay?"

I nodded. "Yeah."

"Well, you look good."

I poked him in the chest. "So do you."

For Ash, good was an understatement. Somewhere in the back of my mind, I'd hoped I'd lost my attraction to him, but he was still hot.

"I'm at work, so there isn't too much going on."

It'd look desperate, but the worst I'd hear was a no or forced yes. "Do you get off soon? I'm just around. Wouldn't mind having a Starbucks buddy."

Asher hesitated, and his body language said more than a no would've. Only thing left to do was laugh it off as a joke. "It's okay if you're busy," I said as I diverted my eyes, rubbing my arm, showing my anxiety. "Forget I asked. It was nice seeing—"

He pulled my arm before I could go any farther toward the exit door. "Wait. It's not like I wouldn't want to. But I don't get off for another hour. I'd hate to keep you waiting just for coffee." His expressive eyes were sincere, but I still wasn't convinced. "I tried texting you. But I figured after...I don't know. I didn't think you were fucking with me anymore."

I tried to think of any times he'd texted and I missed it, and it came up empty. "Well, if you're serious about it, I can come back. Did you bring your bike here?"

Asher shook his head and went into a minute-long explanation about his recent bike trouble.

We exchanged a few words, before I excused myself to hit up the public restroom to check on myself. I did a mirror-check to make sure I looked all right. I hadn't in the car, and I just wanted to see how I looked to people.

Acceptable, I guess, for just denim shorts and a tank top. I twirled to see if I at least gave something to stare at from behind. I passed by Asher again on the way out. He was talking to a customer, so I darted past him so he wouldn't feel obligated to small talk.

I know I said I'd come back, but it seemed like a waste of gas to drive around, so I sat in my car and listened to music. J. Balvin had me so hype and in the zone, I jumped when Asher opened my passenger-side door and hopped in.

"You look surprised. Was I supposed to say no?"

Definitely more anxious than surprised. I told him there was more than enough room for his skateboard in the backseat and then made our next destination latte heaven.

"What have you been into? I haven't seen you in, like, forever," I asked, hoping to end the awkwardness.

"Nothing. Same shit, different day."

"Aw. We should hang out more. Give you something to do," I joked.

"You've always known where the find me."

"Communication works both ways, Ash," I added, taking a right into the plaza parking lot.

"Kinda hard to get up when you don't hear from someone. Just assume someone else is taking up your time. No big deal," he said as he drifted off, glancing out the window. He was calling me on bullshit. Some of it true, but not a complete reflection of me.

"I'm just going through stuff. Texting isn't always a priority."

"Fair enough," he said, scratching his face. "But sometimes it's just easy not to, that's all."

We got to Starbucks and browsed the seasonal blend menu. It wasn't a hard decision to get iced lattes with Miami's weather.

Even though I was content with my Caramel Flan, he had me curious about his Tiramisu.

"You know you missed my exit, right?"

I hadn't been paying attention. My brain just seemed wired to go straight to my condo. I promised to turn around and go the long way.

"Nah, I can take the bus or walk from your place. Appreciate it," he said.

By the time I pulled into my parking lot, I was ready to switch off a sip from our lattes, but he finished the last sip before I asked.

"You suck. Now you know I was gonna ask to try yours."

Asher shrugged, laughing me off with a closed-mouths-don't-get-fed type of comment. There was more than one way to taste it. Before he could object, I leaned in and kissed him. The after-taste wasn't strong on his lips, but as I gently slid my tongue in his mouth, the remnant of espresso was still there.

"It was all right," I said, leaning out.

Asher looked at me with a slack-jawed expression. Maybe that was too soon. An awkward silence lingered as we reached to unbuckle our seatbelts. I figured an apology was in order, especially because I hadn't asked. I didn't even know if he was seeing anyone. Before I could, his lips advanced on mine in a hungry, enticing game of tug-of-war.

"We should go up to your apartment."

I agreed and lead the way to the entrance.

* * *

*Asher*

It seemed right in the car. But the wrong head was leading the way. Now that I was here, I had no idea what I was doing. I kept letting my history with Teddy cloud my judgement. It felt weird being in her apartment now. We'd always been high off of weed or each other in the days of our Teddy-Asher past, and the thought of chilling here sober…

Teddy drew a finger along the space between my ear and neck. Heat prickled at the lines and shapes she traced against my skin.

"Is this new?"

Referring to the ink that hadn't been there before she left. I nodded before falling back, slumped onto the couch. She didn't take long to join me, locking eyes from across the couch.

"What?" I asked to break the silence, but I knew what it was.

"Nothing. I just missed you."

I laughed under my breath and ran my hands across the fronts of my jeans. "I really don't think you did."

Teddy tapped her hands up and down the sofa cushion, a sure sign of her anxiety. "Ash, I don't think there was a person I missed more than you. You're, like, my best friend."

"You could've fooled me. I kept thinking of the weeks of not hearing from you. That's not very friendly."

Teddy held up her hands in front of her in a defensive manner. "In my defense, I didn't bring my phone."

Leaning my arm closest to her point on the sofa, I reached over and played with the ends of her hair. Clearly annoyed, she pushed my hand away, and lightly tugged at my fingers until she interlocked hers with mine.

"I guess they don't have phones in Minnesota."

"What—did you want me to call you to tell you how horrible I was doing? I wrote you telling you that."

She was really going to make me go there. "Okay? Two letters. One of which was one sentence. I get what you were going through, but, an 'I'm not dead' phone call would've been nice. But that type of thing never seems important to you."

She brought her lips to the palm of my hand. If her lips were good for nothing else, they made me feel things. Mostly good things. Sometimes bad things that felt good. But never a feeling I didn't want.

She took two of my fingers in her mouth, slowly running her tongue up and down them. By the time she stopped, I wasn't thinking straight. She hid behind vague brown eyes, kissing and nibbling the skin and smiling because she knew I liked it.

"You don't make things easy for me."

Teddy climbed onto my end of the couch and straddled my lap. She leaned in, kissing and nibbling on the lobe of my ear, sending more bad thoughts into my head. "Well, you don't try very hard."

She took my hat and threw it on the coffee table. We studied each other one last time.

"Sometimes I don't think you want me to."

Teddy edged in closer to me but paused. She licked her lips, like she'd considered kissing me but thought against it.

"Fuck it." I went straight for her lips, pulling her closer to me. She trembled up against me as a moan vibrated from her mouth to mine. The scent she gave off was rich of coconut, and I couldn't tell if it was lotion or something in her hair, but it drove me bonkers.

She took turns between caressing my face and chest. When she'd had her fun tracing her fingers along my stubble, she stretched her fingers across my henley, the sensation through the fabric making me burn for more. This hadn't been the plan. I hadn't meant for this to happen, so I wasn't carrying. I wanted to go further, but if this wasn't meant to happen, something would shut it down.

"Maybe we should slow down."

"Why?"

"I don't have any condoms," I said, defeated.

Teddy laughed under her breath. "Unless you just don't want to, I have some. We don't have to." She bit her lip, with that look of wanting me to put it on her in her eye.

"Well, when you look at me like that…"

She reached back in and nibbled my lower lip. Her tongue traveled to the corner of my mouth where my spider bite rested, sending a tingly sensation all over.

"You play dirty," I said with an unexpected groan to my voice. I leaned in for a real kiss as she pushed against my chest and whispered, "Let's go to my room."

She peeled herself off of me, taking my hand as she led me back to her bedroom. I got comfortable, watching her slide out of her boots, checkered shirt, and tank top. If I'd ignored it before, it was hard to ignore the weight loss once her clothes were off. She didn't look fragile, but that fifteen pounds she claimed to have dropped looked more like twenty-five. Her once pillowy-soft stomach'd been replaced with one that was flatter, but not in a hard way. Her ribs were more pronounced than they'd ever been, and she wasn't sucking it in. She straddled my lap again, bit her lip, but not out of confidence like before.

"I see how you're looking at me."

I pushed her away, so she could see me tell the truth. "How am I looking at you?"

She collapsed into herself, reaching for her tank top on the floor. "I can put my shirt back on. I can tell you weren't expecting this—"

"Teddy. Seriously. Shut up."

A laugh left her, even though she wouldn't go further before sending a friendly "fuck you" my way.

I flipped her on her back, letting my hands trace over every inch of her. "I'm about to. I think it's about time you got reacquainted with someone." I wiggled my tongue, the piercing on full display.

"Mmm…you're so nasty."

"Tell me you don't like it, and I won't be." But she couldn't. She knew that's what she liked about me. I wiped her shorts clean off, working my way toward teasing her to insanity. She was thinner, but…by no means was her body no longer sexy. She was still thick for her frame, and even though I'd miss the former curves I'd had so much fun with, her body would always turn me on. Because it was *hers*.

I thought she planned this until I saw her brown-and-purple polka dot panties. Her undergarments usually matched if sex was her intention. I could promise they wouldn't be on for long. I kissed the outside of her panties, and it caused the sexiest, breathy moan. She sat up on her elbows, anticipating every second. "You okay? You seem anxious."

"It's just been a while," she said, chewing her lower lip.

I pulled on her hips and upper thighs, beckoning her close to my face. I shifted her panties to one side, running my tongue against her exposed skin. Her eyes glassed over as she balled both of her fists.

"Mmm…I hate when you do that."

Even though her body and expression betrayed that entire sentence. It'd been a long time. Too long. I wasn't about to rush it just yet. I held back her panties again and teased her lips open with my tongue.

"Oh my god, I just want to come already," she cried, letting out the breath she'd been holding onto.

I continued to lick higher and higher, bit by bit, until the tip of my tongue was right underneath her clit. She begged me to make her come, fed up with all the teasing. I told her she asked for it, as I peeled her panties completely off. I almost fainted when she spread her legs wider for me, just the way I liked her to be.

I dove in tongue-first, as her trembling body vibrated against my mouth. The entire length of my tongue tasted her, as she matched her hips to my rhythm. I bobbed my mouth all over that pussy, and she moaned in that sexy voice of hers how she liked it just like that and that she'd come all over my mouth if I kept it up.

Her closed eyes forced back open, and she locked eyes with

me, tugging my hair on carnal instinct. She pushed the back of my head, so I'd be in it face-first, her legs shaking at every stroke, lick, and flick.

"Asher, I'm gonna come."

I took hold of her thighs and concentrated my tongue, mouth, and ring on one spot, getting hard just listening to her come all over my mouth. Her inner thighs constricted tighter around my face, until her voice caved uncontrollably. She gently pushed away my face and held out her hands for me to grab hold.

She kissed me and didn't stop kissing me. She tugged at my shirt, in between breathy whispers on how she missed me. Her arms wrapped around me as she held me tight, like she was afraid to let go.

"I wish we could have sex like this."

The only drawback to being so tall, especially where her hips and mine started. Made it nearly impossible to be directly face-to-face unless she was on top of me. I joked that it gave me the best view of her beautiful body, and she was more than okay with that answer.

Before I could object, I was tossed onto my back, all my clothes on the floor in a heartbeat. She wouldn't have to do much. My body was like a rocket—it'd take everything in me to prevent coming too soon. She knelt over and brought my cock as far as she could take it into her mouth. My toes curled at each inch her mouth re-took of me.

"You're seriously gonna make things harder if you keep up like that." I tried to keep my mind centered on everything but busting a nut. The glassy look in her eyes. The way my dick disappeared between her full lips. Her tongue swirling circles along the shaft of my cock. I should've told her to stop. I wanted her to. But when she wrapped her fingers around me and jerked with just the right amount of pressure, saliva, and suction, my dick exploded without warning.

"Shit, Teddy. Fuck." Her jerking hand was full of saliva as she finished off what was left of me. "C'mere."

I pulled her closer to me and kissed her, lips raw and soft from giving me head. She crossed her thigh between mine, awarding me the chance to caress her ample softness. "Just give me a minute to warm back up. I'll last longer for another round."

"No rush," Teddy mumbled between kisses.

Making out made you lose track of time. An hour of locking lips felt like five minutes when you were lost in it. The only detail that was off was the moment I went to unbuckle the band to her bra. I wanted to feel all of her, and it was the only thing she hadn't taken off. I didn't press it when she pushed my hand away, but nothing'd be able to push me away forever.

She fought for control on top of me, gliding and sliding the wetness of her all over me. I reached for the front of her bra, taking her nipple between my lips. She cried for me to stop but didn't try that hard to make me. I unraveled her other hidden breast, gently pinching it between my finger and thumb.

"I want to make you come while you ride me."

Teddy got the message, reaching for a condom in the dresser a few inches away.

My dick was getting there, watching the sight of her naked thighs sprawled over the mattress. She leaned over, playing with my cock until it was hard enough to slip the condom on. A mutual exchange of strained groans left our mouths as she lowered her slick, wet body onto me.

"Let me get to those tits," I said, pushing her bra back down to face me. She was seconds away from fighting me not to, but I was already tonguing down her breasts. Her body sprang up instantly.

We soon moved to the rhythm of one another, me pushing up inside her as her body gently rode me up and down. She became wetter with every whisper of how deep I was inside her, how good she was riding it, and whether or not she wanted to keep going this way. In a tangle of hips and legs, Teddy positioned her back to me. She leaned over my lap, allowing me to enter her from behind. I scattered kisses along the back of her neck and shoulders, watching her body perk at each fold of exposed skin.

"You want me to fuck you?" I asked in a raspy, husky tone.

"Mmhmm," was all Teddy managed to articulate.

Taking hold of her arms, I proceeded to thrust into her all-too-willing body. Convulsive moans and cries of ecstasy echoed throughout the room. My skin up against her skin. My body joined in hers.

"You like that, baby?"

"Yeah." Her voice shaken, breathless, and trembling at each plunge into her warmth.

"Yeah?" She made me want to delve faster, harder, and deeper with every breathy reply. Her body sent an electric sensation through me, and before I knew it, my hips were out of control and selfish. She started egging me on in Spanish with phrases I couldn't understand. "Hazme que me venga" and "Metemela duro" came out in silken, burning sighs. My groin tensed with bursts of quick, volcanic spasms. I thrusted one last hard pump, before pulling out and wrapping my arms around her.

"Teddy, did you come?"

She nodded, but I wasn't so convinced. She giggled and gasped at each claim of her skin with my lips. "Mmm...I love you, Asher."

There was a heavy drop in my stomach, and I sat back. A short bout of silence made things awkward before Teddy got up, said she needed to take a shower, and excused herself from the room.

* * *

*Teddy*

We only get one body. No matter how it performed, how it

looked, how it looked to other people, you had to be grateful for it. I was really trying to be. Really. But there was so much I didn't recognize about myself.

I guess I was still sexy. I still thought I was. But the weight loss made my boobs sag lower than they should. They'd never been perky to begin with, but at least they'd looked nice. Then the stretch marks. I'd had them for a while, but they just seemed more noticeable to me now. You never noticed more about your body when you were looking at it naked in the mirror.

My hair did okay. The edges were thinner than I wanted, but it wasn't as noticeable when I fluffed it out. A concoction of peppermint and castor oil would have to do. I grabbed the bra I brought with me and buckled it around my tummy. I spun it around and up my ribs, securing it over my shoulders.

My clothes didn't fit the same. My body didn't look the same. My hair was just… I don't think things could've been more solidified than through Asher's first impression. He'd hid it well. Shock. Pity. Disgust. They all looked the same at this point so I couldn't tell which one. I hid underneath a robe, braided my hair in two French braids, and prepared to face the outside world.

I half-expected Asher not to be there—not that I wanted him to be—so it surprised me that he laid there, watching me search for a pair of panties in my underwear dresser and something clean to change into. I looked over my shoulder, waiting for him to say something.

"You don't have to stay if you don't want."

Asher edged up, resting on his elbows. "You're really going to ignore ten minutes ago?"

I shrugged. "So just because I tell you I love you, you're entitled to me now or something?"

"No, it's just…" He sighed deeply, reaching for his shirt as he rustled with his jeans. "You're confusing as fuck, Teddy. I wouldn't have even done this if I knew you were going to act like this."

"Act like what?" I entertained.

"Like you don't give a fuck about *anything*. I'm trying to deal with it, but you keep… You don't get to just tell me you love me and then tell me to fuck off. There's a lot of shit I'll deal with, but that's not one of them. I'm tired of the games."

Asher snatched up his sneakers and hightailed it out of the room. I took the opportunity to make myself comfortable at the corner of my bed. Asher wasn't gone—I heard his footsteps travel all over the apartment, so when he stepped back into my room it didn't surprise me.

"Did I leave my phone in here?" I didn't notice it until after he asked, but it was sitting on my dresser, a few inches from eyeshot. I pointed to it, and he crawled onto the mattress, reaching over me to retrieve it. He should've been history by now, but he joined me on the bed, laying a hand on my shoulder.

"Teddy, I'm scared as fuck to want you. But here I am, wanting you anyway," he said with a hint of frustration. "It can be as your friend, or it can be something else, but I'm not gonna… now you're rolling your eyes at me. Seriously, I'm done."

He stormed out of the room before I could defend myself. It was good that he left. I was so used to being alone, I didn't know how not to be.

* * *

*Asher*

If there was something I did *not* need, it was food. My stomach was about to burst all over the floor. Since we'd lost Claude a few weeks ago to live with his girl, we'd been stuck without a roommate for close to two months. Splitting his part of the rent with two other people sucked, so it was a relief when Jesse moved in a few weeks ago.

He was probably trying to show off, like he was a good roommate and shit. One of his first weekends here, he volunteered to grill up steaks and burgers on the patio, and I wasn't turning down shit. Between downing five beers and smoking weed, I was done, and I didn't need to do more than chill until it was time to sleep.

My room was humid as hell, and that portable fan in the corner was no A/C. But I was comfortable and too high to worry about bullshit. My phone'd been resting in the charger since I got home, and I wasn't trying to kill my high. I didn't go to sleep before checking updates though. IG was popping. Facebook, Tumblr, and Twitter all sucked. Two text messages from Analise. Kinda wish she'd get the hint. A message from Reggie. Sure it wasn't important, but I'd text him back later. One from Elias. Hmm…a sext. Suddenly *very* interested.

*Teddy King added you*

My Snapchat profile lit up. When it came to anything Teddy, I was reluctant to even fuck with it. How many times did I have to get played to learn my lesson right? I wasn't done, but…it was hard to be sure where I'd go with her at this point. I let go of the breath I'd been holding onto and clicked on the notification anyway.

I burst out laughing when I caught wind of her profile pic. A series of cute, funny faces roared at the screen. I wasn't petty enough to be mad at that, but it didn't mean I wanted to keep the conversation of *us* going.

*Teddy King is typing…*

I opened her first snap. I barely had time to read it before it disappeared into thin air. She was new to Snapchat, otherwise she'd have known how to use it.

"I can barely use this thing!" she sent back a snap with a surprised look on her face.

I held down on the circle button and recorded a reply back. "You might wanna hold down on the circle. It makes the messages longer."

*Teddy King is typing...*

"I still don't get this!" she replied, with a longer video this time. It'd notify her either way, but I played it back.

*Teddy King is typing...*

She sent another video, but it didn't engage long. She mouthed, "What you doing?"

I sent a snap with the reply, "Snapping you." She was getting the hang of it. She sent another picture snap, with a caption asking, "*Are you mad at me?*" I wasn't sure what she wanted me to say. I wasn't mad. Just tired. Confused. Maybe even a little used. I couldn't stay mad, but I wasn't sure of anything with her. I sent a snap with a passive look and the text, "No. *But we should prolly chill.*"

*Teddy King is typing...*

She sent a pic of her holding her face, wearing a glum expression with a caption that said, "*Check your messages. Pls delete.*" My text notification informed me I had a video text waiting. Hopping off of Snapchat, I checked out the video she'd sent.

I'd never noticed how long her hair was until now. This video marked the first time I'd ever seen it straightened—or close to it since her hair was so tightly curled. She shook her hair out, pulling a few strands away from her scalp in some areas, highlighting where her hair thinned in certain areas. There was even a small a patch in the back where there wasn't any hair.

She scratched her nose, then the video went blank. "*Pls delete,*" she texted again. I went back to my text thread and replied.

Me: *What was that all about?*

Teddy: *I just wanted to show you while I didn't have to watch your reaction :/*

Me: *Is this about earlier?*

Teddy: *No. Kinda. Idk.*

Me: *You don't need me to tell you you're gorgeous. If you want me to, you're gorgeous. But...if you're gonna play games, I can't be that kind of friend.*

Teddy: *A friend that still has sex?*

Me: *Yeah.*

Teddy: *So why would you still want to be cool with me?*

Me: *Because. I know you're going through a lot. I don't say it, but I see it. I notice. If I were in your position, I'd want someone to be there for me. Even from a distance.*

For a half-hour, nothing. Probably not the answer she wanted to hear. She almost snapped me, but a snap never came. Instead I received a text.

Teddy: *Was gonna snap, but I forgot how to use...*

I waited, and a few minutes later, a reply followed after it.

Teddy: *The thing is, I'm gonna be miserable sometimes. I'm not gonna know how not to be. I like the way you make me feel, but I don't think I can be happy all the time...*

Me: *I don't expect you to be...*

Teddy: *You deserve better than me :/*

Me: *Can't think of anyone better than you punk :p*

Teddy: *I meant what I said :/*

She'd said a lot of things. But I knew her well enough to know which one she'd meant.

Me: *Good to know. That I could work with.*

CHAPTER FIVE

**Teddy**

After a few weeks of apologizing, I finally let the beef between me and Reggie go. It seemed silly to let it go on as long as it did, and I still wanted to be friends. It'd be awkward not to if he found out about me and Asher, and I would've rather him find out as my friend.

We weren't dating…but we weren't *not* dating. We weren't more than what we were, but we were only that with each other. Who knows? Maybe. I didn't need someone who was going to baby me, but I wanted a friend who was supportive. Asher was all those things, and we were trying to hash out a way to tell Reggie. We didn't have a plan, but for now, we thought we'd get him *used* to us.

I'd even invited Reggie out to hang, with the intention of inviting Asher along out of the blue. They were both working today, so the timing couldn't be more perfect. PriceSlash was one of those grocery stores you came to for the savings, but hated the wait. The lines were always to the aisle on the right day. I was so glad I didn't plan on buying anything.

Reggie stood out, with a hightop that was reminiscent of Chalky Studebaker. Even with that dingy-ass apron, he was still handsome. I hated that in the time he was gone he chopped all his sexy dreads off, but it wasn't hard to remember why I thought he was so cute. I tapped him on the shoulder, and he held his arms out to invite me in a hug. It didn't make sense to argue now. He'd spent two hours sending "I'm sorry" texts, and I had more to be sorry about than him.

"So what's good with the aquarium?" I'd lived in Miami all my life, but never gone to Seaquarium. It seemed like the best spot to get back into the swing of things without pressure.

"You know I don't get off until five. And I was seven minutes late, so I might be clocking out at 5:07."

"See you didn't say that over the phone. Got me waiting on you." It was a quarter to five, so it wasn't a big deal, but I couldn't help but notice Asher clocking out. It was my bias speaking, but how did I ever let a cutie like Asher slip through my fingers once? The tattoos, the piercings, the intensely-sometimes-creepy-most-times-sexy gunmetal-blue eyes? A girl's knees were giving out just thinking about it.

I pretended not to see Asher sneak up behind me before he used his hands to cover my eyes. I heard him *shush* Reggie, like it was a surprise or something. I rammed my elbow into what felt like Asher's stomach, and a loud "ugh!" followed it. Ash was amping it up for show. It wasn't *that* hard. When he released his hands from my eyes, he smiled like it was the first time he'd seen me in months.

"What's up, shawty?" he joked.

"What's up, moose?"

He brought his hands down to his stomach and faked a laugh. "Oh. I see you got jokes," he said before he offered his hand for me to high-five him. I brought my palm toward his, but just to be petty, he did a bait-and-switch and pulled his hand away. "I'm just playing." He held out his hand again, only when I tried to slap it this time, he raised it over his head, a good seven inches past his six-foot-two frame.

I jumped twice but couldn't reach it, and it wasn't until I hopped on his back and brought it down before I stood a chance. "Damn, all that for a played-out high-five?"

I hopped down, waving him off as I proceeded to head to my car.

"What you guys about to get into?" Asher interjected before I was through the exit door.

"We were about to hit up Seaquarium, but this fool don't get off for twenty minutes."

"You trying to roll?" Reggie interjected, surprising the both of us.

"To an aquarium? Not trying to cramp your style," Asher said, dragging his feet.

Reggie shrugged. "I mean, it's up to Teddy since she's the ride. But I don't care if she doesn't."

I gestured between the two, pointing my finger to get my point across. "I don't mind as long as both of you chipping in for gas."

"Well…if y'all invitin'," Asher said with a toothy grin. It wasn't a long time, waiting for Reggie to clock out. Asher and I sat at the bench near the exit, keeping to small talk in case any onlookers were nearby, including Reggie. We had our own history. It was best to avoid topics that sounded too familiar.

Mostly Ash talked about what he did at his job, how long he'd been there. My phone rang with a familiar number, and Asher just happened to peek over. "Why is PriceSlash calling you?"

I hopped up, heading outside to take the call. I'd just applied two weeks ago, but I was sure I wouldn't hear back since I didn't have any real job experience.

Whoever I spoke to let me know they were only looking to hire a few people and my open availability was the main reason they'd called me. I almost hadn't put that. Didn't make sense putting I could work all day every day when I didn't expect to get a callback. It was a small place, so they weren't as professional as the places I'd applied to in the past, but they called me back and were willing to interview me toward the end of the week.

"What was that all about?" Ash asked with confused eyes.

"I talked to someone named Julie. They want me to come in Thursday? Is there anything I should expect?"

Asher thought it was cute I was serious about trying to get a job here, but it beat going to New York or D.C. The only way I could pay for school here was to get a job fast. At this point, I didn't even care where I worked.

"Just be yourself. Tell whoever interviews you good things, with one bad thing, just so you don't sound perfect," he teased, talking with his hands.

Reggie materialized out of nowhere. "You guys good?"

"I know you're not talking. With your clock-out-at-5:07 ass."

"Says the girl with no job."

"Says the dude with no car." It was nice to get the last word. Reggie's lips curled and matched his smug expression, and they followed me out to the parking lot. "I'll let you guys figure out who's riding shotgun." I tossed it out to see who would bite. It was a no brainer, but if I suggested Ash, Reggie would have something to say. It was better to let them duke it out.

"You even have to ask?" Reggie said as he parked himself outside the passenger side door, waiting for me to pop the lock. Asher didn't seem slighted, but eventually we'd have to figure out a way for his upgrade not to seem obvious. He hopped in the backseat, kicking the back of Reggie's, asking to push up Reggie's seat.

"Dude, for real. I'm not playing. I got long legs."

"So? Tall people always want everybody to accommodate them. Why don't you sit behind the driver's seat?" Asher kicked the seat again, and there was no way I was letting this grade-school game continue.

"Asher, you do that again, it'll be the last thing you do," I said, then geared up to spit the rest of my venom at Reggie. "And you? Just push up the damn seat, otherwise you can both sit in the back. I didn't know I'd be babysitting today. Damn."

The car was awkwardly silent as I pulled out of the grocery store's parking lot. It was as good a time as any to blast that playlist I'd spent three hours organizing. Between ChocQuib-Town, J. Balvin, and Voodoo Souljahs, everything in Spanish worth listening to was coming from Colombia. I knew Ash and Reg got sick of the rock and pop music, so this was as far as I was willing to go to accommodate their preferences.

I did like everything they liked, but given the chance, I knew neither would play a song from one of my favorite artists. While I was DJ of *my* car, ChocQuibTown it was. I didn't bother peering over at Reggie. He'd be annoyed by three songs, but at least I had the right music to drown out his sighs.

I took a short detour to a Starbucks drive-thru, and all was forgiven. It was a good thing, too, because when we got to Seaquarium the parking lot was nearly empty. It took asking a group walking to their car to find out the place closed at six, and it was fifteen minutes shy. Between waiting on Reggie, a field trip to Starbucks, and jumping on 95, we'd missed our chance.

"You just had to go to Starbucks?" Reggie said, as if he was objecting when he ordered that Caramel Macchiato.

"Reggie, I know you're not talking. No one thought to look online while I was driving to see when they closed? Probably looking up everything else. Damn, what a mood ruiner. I was looking forward to this."

Asher leaned up in the backseat, speaking between us. "You guys are welcome to chill at my place—"

"Why don't we just head over Teddy's? She doesn't live with people." Reggie said at the same time.

"And do what? It's not like I have any weed," I fired back.

"Listen. My roommate has a PS4. I have beer and shit. It's not an aquarium, but it's something to do."

"I don't know how to play video games." It was true. I was familiar with some classic systems due to cousins growing up, but I never found time to play them much.

"Who doesn't know how to play video games? That's silly as hell," Reggie said, adding in his two cents.

Asher asked if it was cool once more, before I turned the car around and headed for his round of way. I'd dropped him off here a bunch of times, but I'd never asked to come up or vice versa. I was hung up over the fact that his roommates could unintentionally snitch if I came through, not knowing Reggie and Ash hung out a bunch of times. All it'd take is *"Where's that girl Teddy you were messing with?"* to blow the cover, so I'd always opted not to come up.

Wynwood's cost of living was getting higher every day, so it didn't surprise me he shared an apartment with three other guys. What I wasn't expecting was for it to look so clean. There was a minimalist Ikea feel to the setup in the living room that brought attention to the big screen in the room's center. When Asher told us to make ourselves comfortable, I did just that.

He knocked on a bathroom door not far from the living room. "Oh, now he's going to act like he can't hear me."

"How do you even know he's even in there?" Reggie asked, leaned over the arm of the couch.

"He's the only one blasting Kinito Mendez every time he gets ready for work—"

Suddenly the door flung open, and a guy emerged about Reggie's frame, but with a Miami kissed complexion.

"Damn, what? You hear I'm getting ready for work?" His accent was American, but I knew he was Puerto Rican. Call it a sixth sense.

"What's good with that PlayStation?"

"You mean *my* PlayStation?"

Asher pointed toward us, trying to gain sympathy. "Come on, you see I got company over. I owe you if you hook me up."

His roommate tilted his head out of the bathroom, inspecting us with suspicious eyes. His eyes widened for a second, and then he disappeared in the bathroom. "Damn who *that?*" he asked, not even trying to lower his voice. Neither of them were fooling anyone when Ash stuck his head inside the door.

"My homegirl Theodora."

"Damn, she single?"

"You gonna have to ask her." Asher laughed, as their back and forth ended up in Asher closing the door behind him.

I rolled my eyes at the exchange, speculating on what was going on behind the muffled door. "Just thirsty."

"Damn, you're getting mad because a dude thinks you're bad?"

"Can I exist without giving a fuck whether someone does?"

Asher emerged from the bathroom, stalking in front of the TV. He brought his hands together in a clap to give the good or bad news. "Here's the deal. He's gonna hook us up, but we can only play the internal games. That gonna be an issue?"

"What the fuck?" Reggie deemed it necessary to add.

"Favian collects the discs, so he doesn't open them. But it's cool, he's a game addict, so he's got like two hundred games on that thing." He pointed to me, killing me with that flirtatious grin. "By the way, he seems like he's got a crush on you."

I faked a smile, hitting Reggie on the shoulder when he laughed at me.

Asher hooked up the system, which from here looked like it was cleaned daily. Reggie and Ash fought over which games they were trying to play, and I didn't know *Metal Gear Solid* from *NBA 2K*, so I figured I'd watch and wait for the offer when one of them got bored.

Big mistake. Between all their trash talking and control hogging, they barely noticed I was there. If I hadn't had my phone, I would've sat there for two hours straight doing nothing but watching them play. I stopped counting how many times either of them won or lost, taunted one another, or challenged each other to another game before they moved on to something else. I was feeling like the ride and nothing else.

My phone was at the ready, and I texted Asher, hoping his ringer was on low. Just in case, I turned my ringer, vibration included, off. That way, it'd only appear as if I were studying my phone screen or playing a game.

Me: *I'm bored* 😗

Asher's phone vibrated, and without missing a beat, he shuffled around the couch to pull it from his pocket. His attention didn't divert long from the TV screen, but in a few seconds, he managed to reply a weak text, then went back to his game.

Asher: *y*

The text alone pissed me off. I didn't like being ignored. If they didn't care that I was there anyway, I was going to take my ass home.

Me: *If you have to ask, I swear I'm walking right out that door*

When his phone chimed this time, it was heavy in the middle of a death match of *Mortal Kombat*. Preventing a Round III was hard enough. He looked as if he were about to ignore the text altogether, but the time between the rounds gave him a chance to read the reply.

"What time is it?" Asher asked, bringing Reggie out of his mind warp.

"Bruh, who cares? Play the damn game."

The game screen froze as Asher held out the controller in my direction. "Were you trying to play?"

"First of all," I said, directed toward the both of them, "both y'all are rude as hell. If I knew I was just the ride, I would've let you stay at Seaquarium and made you both take the bus home."

Asher averted his eyes, sitting on the couch. His cheeks burned red, but they did all the time anyway. Reggie was on the defensive as always, clucking his teeth and adopting a dismissive tone.

"It ain't like you wanted to play."

"I said I didn't know *how* to play. There's a difference."

Asher gestured for me to sit closer to him, but I instead opted for his controller. "See, if we were playing old school *Street Fighter*, it'd be no issue. These new controllers have, like, four buttons you don't even need. PlayStation ain't SNES."

Asher's mouth curved into a dopey smile, the kind I'd never admit to melting over, as he stood behind me, guiding my fingers on the controller. "I don't know. Super Nintendo is more for nostalgia. It's hard to fuck with Sony's graphics. They're friggin' tight." He instructed me on which buttons to press, and I played against the system's computer. His imperiously long fingers closed in around mine, forcing my hands where to go and what to press.

"I nned to use the bathroom. Which one is yours again?" Reggie stood, pep in his step from sitting on the couch. Asher lifted one hand off the controller, pointing him around the corner.

"Door between the hamper and Mika's room, one room from mine."

Reggie paced around the corner, confirming his location once he closed the bathroom door. Asher's guidance turned into an embrace, and I tilted his ear to me, whispering under the punches and blood splatter of the game's special effects. "I want to suck your dick."

He bit his lip, a low rumble vibrating at the back of his throat. "We should tell him." he whispered back. Asher planted a kiss on my shoulder and grabbed the other controller when the door around the corner creaked open. He entered the game and threatened to murder me in the process, Reggie none the wiser upon his return.

"Go easy on me. I just started," I said, trying to apply the little he'd taught me in a deathmatch to prove myself.

"The lesson is over, homie. I can't hold your hand the entire game. Reggie sucks, maybe you'll get a better chance at winning against him."

That was the last straw for Reggie. He snatched the controller out of Ash's hand, spewing more trash talk. "Give me that damn thing. Probably ain't teach you anything useful this whole time. Don't be too disappointed if you can't win against a master."

I admit, I wasn't as good as they were, but I found my niche, repeating the same move that served me well.

"Why the hell did you teach her that move?"

But Asher wasn't paying him any mind. He was too busy screaming in the background at me, like he was watching a game or something. *"Grab him." "Block." "What are you doing? You had him!"* He repeated it all so many times, it seemed like he was more involved than me.

"Damn, Ash. Am I playing or you?"

"I can't help it. My progeny is making such basic mistakes." Ash collapsed onto the couch, pulling at the root of his hair. Now I see how they wasted hours playing this thing. It was actually kind of fun. You got used to the trash talk—it just became part of the game.

"I'm hungry as hell. We should've got something to eat before we came here. It's like some lock-out-tag-out shit over here," Reggie said. That must've been an inside joke, because Asher laughed but I had no idea why.

"I'd order out if you guys are bumming it. Everybody got cash?" I really hoped one of these fools would say yes. Neither one of them had more than a debit card, so if we wanted to eat, it meant I'd be driving. *Again.* I didn't mind. Or I should say, did I really have a choice? Some online takeout places at best let you split a bill two ways, but three? So no one had to pay for someone else's food, the only option was to go out.

I sighed. "I guess I'm driving."

"We better go now, otherwise nothing will be open with exceptions for McDonald's and diners," Asher added, before we all went into a debate on whether to go Peruvian, Jamaican, or Chinese. Kitchens would close soon, so we didn't have a lot of time to disagree.

* * *

*Asher*

Since we couldn't agree on an individual spot, we ended up going with a Brazilian buffet. Me and Reggie liked meat, and Teddy…liked whatever else they were serving. She seemed impressed by some passionfruit mousse they made here. Reggie just watched her gloss and consider vegetarian options, and I hit him over the shoulder to snap him out.

"Dude, stop pitying her. She's not dead."

Reggie shifted, crossing his arms toward his waist, before letting them fall to his side altogether. "I'm not trying to. What would you do if someone you knew told you they had cancer?"

Probably the same thing I did with Teddy. Tell them it sucks and offer them a cigarette.

"Not mope, that's for damn sure."

We were out of Teddy's earshot, but Reggie felt the need to mumble. "I was looking that shit up the other day. Hodgkin's lymphoma is some serious shit."

"So you plan to baby her? Treat her like a kid?" I wasn't trying to be insensitive, but I'd gone through the motions with Teddy before. It was the biggest deal that wasn't a big deal.

"I don't know. I just don't know anyone going through that. Especially not someone I wanted to be with."

I could've gone all day without feeling guilty until now. It sucked. I'd sat through too many conversations about what he'd gone through with Teddy, so while his feelings had authenticity, I wasn't about to compete with him again.

"I don't know what to tell you, kid."

Teddy sandwiched herself between us, deciding between the only other options that weren't pork or beef. Once everyone was well-equipped with a full plate, we sat at a small booth in the corner of the restaurant.

They were all out of linguiça, a divine sausage that was only fit for gods and the sole reason I even agreed on this place. I was forced to fill my plate with picanha, costela, and white rice to make the trip worth it.

"Damn, Ash, how much barbeque sauce does that strip need?"

I paid Reggie no mind, making sure he knew it as I flipped him the bird.

Reggie examined Teddy's modest plate, terrible at hiding his discomfort. "Is that all you're going to eat?"

Even from the journey to the grill alone, he couldn't stop commenting on her weight loss, her eating habits, or just about anything else he noticed. I thought her plate was pretty decent. She had a few small chicken pieces, mostly sides of vegetables. Basically what a balanced plate should've looked like. It was twenty-three bucks a person, though, so I didn't give a fuck about balance.

"You're gonna ask that now?" I asked, trying not to sound defensive.

"I haven't asked you anything. And you haven't brought it up. If I don't ask, I'm never going to know."

Teddy just rubbed her face, like she'd been preparing to have this conversation for a long time with him. "Reggie, you can relax. I've been going through this stuff for a while now. It's been rough, but for right now, I'm okay—"

"Right now?" he interrupted. She wasn't selling it well either.

"It's so hard to tell. Which is why I'm not shouting my business out to the world. *'Are you okay, or aren't you?' 'Are you sick, or aren't you?'* Truth is, most days I feel okay. Just okay, but okay is a lot better than most things. I don't have control over whether something could come back. But if I'm telling you today I'm fine, then I'm fine."

I joked about the shift in mood, in an effort to change the subject. It worked for the time being, but I knew there were some things Reggie wouldn't ask while I was around. I excused myself to grab more food and let them talk. On occasion, they'd lean into each other's space, so I knew they were talking about some deep shit. I wasn't going to be in the middle of it, so I'd need to know tonight what we were going to be.

Me: *Tonight...we talkin'?*

It was a good thing Reggie lived out of the way. Even though he argued to be dropped off last, Teddy made it clear she wasn't a taxi cab, and that by living closer to each other, it was more convenient to drop Reg off first. I let my mind wander and waste away on neighboring Wi-Fi and phone apps until she was in front of Reggie's house. I tried not to look uncomfortable when he asked her to call him, and then she scolded me to the front seat because she wasn't my chauffeur.

I waited until we were far enough away from Reggie's house to get to business.

* * *

***Teddy***

"So are we gonna talk? Let's talk." Asher rubbed my free hand with his, but diverted his attention out the window, like he wasn't looking forward to it. Why should we? Neither of us knew what was coming. This was something new for both of us.

"I think there's an us. Ever since that party, there's probably *been* an us. But I don't think we're hiding anything because we don't tell Reggie. There's nothing really to hide when we're just friends."

Asher's attention was caught. Despite my eyes on the wheel, I knew his gaze was centered on me.

"Teddy, we sleep together. *A lot.* But just because I'm feeling you, doesn't mean Reggie stopped, unless you give him a reason to. I know you guys get into it a lot, but even with your history, no one deserves to be in the blue that long."

"I never said he did. I'm just saying. You sound like you want to rush into telling him something we're not even sure of. It's not like you consider me your girlfriend—"

He took my hand and kissed it. "You don't know what I consider you."

I didn't know what to make of that statement, but at least his lips brought warmth to the outside of my hand. "So what do you consider what we're doing?"

Asher's eyes widened, and he shuffled in his seat and shrugged. "Fun."

Not exactly the answer I was looking for. "Okay…"

"I'm about to get one hundred percent honest with you." He let go of my hand so he could speak with his own. "At this point, lying to Reggie sucks. I can't kiss up on you. I can't touch you. I can't acknowledge you in all the ways I *know* you like to be as long as he's in the dark. I'm not asking to be your boyfriend if you don't want one. But you're not my dirty secret, and I hope I'm not yours."

He wasn't, but I hated how the shift in our friendship changed whenever we were around Reggie. We couldn't make inside jokes or mention old times. Our history was erased when we were all together. I wasn't against telling Reggie, but if we were going to say something, I wanted it to be the *right* something.

"Have you ever been in a relationship?" I asked out of curiosity. I'd had my fair share, but none that had been as successful going in as walking out.

"Yeah, but they haven't always been monogamous," he joked.

"But I can be a relationship person. I can be if that's what *you* want. And I don't have to be if it's not what you want."

Our history was about the same. More flings than actual relationships. Situation changes—back to being single again.

"Are you looking for monogamy?"

I shrugged. "I don't know. I'm looking for a you. And a me. Anything else, I don't know."

"I can dig that. But I should also say, I think we're compatible. Reggie's my boy and I'm jacked up for saying this, but I don't think you and Reggie were in that way. Otherwise we wouldn't have fucked with each other. And I don't just mean sex, though the sex is a pretty big plus." He laughed into his fist and used the same hand to rub my thigh.

"I guess I just don't want to lose you as a friend. Like the way we are now."

"Teddy, I don't need to mess with you to be your friend. No-sex-Asher is the same Asher. Regardless of what happens, you won't lose me as a friend. But I need to know—am I messing with other people? Am I only messing with you? I just want an understanding. It doesn't mean I'm your man. But a babe, a boo, a bae. Something. Let me know where I stand with you."

It was realest conversation I'd actually wanted to have. There wasn't any pressure, just figuring things out. It might require a little work, but slowly we'd figure things out.

# CHAPTER SIX

**Teddy**

If Asher hadn't had to work early the next day, he would've stayed over and I could've dropped him off. But sometimes after he got off, a game of phone tag ensued. Eventually we'd have to get up.

Asher: *What's up, gorgeous?*

Teddy: *Chilling. At work?*

Asher: *Got off a half hour late. You know how it goes.*

I really didn't, but I joked on with him anyway.

Teddy: *Better get the alcohol* 😎

Asher: *Not that serious...wyd*

Teddy: *Nothing. Home. In bed.*

Asher: *I'm in my bed. You're in your bed. One of us is in the wrong place.*

Me: *I have something for you.*

Asher: *???*

Me: *More like for us. But you'll have to wait to see it. Hard to explain via text.*

It wasn't a big surprise, but it really was one of those things you'd have to see in person. Otherwise, you'd burst out laughing.

Asher: *Hmm...I hope it's a good surprise.*

Me: *Be up tomorrow and I'll pick you up.*

Asher: *Ok*

Me: *:)*

Asher was a marathon texter. It usually took a phone full of numbers to be this busy with replies. Asher read me right. He'd never let an hour or two go by without saying something. A *"Hi cutie," "I'm alive,"* or at least a cynical *"Let's rob a bank."* At least it made me laugh. At least he'd be a good boyfriend. Was he my boyfriend? The term never leave my mouth. Not all at once.

I didn't want anyone else but him, but for now it was easier not to break, should something ever go south. That way, no one was ever too knee-deep in something they didn't want to be in. I was head over heels for the dude, but it didn't mean I wanted my vulnerability out there all the time. As long as Asher didn't exploit that, I was all his.

Asher: *Sweet dreams*

Me: *Can't sleep*

Asher: *Me either... Let's can't sleep together*

* * *

He was probably cheating. It was hard to make sure his eyes were covered and pull him forward at the same time. He was tall enough where it wasn't an easy feat for me, so I opted only to make sure he didn't bump into the wall on the way to my room.

"Why don't you just tell me what it is?"

"Because you're going to laugh. It makes more sense in person." I'd done the honors of setting it up before he got here. Even with proper placement, it didn't look any less silly. "You can open your eyes now."

Asher's smug expression lit up as he examined the pillow

wedge on the middle of my mattress. A silted laugh, followed by a mumbled, "What the fuck?" I plopped down on the bed, pulling one of the pillows apart.

"It's a pillow wedge."

"I know what it is, Teddy. Why is this for us again?"

I took what I remembered from the instruction manual. "It's like a sex wedge. It helps with height differences. You always say you hate getting off the bed just to do doggie-style. With this, my hips would lift so you don't have to." I laid my body out on the higher end of the wedge. It felt like I was in a shorter downward-facing dog position, but I didn't have to hold myself up with my arms.

Asher joined me on the bed, crawling behind me as he held onto my hips. "I guess I can see how something like this is useful. I'm not sure it's worth—" He pulled out his phone, lying on my back and bringing the screen to both our eye-level. Several price ranges came up, none of which he could believe. "A hundred and eight bucks? For a fucking pillow that has, like, two uses?"

"Get up."

We both sat up, and I brought the smaller end to meet the taller pillow in an uneven pyramid. I gestured for him to sit his back on the lower end, and it brought his hips on the higher end. It confused him when I crawled over him facing the opposite direction. But when I tapped his crotch with my lips, he gained full understand. "Okay, I'm listening…"

Up until this point, we'd never successfully 69ed. If I was close enough to him, he was nowhere near a point to do any damage or vice versa. His torso was too long for me to reach him comfortably, and even though he'd often improvise with his fingers, it just wasn't the same.

I flipped through a book of positions provided in the package, and with a little adjustment, Asher managed to stretch out on top of me, staring me face to face.

"We did talk about this. Personally, I get the best view from here," he said, sitting up and pulling my thighs over his hips. He leaned back in and kissed my lips, neck, and face, getting his point across. "But I get to kiss you all over now because I know you like that."

His lips sent me into a fit of giggles, until he drew them closer to mine and our mouths closed in for the kill.

"I wish we could use this right now," he managed to say without taking much time from my lips.

"Why not now?" I asked, hoping the occasion would last more than a moment.

He pulled his mouth from mine, hovering over me, his bleached hair falling in piles over his eyes. "When you told me you had a surprise, I didn't know what it'd be, so I wanted to give my own surprise." He scooted over, resting the back of his head on the pillow.

I took my rightful place on his lap, leaning in for a peck. "Like what?"

"It requires an open mind."

"Damn, what is it?" Last time something required an open mind, I was licking his face, telling him it tasted like ice cream. I'd need a little more information than that.

"You've mentioned wanting one."

"Now I'm curious."

Asher hoisted me up as he stood and placed me firmly on my feet. "You usually need an appointment for this kind of thing, but I know someone. They said they'd hook me up."

We didn't take much time at my place to rest before he convinced me a short ride downtown was the only way to claim my gift. I knew my way downtown well, but he had to direct me to the little hole-in-the-wall spot he was so eager to get me to. When we got there, it made more sense.

He'd taken me to a tattoo parlor. I'd always wanted a tattoo. Everyone seemed to have one but me. I wasn't as brave as Asher who had a half-sleeve on one arm, a full sleeve on the other, and a load of others everywhere else. I wasn't ready to have my body covered in them. His were so a part of him, he wore them with an elegance that was an extension of him. I wanted something with that feel, but from just one or two.

It was a small place not far from Little Havana. It hadn't been his first, but since then he'd researched better tattoo artists and didn't trust anyone but an artist who went by the moniker MacGyver. Apparently they could do *anything* with an ink gun.

"See anything you like?" Ash and I studied the walls of sketches. I was drawn to anything cutesy, but I decided against living with designs like that forever.

"Nervous?" Asher asked, taking my silence for fear.

"I don't know what to expect. Does it hurt?" He wasn't the right person to ask because he had a high threshold for pain. I didn't want something too big, but I wanted it to look pretty. I was drawn to an example on the wall of white ink on fair skin. Asher advised against it, since white ink faded quicker and didn't show up as much on darker skin like mine. He told me if I absolutely wanted a white tattoo, the best bet would be to allow a black tattoo to heal and paint white over it, since a fresh tattoo just absorbed the ink.

"This is all so much information!"

"You'll like it, I promise. I'm just curious where you want it, though."

I didn't have a lot of time to think, but I'd considered options in the past. "I was thinking an ankle or a foot tattoo."

Asher's face stretched into a clown-like grin, his fingers straightening his messy quiff. "You must be trying to drive me insane."

"Why?"

"Because I love placements there. But it's going to be sore for a few days, so I can't do anything about it."

Which is why I wanted one there. I knew Ash had a thing for feet. I wanted one on my back, too, but I was still feeling things through since Ash mentioned I had to be careful sleeping on it or it'd break.

I didn't know what I was expecting from MacGyver, but it definitely wasn't a five-foot-tall androgynous Latinx. They reminded me a little of that cutie who played Sam on *Scream Queens* (figures the only Asian chick would get got). They were even Cuban like me. There was too much Brooklyn in their accent to confuse them for a Miami native, but their Spanish was reminiscent of someone born here. They spoke Spanish better than I did.

"¿Que bola asere?" they said in a rich, creamy voice.

"Ahí, voy tirando."

MacGyver laughed and probed with questions on what I wanted to get. "¿Sabes lo que quieres?"

I went on to explain that I wanted two, but Ash was only paying for one. This made them curious.

"¿Es tu chillo?" trying to see if they were my man or not. Nosy, but cool. I almost felt bad Asher was just sitting there, waiting for us to speak English so he could join the conversation. He needed a Spanish lesson ASAP.

It took almost two hours, but when I decided on a family of feathers on top of my foot and a trail of small stars on my shoulder, I didn't regret my choice. My skin was raw and red around the surface, but I'm sure it'd look awesome when the swelling went down. The sensation on my foot was a little intense. I walked with a limp from the register to my car, hopping into my front seat. Asher's hand brushed across my right thigh, smoothing over my skin. His palm was so warm, the heat transferred, sending tingles from my thigh to my knees. The moment was ruined when his phone rang, and my dumb ass told him to answer it.

"Yo…" His posture and expression changed, as his eyebrows furrowed and he rubbed the side of his face. "That shit was tonight? … I'd have to see first. … I don't wanna just say yes. Can

I hit you up later? … I had something to do." Even before he hung it up, I knew it was Reggie.

"What was that about?"

"He wanted me to hit up some party with him. He asked me last month, and back then I was down, but obviously there was no this." He gestured between us. "So…"

"He can't go by himself? Why does he need you there so bad?"

Asher leaned back in the passenger seat, covering and rubbing his face. "I'm kind of his wingman for shit like this." That didn't surprise me. It was only a few months back at that club Heat that I'd bumped into Asher and Reggie *happened* to appear out of nowhere. "He's trying to hook up with this chick who doesn't go anywhere without her friend. The chick's feeling me, but she's not really my type. Basically, the only way he can get up with this girl is if I keep the other one company. And he'll probably think something's up if I don't."

"It's not my job to tell you you can't go."

"I just don't want you to be mad. And it'd solve more problems than one if it worked out."

"Why do you say that?"

"If Reggie is feeling some other girl, he's not worried about you. I feel like I'm getting the better deal. I kind of owe him at least this."

I felt bad, but I didn't think I owed Reggie anything. I just wanted him to be happy. I swallowed my pride, embracing solidarity.

"Okay. I'll just sit home. Bored as ever."

Asher licked his lips, caressing the upper part of my thigh. "I won't have fun if that's what you want."

"Have fun. But we have to figure out a way where all three of us can chill. I hate feeling left out."

* * *

Reggie spent most of the car ride talking about finally getting up with Ari, this Puerto Rican chick whose curves were ridiculous. There wasn't anything wrong with her—I just wasn't attracted to her face. But he did get bragging rights for her ass alone, so it didn't matter. He'd met Ari through her best friend Serena, who met through me.

Serena was cool, but she seemed like a good girl *trying* to be bad. She was cute—she just never seemed herself around me. Most people would probably kick me for saying this, but for a pretty girl, she wasn't that interesting. We were cool when we saw each other at parties, but other than that, I'd never crossed that line. She seemed like the clingy type.

The party was smaller than I thought, but sick. It made entertaining Serena more awkward, but there was plenty of beer and weed to keep me stimulated. Reggie flirted his ass off with Ari across the room. She didn't even seem put off by him kissing her skin or touching her in places I wouldn't want someone I was with to be touched. I was surprised I was even paying attention. Every time my phone went off, I checked it just to make sure it wasn't Teddy.

It must've looked rude because Serena excused herself, prompting Ari to follow her. When Ari returned, Serena wasn't with her, and she seemed to give Reggie an earful. When he approached me, I had a feeling I knew what it'd be about.

"Ash, let me holla at you for a second."

I played dumb until we were outside, when I offered him a smoke.

"What's good with you and Serena?"

"We're cool. But I'm helping you out. I'm just not interested. That's all."

"I don't know," Reggie started in a deadpan tone. "From what Ari said, she stay trying to get at you, but you always seem bored."

I was more distracted than bored. Every time my phone vibrated, it was habit to reach for it to reply.

"Look like you been on your phone all night."

"I was just planning to meet up with someone."

"Damn, you wifed up?"

"Nah."

"Hubbed up?" Reggie asked for clarification.

"No. It's a chick, but we're not together like that. But she seems like she's feeling me. It's nothing against Serena."

"It's just her?"

"Is that a problem?"

"You just never seem like the type to mess with just one person."

"Shit changed." My voice cracked in a laugh. I should've prepared myself for the next question because he'd always ask.

"What is she?"

I don't know why either of us had to know. It wasn't important. It was just habit to want to picture what the girl might look like with a little imagination. I'd have to be vague. Teddy's stats were very specific.

"She's Black."

"You smash?"

I shouldn't have smiled. It gave away my answer whether I wanted to kiss-and-tell or not. "No, but I'm trying to get to know her better. She's cool. Anyway, what's good with you and Ari?" I asked, hoping to change the subject.

"She's interested, but I'm not feeling that she just got out of something. So really this is some rebound shit, and the only reason she wanted to get up." No strings attached, what could be better? "I guess it's cool for now. I'm feeling Teddy more anyway, but she's going through some shit. Figure why not fill my plate until she's ready to talk?"

Yikes. This was not where I thought this conversation would go. Anything I said, anywhere I went with it, could be used against me. It was the best time to come clean with the truth. But…

It was selfish to make that decision without Teddy. I wanted to do it; she wanted to wait. I was respecting her choice. "You have to do you in the meantime."

The patio door opened, and out came Ari and Serena. Ari must've been checking for Reg because she went straight to his side and whispered something in his ear.

"I'mma have to see you a little later, fam. Peace." Reggie exchanged a proper handshake before disappearing inside with Ari. It left me alone with Serena. I'd have to spark up conversation otherwise it'd get boring fast.

"What's up, girl?" I asked, trying to be flirtatious. She was shy, but it hadn't stopped her in the past for being bold enough to ask for my number. She was cute. In between races, not quite Black or White. But I felt like I was the kind of guy she wanted to use to piss off her parents, and it was probably most of my appeal to her.

"Nothing," she whined back. She hid behind a nervous smile, the kind that convinced me I was too much for her. "I guess they found something to do, though."

"Hope your girl isn't that good. Reggie be on that stalker shit," I joked, glad to get the first genuine smile from her all night. But that smile disappeared the minute my phone went off and I took it out my pocket.

She raised an eyebrow in my direction, airing out her suspicions. "Lucky person, I guess."

"My bad. Not trying to be rude."

"It's cool if you have somewhere to be. You seem distracted. You have to be. Especially at a place with half-naked girls walking around thirsty for your attention."

"Serena, my eyes don't gloss over that shit. Trust me, I see you. I'm just…feeling things out with someone, and I don't want to fuck it up if that makes any sense." I know no girl wanted to hear you talk about another girl, but after a bout of awkward small talk, she asked me about Teddy. How long I'd liked her? What did I like about her? Was she good at making me laugh?

It wasn't the way I thought our last conversation would go, but she even gave me tips on what Teddy might like, even if they weren't things Serena liked herself. When we finally went inside, we talked for nearly a half-hour about what she liked, what she looked for in someone. She kept hinting with comments *"like you,"* and she liked things about me for the right reasons. I wish there had been a spark there in the past.

It was running later than I thought things would go. Either Reggie was running a marathon or they were doing more than hooking up, and I didn't want to waste Teddy's entire night waiting on me.

"Is it cool if I book it?" I asked, even though it wasn't Serena's decision to make. She wasn't slighted by the thought and even hugged me goodbye when I went to wait outside.

When Teddy finally pulled up, I made a quick exit, since I wouldn't need a ride from Reggie. If he asked, I'd just tell him she was around and hadn't minded giving me a ride. He knew I wouldn't wait all night. But the car ride was eerily quiet and it didn't sound good. Teddy didn't have anything to worry about, but I had a feeling she needed me to tell her that.

She looked cute. Her hair was already in the little French braids she wore when she didn't feel like twisting her hair all the way through.

"I would tell you everything, but there's really nothing to tell."

Teddy gave most of her attention to the road. She didn't look interested in delving further than that. "I'm not asking because it's none of my business," she said with uncertainty in her voice.

It was later than I'd planned on leaving, but I was prepared to make up for it. "I seriously spent thirty-five minutes talking to that girl about you if that helps. She didn't look too happy about it either." I hoped my weak attempt at a joke would help, but

Teddy continued on in silence. I'd better get used to this in case I ever pissed her off. "Are you really not going to talk the entire car ride?"

I unbuckled my seatbelt, reaching over to tickle her legs, tracing kisses over the thigh closest to me. A little nibble and a few sloppy kisses finally got her to open up. "Asher, stop being annoying."

"I guess that's a start." I wasn't about to let her go an entire car ride without saying anything. "If you're mad, you can tell me. If you can't, who can you tell?"

"I'm not mad. I just… I'm gonna look corny when you get to my house. I wouldn't have stayed up if I knew you'd be so long." She rubbed her eyes, a weak attempt to stay awake at the wheel. I offered to drive, and she didn't object. It took pushing the seat a thousand feet back to be comfortable, but her house was just ten minutes away, so I'd bear it. Her eyes were closed when I pulled into her garage, but she just rested them and hadn't fully fallen asleep.

The walk from the car to her building felt short, but it was late and both of us were tired. I wrapped my arms around her once we were in the elevator, and a kiss or two to the neck loosened the clench in her fist.

The guilt was real the minute we stepped in. The place was lit with candles, creating that dope-ass rom-com movie feel. I was whack like that. I knew all the signs.

"Damn, girl, I should've rushed over here if I knew you had it nice like this."

She stripped down to her skivvies, and I didn't waste time doing the same. The candles in her room gave off a low light that made every curve on Teddy's body standout. I almost tripped stepping out my jeans.

"That tattoo looks sexy as fuck on your shoulder." I spun her toward me and brought her into my arms to bring her mouth to mine. Her kiss was light, soft, airy, like she was exhausted but still wanted to try. I didn't plan on keeping her up too long.

I sprawled out over her bed, Teddy on top of me, drinking every ounce of me available to her. "Mmm…you are so beautiful." And I wasn't just saying that because she was half-naked on top of me. I wish she knew how hot she made me. I wanted to make her feel things. Every moment felt too real.

When she asked me to stretch out over the wedge, I knew she meant business. It was just like we'd practiced, too. My hips on the higher end, the rest of me on the lower. Teddy tugged and pulled at my boxers until they were just an afterthought, but I was too busy kissing the back of her thighs to notice. I couldn't ignore the wet of her tongue sliding down my inner thigh, though.

"That feels good." It barely came out as a whisper. I separated her from her panties, and she lifted her body to help me with it. Her scent was so mesmerizing it was like she was begging me to taste her. I kissed the inside of her thigh, and my lips traced in circles closer to the spot that'd make her sing.

I didn't rush. To make sure she was even ready for me, I just ran my tongue over her sweet folds and flicked the hood covering her clit to wake it up. She was busy on the other end, smoothing her wet hand down the length of me, while her mouth encircled around the head of my cock. I smacked her ass as her body jumped, and her thighs widened to make room for me to taste her.

I flicked her clit, light and gentle, and her inner thighs clamped down on my face. It was so exposed at this point, it was easy to lap it up with my entire tongue. I didn't know what the hell she was doing on her end, but each time she swirled her tongue around the head of my dick, I bit my lip, holding my breath at the toe-curling sensations. My fingers dug into her thighs as I urged her to slow down.

"Relax, baby. You're gonna make me…" But I couldn't finish the sentence.

Her small fingers took turns sliding up and down my shaft, all while her lips and tongue stimulated the head. I wasn't new to the sensation, but the different angle made it all the more incredible. It took everything I had to please her at the same time. She was working my body like she wanted to pull my cord first. I really wanted to do other stuff on this damn thing, but she knew how weak my body was when it came to good head.

My body spasmed in quick, rhythmic pulses I could only articulate in swears. My heavy breathing quickly calmed down as she turned to straddle my lap. Our mouths drew each other in, drowning in each other's sloppy kisses. Her body was so soft against mine as my hands spread all over her back, ass, and thighs.

"Sit on my face, Teddy," I said between kisses. "So you can come all over my face."

She didn't stop kissing me or rubbing her body against mine because she knew how good it felt.

"Can you do that for me?"

Her sighs breathed into me, and she opened her eyes and peered into mine. When I fell into her eyes, I fell into darkness. I loved getting lost in that darkness. My hands grazed over her hips until she crawled up to my neck and was inches from my face. I was done teasing. I kissed her outer lips and spread them apart, exploring each shape and curve with my tongue.

She winced, reaching down to caress my face. Her face went into a grimace as I flattened my tongue against her soaking wet folds. I hummed against her body, lapping up every bit of her, watching her squirm and grind up against my face. The pitch of her moans, the bite at her lip, the shake in her inner thighs, all had the makings of getting me hard all over again.

She grabbed fistfuls of my hair and wore a pained grimace before she opened her eyes. She asked if I wanted her to come all over my face, followed by some freaky shit in Spanish I couldn't understand. She matched the rhythm of her hips to the rhythm of my tongue as her grip grew tighter and her body trembled against mine, panting her surrender.

I lifted the hood of her clit, lightly sucking on the sensitive area still throbbing against my lips. She begged me to stop, but not before I had to a chance to plant kisses all over her delectable pussy. She was too weak in the knees to fight that, but managed to crawl off my face as I slid off the wedge. She pushed it off the bed, pulling the sheet over her body and mine, and the only thing hitting us now was sleep.

# CHAPTER SEVEN

**Teddy**

It'd only been a few hours, but my tattoos were still raw from yesterday. It was going to require a bunch of lukewarm showers and a break from my usual scrub, but I'd survive. I honestly couldn't wait for them to set in. They were pretty sweet when some of the swelling went down.

My interview was in a few hours, so it'd require a ton of pinch and primping to make sure I looked the part. I picked out a white button-up but, for some personality, a knee-length emerald skirt and cheetah flats to match. A part of me hoped I didn't get it. Me, Reggie, and Asher all working together? It sounded cool on paper, but what would it be like if we told him?

I tried not to think about it. I needed a job more than my comfort level working with my friends. Six interviews with no success? The sooner a place hired me, the sooner I could evaluate which semester I'd be going back.

I passed my mirror on the way to the bathroom and was grateful I hadn't forgot to stretch out my hair. I'd probably pay for not using a wrap or silk pillowcase, but it was only a day. I planned on wearing it in a puff anyway, and I scoured my place for some broken pantyhose.

I'd woken up in the middle of the night to blow all my candles out, otherwise one wrong move and my apartment was toast. But the air was still coated with the smell of vanilla and cinnamon, lingering in my room and hallway, reminding me how silly I'd felt waiting up.

I was too distracted to worry about it, though. Somewhere around this room had to be some broken stockings. Seemed like I found everything but them. A crumbled dust jacket. A half-open pack of highlighters. A Polaroid 600. A dictionary. Basically nothing of use to me.

Asher tossed around on my bed, passed out from last night. He'd probably go ballistic if I took his picture in his sleep, which motivated me to do it more. I was into that vintage Polaroid look, so I had one for more interesting moments. The sound of a few snaps must've startled him because he poked his head out, burning his intense gaze through my skin.

He mumbled "C'mere" in a drunken state. No one liked their picture taken that vulnerable, especially with a friends-with-benefits, so I assumed there would be a fight over the camera. When I approached, I held the camera far away from him, but all he did was kiss me on the cheek and bury his head back under the sheet.

I finally found a broken stocking and rushed for the bathroom to secure my hair. I unbraided it, unfluffing each coil for the most shape I could get. The broken pantyhose was the only thing my hair didn't break when I wore it this way, and I hid the lines under strays. Asher stumbled in, asking if he could use my shower.

I'd already taken one before he woke up, so he'd be at it alone. But at least I could be a perv while he did. Once he was clean and out of the shower, he had a good hour before work and felt a different set of clothes were in order. Reggie'd be there, and he was just that nosy to notice him wearing the clothes he'd been in last night.

From the short ride to his place, he'd just about to got to the door to his apartment building, when he stopped and asked, "Do you want to come up?"

I thought about the last time Reggie and me were over. Asher disappearing to say something privately to his roommate. "That depends…what did you tell your roommate?"

Asher dropped his face in his hand, trying to hide the smile that formed. "You really wanna know?" I nodded. "I said we were both feeling you, but I was feeling you more. And I wanted to use his PS4 because I just wanted a reason to be around you."

I took it as an acceptable answer and followed him up. Even though he lived with people, they worked opposite times of the day, so outside of two shared bathrooms, it wasn't dangerously messy in their apartment. I'd never been in his room until today, but aside from some piles of clothes, he was cleaner than I thought him to be.

"My bad with all the clothes. I swear, when you come over again, it'll look way better than this," he said with a laugh.

I examined his book collection and noticed it hadn't grown much since the last time, but it was still bigger than nothing. He was already halfway through *The Fifth Season* based on the position of his bookmark. I'd read it in, like, 5.2 seconds, so I was butt-hurt he was weening it.

When I got tired of standing, I moved toward the bed. "Before I sit, anything I should know?"

"Eff you, Teddy, my bed is clean."

"Just checking." His full-size mattress seemed small in comparison to mine. He took up so much room, I had a hard time imagining him getting much sleep with anyone else on it with him. He changed into something quick and light enough for an eight-and-a-half hour shift, wiggling his legs through a slim pair of skinny jeans.

"I just love how you wear boxer-briefs instead of boxers. Boxers are so played out."

He looked himself over, pulling a belt over his hips. "To be honest, I prefer boxers. They're roomier. But these jeans are tight as fuck. It looks stupid trying to stuff them in tight-ass jeans."

"You could always wear baggier jeans."

"Then I'd look mad nineties. Who even wears baggy jeans anymore?"

Hmm…any dude over forty. Any dude that just got out of jail. And any dude that didn't listen to hip-hop made after 1998. I kind of liked skinny jeans on dudes. It seemed made for leaner bodies like his.

Asher left the room for a second and returned with a bowl of cereal.

"You're really goning to pour yourself a bowl when you know you owe me a box of cereal?"

His warm smile lit up his face. "That's right. I owe you some Oat O's. My bad. I can bring you some after work."

"Do you want a ride?"

Asher took several bites before answering with a full mouth. "If I get one from you, I'll either have to bus it home or get a ride back. Plus Reggie's working. In the instance Reggie might be *just* around, he's not stupid. He can put two and two together if we keep giving him reasons to. Which is why we should just tell him."

"I know we should. I just don't want him to flip."

"Trust me. The longer we wait, the more he'll flip. A few weeks is easier to get over than a few months."

"Well, why don't you ask him how his night was first? I'd feel a little better about it knowing he's not even thinking about me like that."

Asher shifted, leaning on a dresser in the corner of the room. "If you're worried about that, then you have a lot to worry about."

"Why? Did he say anything?"

"Just that he just wanted to give you time and space because of what you were going through. I was *this* close to telling him, but I figured you'd get mad."

I don't think I saw it the way Ash did. He was around Reggie more, so it affected him more. Maybe I was afraid I'd lose more than a guy I used to know. I'd lose a friend, too. I didn't have many lying around, so the selfish part of me wanted to keep each one I had.

"I'm going to ask when I see him at work. You still got your interview right?" I nodded. "Then we should tell him today."

I didn't know who'd lead on a conversation like "I've been kicking it to a girl you used to be hung up over, we still down for ball later?" but he was more confident than me. If he thought it'd be easier to get it over with, who was I to argue?

* * *

*Asher*

"Girl, you're short." I'd counted this drawer three times, not including the two times Deana, one of the front-end supervisors, confirmed by the time I got there.

"This would be my second write-up. I can't afford to have that over a fifty-cent difference."

"It's actually a five dollar and fifty cents difference Amber. I don't know what you want me to tell you. I wasn't at your register. Only you were." Nothing sucked more than the amount of callouts and shortages around this place. I wish I could say it only happened once in a while, but we didn't have high turnover for nothing. Four out of five shifts made you want to knock someone out. I probably would've quit a long time ago if I hadn't become full-time.

Regular check versus being broke? Not really a contest. The job was just annoying. Being the assistant cash office manager wasn't a hard job. It just meant managing a whole bunch of lazy teenagers and folks who thought they were too pretty to ring. I wasn't going to lie. A bunch of them *were* cute. But not that cute. Especially dealing with it every damn shift.

I friggin' flew to the time clock every break. Fifteen, thirty—shit, even five minutes away from this job was better than being on the floor. I was hungry anyway, and Deana hooked me up, hitting some sub place on her break so I didn't have to waste mine getting something to eat.

I was already in the breakroom by the time Reggie walked in, talking to someone over the phone. I didn't bother him, especially since me and Teddy planned on explaining ourselves sometime before one of our shifts was over or before her interview, whichever came first. But he seemed more anxious than usual, so much that when he hung up the phone, I reached out to see if things were all right.

"You okay, man?"

"I can't concentrate. I don't think I can work today," he said in a panicked state.

"Why? What happened?"

"I just got a phone call that someone hit my grandmother's car. I'm her emergency contact, but they won't tell me if she's hurt or whether she went to the hospital as a precaution. And I don't know whether I'm getting worked up for nothing or—"

"Yeah, yeah, I get it." I didn't know a lot about how Reggie grew up, but I knew there wasn't anyone more important to him than his grandmother. "What are you going to do?"

Reggie shrugged. "I don't know. I need to talk to Lanier," he said, referring to the produce manager.

"I'm sure she's all right, man."

Reggie nodded, rubbing his hands together. Clearly he didn't believe that.

*"Asher to the front of the store."*

Oh my god. What the hell did these people want? Didn't they know I was on break?

"Yo, I swear to god, Deana acts like she can't function when she's by herself," I joked, forgetting Reggie was still a bundle of nerves. "Dude, you're friggin' shaking. Why don't you just go find Lanier? I doubt you'll do much working worrying yourself like that."

"You're right," Reggie said and left the breakroom. I stuffed my sub in the bag it came in, dusted myself off, and walked to the front.

"You know I'm on break, right?" I asked with my arms stretched out, waiting for someone to answer me back. Deana pointed out to Joyce, the front end manager looking for me.

"I'll need you in the CBL room at twelve-thirty," she said walking by me, not waiting for an answer. Which meant I didn't have a choice, whatever it was. I noticed Reggie clocking out, and I made my way toward him before he went far. "Find anything out?"

"No. But my sister is picking me up. So I'll find out more."

"Hope she's all right, man," I said, taking him in an outstretched hug. It was just then I noticed Teddy sitting at the entrance. How hadn't I not noticed how funny she looked in business-casual clothes? She must've heard us talking or something because she seemed eager to approach. We were supposed to talk to Reggie, crack a few jokes—soften the blow a little before we told him about us. Especially in case she started working here.

But I only had Reggie's back to me a split second before I signaled for Teddy to abort the whole thing. She caught on quick. She ducked into a cash lane before Reggie got a good look at her as he walked out of the store. That was close. That did *not* work out how I planned it. How was I supposed to predict his grandmother would get in a car accident?

We were going to tell him. But I didn't think this very second was a good time. Fuck us, right?

Teddy walked back to the front of the store, and Joyce came

up to her and lead her away. I didn't even get to the middle of the store before Joyce approached me again.

"You in or still out?"

"Still out."

"Well, when you're in, I got that interview in the CBL room. Don't forget."

* * *

Sigh. Why today? Nothing else was going as planned, so why should this? That regional manager who usually came every ninety days to help with this kind of thing? Miraculously unavailable. Just great.

I wouldn't say I hated interviews. It got me off the floor for thirty minutes if I was lucky, and if they were pushing for a front-end position, I'd get to see what I was working with. But I didn't like that it meant I'd have someone's future employment in my hand. Especially since I wasn't the model employee myself.

Add on that it was one of my best friends? Made for interesting times.

I wish the CBL room had cameras. Just the look on Teddy's face when I opened the door was priceless. A tight-lipped pout that accompanied a scrunched nose and eyebrows that gathered at the middle of her face. I shouldn't have laughed, but she made it too easy.

"Really, Ash?"

I sat down, laying a few folders and her application on the table between us. "Okay, jokes aside," I started, lowering my voice, despite there being little chance that people would hear me. "The person that was supposed to interview you? They had to leave earlier than planned, so you're stuck with me."

She rolled her neck, letting out a sigh of relief, more confident in her posture than she had been. "I'm about to get this job."

I laughed and leaned back in my chair. Just because there was a slight conflict of interest didn't mean I was going to just give it to her. I was almost a little relieved we were in that in-between friends stage. If she were my full-on girlfriend, I'd be too afraid to hire her.

"Teddy, I can't just give you the job. I have to *actually* interview you. And your answers have to be somewhat favorable for me to justify offering it to you."

Teddy sunk into her chair. "For a damn grocery store?"

"Yes, for a grocery store, Ms. I've Never Had a Job Before." Just from our time as friends, you could tell she was spoiled as hell. Never worked and expected getting a job to be easy. "So I already know you've never worked. I'm not even gonna ask you about that. I'm about to ask you questions, so please don't say the wrong thing. I really don't want to *not* hire you."

"Am I allowed to ask questions?"

"Do they pertain to the job?" Her eyes burned back at me, like she was trying to blaze straight through my skin, and I laughed. "Okay, shoot."

"Say I got hired as a cashier." She gestured back and forth with her hands dancing around the air. "Would that make you my manager?"

I loosened the collar of my shirt. Valid question. "Check it like this. There's a front-end manager, an assistant manager, a bunch of supervisors, and right under that are cashiers. Supervisors are kind of like head cashiers. I'm just the assistant manager. I can hire you, fire you, clock you in and out, but technically I wouldn't be your manager. At best, I'd be like…you're head supervisor?"

"So does that mean—"

"No, it means I'm still interviewing you."

She nodded, satisfied with my answer.

"Just so you know, you look like a dweeb. But not bad, you're totally selling it," I joked. She stuck up her middle finger. This interview was about to be lit.

"Okay, so, Theodora King, tell me about yourself."

"What about? The fact that I need a job?"

I gently shook my head, holding in a laugh, but failing miserably. "Teddy, you're making my job so hard right now. Just tell me something you're ambitious about. Something I can write down."

At least that sparked something out of her. She mentioned how her parents' professions inspired her to help people, and I made sure to write that she was bilingual in big bold letters across her application. Could never have enough of that in Miami.

I asked about her goals for the next five years and made sure to emphasize "education-oriented" when she talked about finishing her undergrad. I wasn't so convinced at the answers she gave during the stress questions, but I was positive she'd deal with customers better if she were actually doing so, instead of giving her pretend scenarios on how she'd handle things.

"So…why should I hire you?"

She brought her hands together in a clap. "Because I need a job, Ash."

I shook my head again and fought giggles. "You are so lucky this room don't have cameras. I'm going to ignore that entire answer and ask you again. *Why* should *I* hire *you?*"

Teddy sunk into her chair again, like she was tired of being asked questions.

I laughed. "You better act like you want this."

A groan that vibrated the table came out as she sat back up, counting each answer on each finger. "I guess I'm…friendly"—people person, check—"I show up on time"—punctual, check. Her eyes widened as she searched for the right thing to say. "I don't know…desperate?"

I marked "reliable" on her application and moved on.

"They don't do drug tests here, do they?"

"You think if they did I'd be assistant manager?" The chain of stores was too small and turnover too high for them to waste dishing one hundred dollars a pop for an employee to quit or get terminated a month later. I handed her a new hire employee packet that had the paperwork I'd hated signing when I'd been a new hire some-odd years ago.

"I'm probably going to regret this, but since you have open availability, I'm goint to offer you a position. I'll be honest, I don't think you'll last a month." I held out my hands defensively, as she peered through me with piercing eyes. "But in my defense, I hope I'm wrong. We'll see."

She took the folder and the pen I forked over and let out a sigh of relief. "I'm so glad I don't have to look anymore."

"Why don't you save that enthusiasm for your first day, okay?"

CHAPTER EIGHT

**Asher**

There was only one day between me and the beginning of the month. Want to guess when I got my only day off? Joyce knew what she was doing when she printed out that schedule. Can't complain though. Who really wanted to work the day before the work week of the store's busiest time? I'd have next to no days off once the first hit, but the overtime made it worth it Just left me with little to do up until then.

Teddy: Wyd👀

Surfing the web for porn the last twenty-five minutes probably wasn't the best answer. But I admitted that, she'd want to know what I looked up. I had a wide taste of shit worth banging one out to. Most times, I was pretty 50/50 with attraction. It wasn't uncommon to feel 70/30 sometimes—or even 90/10 depending on my mood.

Things only changed if I were trying to be with someone, and when I define be with someone, I mean we both have side flings.

Right now? I was 100/0 with whatever Teddy had to offer. Porn was cool when you were bored, but if this was a come through text, I'd pretty much fly over her house in exchange for the real thing.

Me: *Not much. Hbu.*

Teddy: *Had training this morning. Didn't see you. Doing hair.*

Me: *Teasing much...*

Teddy: *What are you talking about* 😗

Me: *I want to see you.*

Teddy: *Oh yeah?*

Leave it to Teddy to make me beg for her time. Which with how horny I was, had no problem doing.

Me: *I want to kiss you. All over. Let me come over so you can be bad with me...*

Teddy: 😗

Me: *Is that a nice-no?*

Teddy: *You can come over. But I was planning on heading out soon.*

Me: *Where?*

Teddy: *Drop off some books.*

Me: *Let me know if you need a ride buddy* • •

Teddy: *Boy just come over.*

Me: OMW

Did I really need to be told twice? The only internal debate I did have was whether or not to bring a helmet. Teddy didn't live that far from me, especially on bike. I hated lugging it around if I didn't have to. I decided against the helmet, but grabbed a hoodie since Teddy's apartment actually had central air conditioning and was on the road in five minutes.

If there hadn't been traffic, I would've made it to her place in less than ten. Once I was across the street from her luxury apartment building, I drove around until I could find a park that didn't require a meter. With just a street down, a few hundred yards away, I made my way back to her building as she buzzed me in upstairs.

By the time I reached her apartment door, she'd left the door open so I could slip right inside. When I finally did run into

Teddy, she was in parked in front of her mirror, brushing a small bunch of loose hair.

"Hey, babe." As I rested my hands on her shoulders and reached into to kiss the side of her neck where her hair was braided.

"Hi, Ash." She replied back, with just enough attention to meet my lips in a light peck before I collapsed on her bed. There was a quarter of her scalp that wasn't braided, and I didn't want to bother her since I didn't know how long that usually took.

"Why do you use fake hair when you already have hair?" When Teddy stretched her hair, it was like—massive. Maybe I was too much of a guy to understand, but I'd always assumed extensions were for short hair. By the pause in between the sound Teddy's mouth made, a combination of a laugh and a sigh, I assumed she didn't intend on answering.

"Ghana braids don't look as full unless you add hair."

There was a book on her bed, that I'd tossed between my hands a few times before I threw it back on the mattress. "Sounds heavy."

"It's not. I use the soft braiding hair. As long as I don't get it wet, it's fine. I would've done this last week, but I had that interview. I didn't want to come with my hair braided."

All of a sudden, that book on her mattress became interesting again. "I always notice girls do that. Come to the interview one way. Then the day they start—"

"Well, if I'd known you were interviewing me, I wouldn't have cared." She joked, interrupting. She grabbed a thin strand of hair and folded it between her cornrowed crown. "This close to summer, I'm really not trying to do my hair every single day." She added.

"Well, it looks nice." Which wasn't a lie. I liked what her hair looked like in cornrows, or french braids, or any other style that required her hair braided against the scalp. She was not round the way by any means, but they made her look like she was. Plus, they didn't get in the way of anything—on top of being fucking sexy.

Sitting in front of her mirror in a robe brought back memories of soap operas in my childhood. I almost laughed at the comparison.

"Have you ever watched Dynasty?" I should've been bored with the book on her bed, but I kept flipping through it, like I was looking for pictures or something. Teddy pivoted on her stool, however briefly, to show her confusion. "No. Why would I?"

"Heh, doing your hair. In front of a mirror, like a little diva and shit. It reminds me of this show I used to watch."

Teddy brought her attention back to the mirror to bring the braid down until it required the loose hair. "What was it about?"

"I don't fucking know? It was a soap about rich White people with nothing better to do than dislike each other. I'm surprised you never heard of it. It was popular as fuck in the 80's."

Teddy's voice broke in a light laugh. "Why were you watching an 80's soap? Doesn't sound like your thing."

"Don't act like your parents never hogged the tv and shit. My mom's disabled, so she didn't really work. So she just watched her stories all day. She'd chop your hand off if you turned it, so if you weren't watching, there was no tv."

Teddy didn't reply for a long while, as she got closer to the ends where her hair met, and the synthetic hair started. "Now, I'm curious,"

"About what?"

"Your folks. You never talk about them."

Never talked about them, or never wanted to? "I don't know. We don't have the best relationship. My folks are weird. They have to be like, dying for me to go over to see them." Interestingly enough, just a twenty minute drive to Allahpattah separated me from my immediate family, which compiled of my parents, older sister and 3 year-old niece.

"You must've been a problem child." Teddy giggled, half

expecting me to laugh with her. I guess it wasn't for me to say whether I was or not. But it'd always been a constant push and pull with my parents.

"Look, I only gave what I got." My parents were obnoxious, rude, and 99% of them time spoke with no filter. My dad claimed he just "told it like it was", whatever the hell that meant.

Giving it more thought, I was more than a handful. Most of it came from how my dad treated me, and how my mother never defended me against it.

We definitely had a love/hate relationship—We hated everything about each other, and loved very little. But my dad had always been uncomfortable with my sexuality, especially when he caught me kissing a guy. I was twelve. It was one of those moments that should've been a good memory, considering it'd been my first. But ever since, he'd always refer to me as "his little fairy" and joked that technically he had two daughters.

I'd always been attracted to women, but it just so happened I was just as attracted to men. But after that? I didn't explore my attraction fluidly until I got to high school. It wasn't as if I were afraid to, I just…

My father always made me feel like less of a man because I was different than him. So while everyone can comfortably label themselves proudly, I've just never been into labels because of it.

I could've brought Megan Fox through the front door, and my dad would've still cracked jokes that she was my make-up artist, stylist or something else equally stupid.

He'd never outright said he hated me, but I'd be lying if I said I'd felt the love, either. "I barely get along with my sister. But at least she's popped out someone I actually like in my family. I'm not as family oriented as you Ted."

"Who said I was family oriented?"

I couldn't imagine her not being close to her family. They supported her, in more ways than one. "Your parents must love you more than mine love me. They're definitely not fitting the bill for my rent, or any other bills I have."

"You mistake guilt for love." Teddy's voice lowered to a cold lack of expression, as she concentrated on jelling the loose hair near her crown to her scalp. Now that she mentioned it, she didn't talk about her parents much either. Shit, I wish mine loved the way hers did. They definitely had a lot to be guilty for.

I didn't debate it long before Teddy grabbed a change of clothes and excused herself from them room. In just a few short weeks, I could tell her confidence level was lacking. I didn't think there was a strong need to be, but I couldn't control how she felt about herself.

I knew I was biased, but she was beautiful. I'm a guy, so I was cultured to focus on what visually attracted me first, then to worry about everything else later. Her inner geek, resilience and go with the flow demeanor were what actually made me fall for her, but it was a complete lie to say I wasn't highly attracted to her. But trying telling her that.

At least she knew what attracted me to her. I was decently attractive. I didn't think I wasn't. I wasn't Brad Pitt, but he was no me either. I was comfortable in my own skin, I just didn't know what attracted Teddy when it came to me.

It all became an afterthought once Teddy returned to her room. She came back fully dressed, but my mind went to different places once she came into view. She looked good, but it wasn't just that. I don't know whether it'd been a coincidence, considering the original reason I'd come in the first place, but she was sucking on a popsicle. My mind didn't stay in clean places, considering what I knew her mouth was capable of, and it'd been the first time since I got here, that I'd been motivated to hop off her bed and invade her personal space.

Wrapping my arms around her waist always seemed effortless. The scent and sight of her skin called to me, as I kissed the creak of her neck, rubbing the skin on the back of her hand that held the popsicle.

"Do you want one?" Teddy asked, pretending to be nonchalant. It was hot, but it wasn't that hot.

"Mmm…do I want one what?" I asked, tilting her face to the side in a kiss. She was still trying to play it off, but she wasn't fooling anyone.

"There's more in the fridge." She continued off and on, as I leaned in to steal her lips, watching her take turns between me and the popsicle.

"I'll just have a combination of you, and what you're doing to that popsicle." The first time she betrayed her demeanor since I got here. She giggled from the time it took to move from the threshold of her bedroom door to her mattress. She made me watch her eat that entire popsicle, and all it did was refresh my memory of what it'd been like when her mouth and my body became better acquaintances.

It wasn't long before Teddy climbed on top of me, lips joined to mine. Grabbing her hips, I pulled her close to me, while her hands reached out for the belt of my jeans. I wanted to to tease her in the time it'd take for me to get hard again, but when I reached in between her thighs it appeared I didn't need to.

"Damn, that shit's already wet." I said proudly, rubbing my fingers against her folds. Her small hands worked their way into my jeans, as she stretched her fingers against the inside of my thigh. Teddy felt far away without her lips against mine, but the feel of her touching me made want to reach in and bite the lower part of her lip.

"Mmm…that feels good." My breath caught under a low laugh. Teddy stopped herself midway, grabbing both sides of my face to kiss me. Painful as it was, I pulled away from her, eager lips concentrated along her jaw, face, until I eventually ended up kissing her neck.

A soft moan vibrated against me. She wanted it to—to feel

good. But she pushed me onto my back again, lips leaning in to explore my own. Teddy drove me crazy when she slid her tongue between my lips. One of my many weaknesses. It probably fair to say I liked my kisses like blowjobs. Nasty, wet and sloppy. Leave it to Teddy to be a master at all three.

Between alternating whose tongue got more attention, with a bit of adjustment, she'd managed to pull my shorts down just enough and slip a condom onto me. I slipped her panties to one side, as a combination of her easing onto me and my cock burying deep inside her, ensued.

"God damn, girl. That pussy just open up."

In the last week or two, we'd benefited greatly from that stupid pillow wedge she bought. The game was changed once I could fuck her in any position I wanted, but her being on top of me was a classic. As if watching my dick disappear inside her wasn't enough, I got to touch and feel all the places I couldn't once the role was reversed.

Don't get me wrong, missionary was still fun and all. Can't say that I didn't prefer to be in the driver's seat most times. But the way Teddy took control gave me the opportunity to multitask. Who'd want to screw that up?

Maneuvering her out that bra wasn't as easy, especially since she guarded it like it was Pandora's Box. But I made every attempt to, especially since they didn't look much different to me. They were still the same breasts I licked, sucked and tit fucked whenever she'd let me. Plus it was more important to me how it felt to her, than how they looked. Which was still fucking amazing.

The challenge was getting to them. Not to mention being distracted by the rhythm of her bouncing up and down on my hips. Her body felt way too inviting for me to keep up at that pace but I had to smack the outside of her behind catch her attention. "Slow down, baby. I didn't jack off at all before I got here. Keep that up and you'll be mighty disappointed."

Teddy laughed me off before leaning into kiss me. "I like it when you're vulnerable. You're so cute when you can't help it."

"Take off this bra, and I'll show you how vulnerable you can be." Reaching in to kiss the skin above her chest. She arched her body away from mine, readjusting the straps like she expected me to tug at them. I sat up on my elbows, with a grin so big I'm sure Teddy could see all my teeth. "You don't want me to, because you know it'll just make you sing," I joked.

"You're talking a lot of shit to the person in control of your dick right now." She said, pushing my back against the mattress again.

"Teddy, you are one flip away from your legs up over my shoulders. Don't get cute."

"Oh, yeah?" Teddy taunted, increasing the speed of her rise-and-fall hips from mine.

"Now you're playing dirty." I dug my fingers into the skin on each side of her thighs, but it didn't stop her. I didn't like to come before Teddy if I didn't have to, but my body was too responsive to how good she felt, and she wasn't playing fair.

"You like that?" Teddy moaned back. She'd studied my expression enough to know when I was on the verge of exploding. Now she was just tormenting me. I had no intention of giving up much of a fight. My steady beating heart was only rivaled by my shortness of breath. All the blood in my body rushed to the single part of me that was difficult to control.

"You are riding that dick," I managed to say through clenched teeth. I was helpless once I got to this point, and I was so close to the point of no return that I ignored my skull banging against the headboard. Every muscle in my body tensed, which brought an intensity to my groin explosive like fireworks. I pulled her body close to mine one last time, smashing her lips with my own.

I felt her chest beat against mine, even through the fabric of the hoodie, as she leaned out and kissed my cheek. Short of breath, she whispered, "Your face is so red right now."

"What'd you expect? You just rode the shit out of me." I replied under a laugh. Teddy leaned in again, with a light peck on the lips before climbing off my lap to readjust her skirt. I was about to throw the condom in her bathroom's trash when Teddy zoomed past me in the hallway to her apartment's front door. She slipped on the sandals facing a box full of books. "Going somewhere?"

When she bent over for the books, she gave a light struggle. It must've been heavy. "Didn't I text you that earlier?"

With my one track mind, who knows? Maybe. I didn't register much of what she'd texted when I was that horny, but I'm sure it had something to do with books. "Something about a bookstore?"

With Teddy's swelling bookcases, her place might've as well have been a bookstore. I can't imagine she's read every single one of them. Probably didn't even put a dent in her bookcase, either. I haven't finished five books since I met Teddy.

"I'm dropping these off at Kendall's."

"For what?"

"They're a new and used book store. There's a really good book exchange there, and I'm not going to hoard books I don't like."

So wait, people just give books they paid for away? "You're just giving them away?"

"No. I'm exchanging them for store credit. So I can in turn, get more books. It's kind of a never ending cycle." A majority of the books didn't look like they'd been read. What was the point of buying books to give them away? "You should let me see if I'd want any of them."

Teddy shrugged, heading back toward her front door. "You can look if you want. You can keep anything you'd actually read. I just wanted to walk and talk. A bunch of places close by a certain time, and I wanted to go to all of them."

There was no debating this. I slipped back into my own shoes, as I followed her into the hall and helped her lock her door. We could've taken our time getting to the elevator—whoever was on the eighth floor took forever playing on it. But it gave me enough time to inspect her box before she got too attached to anything.

Leaning forward over Teddy's shoulders, I reached in to examine the books inside. Cover-wise, they were eye catching. Pretty if that type of thing mattered. I'd only sampled a small piece of her taste in books, but I knew from older editions, attractive covers didn't matter much.

I kissed the back of her neck, as she coiled at the exchange and laughed. "I thought you were looking at the books."

"I am." I defended. It took the elevator nearly three minutes before the door opened, and by then I'd already made my first consideration. "What is *Court of Thorn and Roses?*"

"A corny ass young adult book."

For some reason, she thought I knew what that meant. She even went as far to admit ten out of fifteen of them were young adult, and it was why she was donating them. I continued on with my search until we reached her garage, and she handed me the box. The walk to the car was short in comparison to the winded wait for the elevator. Once I was outside the passenger seat door, I placed the box on the hood, pulling out another book to inquire about. "What is *The Diviners?*"

"Didn't I tell you that box was full of young adult books?" She popped the lock on her end, as I took the box and brought it to the floor once I got inside.

"Is young adult bad or something?"

Technically, no. Or at least from her description of it. It was more an age category than anything, but that normally, it was meant for teenagers unless there was crossover appeal. The term Mary Sue got thrown around so many times, I thought it was a name of one of the books.

The ride was shorter than I thought, so I hadn't even combed through half the box before we were in the parking lot of

Kendall's Book Exchange. I wasn't good at choosing when it came to this kind of thing, so I decided against every book. Best to go off of recommendations.

There only reason I went to bookstores at this point was because of her anyway. Back in February, it'd taken me eight stores and a failed trip to Ebay to find the first editions of books she liked. Lucky for me, Dunbar Old Books over by Coral Terrace had them.

I guess I was dealing with the real world too much to worry about fiction, but I liked that Teddy liked it. It meant I didn't have to drown in a pile of thousands of suggestions I wouldn't like. But boy, I wish I would've known she was one of those shoppers who could live in a bookstore.

When she claimed to want to go to a number of places, what she'd really meant was hours of browsing. Teddy had to go to four bookstores before she was satisfied no place in the area had what she wanted. And she claimed she wasn't a hoarder.

Three Barnes and Nobles later, aisles started looking the same. I don't know how she didn't get exhausted—shit, I was exhausted. If there hadn't been a Starbucks inside, I would've collapsed off the lack of caffeine. But our journey didn't end there. Luckily, she was willing to spend more than just a few minutes at Second Edition Bookshop.

At least they had tons of chairs to sit on, even if they were made for freaking twelve year-olds. I don't think people knew how precious a chair could be, when it actually accommodated you. One can abandon the idea that with long legs, you'll ever fit comfortably in the backseat of a chair, or plane. But even seats at the movies, or swivel chairs at work were uncomfortable if they weren't purchased with long legs in mind.

It was like sitting in a children's chair when you were a regular height, which sounds just as uncomfortable for you as a normal chair felt for me. I was about to stretch my legs a bit, before Teddy approached to sit on my lap. All of a sudden, things got much more comfortable.

"These chairs are fucking low." I shuffled back and forth, attempting to make sitting down more comfortable.

"You think everything is too low." As Teddy stretched two books across her lap.

"I can't believe we've been out for three hours just at bookstores." I thought out loud.

"You know, you didn't have to come. I told you my plans beforehand. I would've dropped you off if I knew you'd be bored." Ah, the taste test. That moment of truth when someone was secretly testing you—just to see if you'd fuck up and say the wrong thing. I studied Teddy's dark brown eyes. There was nothing off base to give what went on in her head away. I just leaned in and brought my lips to hers for a whisper of a kiss.

"Never that."

* * *

Sometimes I didn't know about this girl. I swear, if I didn't love her I'd swear she was a psychopath. I made the mistake of admitting I'd never listened to an audiobook. Hell, I didn't even think they counted. So once we got back to her place, she deemed it her mission to get me hooked on audiobooks.

But if you thought books were dark when you read them, they were even weirder when you listened to them. The idea of audiobooks seemed appealing at first—finishing a book while I wash the dishes? My backlist was bound to shoot up in no time.

Little did I know, that a creepy book was only creepier with narration. I'd give Teddy this—no one was fucking with Octavia Butler. I didn't have to like everything she wrote to feel something, even if it were plain disgust. I just didn't know how much I could take of the audiobook in question.

Stretched out along her queen size bed, between take out and my sudden outbursts, she'd spent two hours trying to catch me up on Parable of The Sower. I burst out laughing every time something crazy happened. This book was an acquired taste, and more violent than I expected. I'm talking body count high as fuck more violent. Once we got to the point of dogs eating babies, I had to tap out for a second.

"What's wrong baby?" Teddy asked, clearly unaffected since she'd already read it.

"Damn Teddy, *are we listening to the same audiobook?*"

"You don't like it?"

"I didn't say that. It's just…this is on some Walking Dead shit. I can't even watch that without constantly checking outside my window, praying the coast is clear. To say horror and me are friends would be a great overstatement. I might have to be high for that next chapter. Calm my ass down."

Inside my wallet hosted a joint I'd actually wanted to smoke earlier, but hadn't anticipated being out most the day. Man was it good timing, it was made for moments like this.

The best thing about messing with someone who smoked, was that they always had a lighter.  Even if you didn't. The joint was by no means meant to be more than a quick session to get a few drags out of. Teddy paused the book and lit the end. I let her take the first smoke, as I reached over and kicked my shoes off the bed.

Stretching out back on her bed, she handed me the joint as we took turns going through it. Now I was ready to go back massive death sprees. My mind was much more open under the influence. Teddy stretched out alongside me, as we took both our headphones with a splitter.

I can't tell you what happened from then until the time Teddy woke me up, but weed must've made me too relaxed. I felt her poking and probing, but I wasn't motivated in the slightest, until I felt her lips on mine. You'd be surprised how quickly your senses wake up after that.

By now, I was more eager to fulfill my own fantasy, than read some book. Dragging Teddy closer to me, I didn't let go the deeper the kiss got. She'd only been doing so to wake me, but man did it work. "Asher, I was just seeing if you were awake," She said between kisses. "Wasn't sure if you wanted to leave or get comfortable."

Now that I was up, my clothes did feel a little constricting. It was too hot not to take advantage of the central air in her room, so I settled out my hoodie and shorts, left with the boxer briefs and Hanes shirt I had on underneath.

Teddy opted for a similar look, but I can guarantee it looked way better on her than me. Just the sight of her bare legs made me want to reach out and kiss them. A half an inch away from me made it that much more accessible.

I dropped her head to the pillow, but I had way more on my mind than sleep. Running the tip of my tongue along Teddy's outer thigh, I kissed the skin aiming for the outside of her hip. She just smiled, pushed me away and said, "It's one o' clock in the morning."

"You owe me kitten."

"Excuse me?"

It took more than one time to sleep with them to know when you didn't get someone there. I'd studied Teddy's reactions enough to know when she came. Can't say I could tell when she was faking it, but at least I could tell when nothing happened at all. "Don't even pretend like you came earlier. I'm going to be thinking about that all night if I don't handle that."

"It can't wait until the morning?" Teddy giggled.

"By then I'll be a lot hornier. Right now I'm a lot less selfish." As I kissed the top of the meanest part of her thigh. "Just let me eat it. I kid you not, I'll be tired after that."

"I'm exhausted," Teddy went on to say, as she rubbed her forehead. "But you're lucky I kind of want to." She finished in a tired state, sliding her back further down the mattress. I crawled onto my stomach, burying my face between each side of her thighs, gracing each one with attention.

I kissed the outside of her panties, and the scent of her drove me off the wall. If she hadn't been so tired, I could've gone another round. But I was content with the alternative. Oral sex was one of the few times I had complete control over how Teddy felt, if only physically.

For now, I just didn't want her to fall asleep on me. But most times I could tease her enough to make her beg for it. Other times I could lick her so good, it'd make her scream. I focused on kissing the area outside her panties, before I lifted her up and swiped them off all together.

Once she was exposed, I didn't hesitate bringing the tip of my tongue to her delicious folds. Slow, light, feathery lips worked wonders in her dizzy state. Her fingers already began making a home through my hair, her pitch of breath changing at each kiss, lick or flick.

Deep, long strokes forced her inner thighs to close in on my face, and it was only then I knew how much she liked what I was doing. I lived for that twenty second grip against my skull, until she usually passed out from exhaustion, and she was just about there by the way she grabbed onto me. "Keep doing that Asher. I swear, I'm going to come so hard if you keep doing that."

Nothing like a little motivational speaking to boost one's morale. I wanted nothing more than to do just that, so continued on what she moaned she liked most. She lifted her hips deeper as I got into it. It didn't take long after a few strong seconds of rubbing my face against her that series of strained moans finally left her mouth.

She'd made her best efforts to push me away, but I didn't intend on going anywhere until her throbbing went down. "Baby, stop," She said jokingly, trying to pull away from my mouth. I kissed her lips one last time, before stretching up and wiping my mouth off.

"Mmm…you taste blazin' as fuck."

She ignored me, reaching over to slip back into her panties and underneath the covers. "Can you turn down the a/c? I'm freezing."

It wasn't that cold to me, but I kept forgetting. My body heat was natural, so I was hot even when it wasn't. I hopped off the bed to adjust the a/c, but it was only on the seven node, and there was no way I was turning it down any lower. Instead I cranked it to nine. I knew she'd be too tired not to take my word for it, and she'd get so cold she'd want to cuddle. Which in itself was a win-win. I crawled back into bed, as she popped her head from the blanket, curious eyes squinting.

"Did you turn it down?"

"Duh!" I defended. But after a few minutes, my master plan worked. She crawled into my space to bask in my natural heat, and I wrapped my arms around her. I needed more than a minute to fall back asleep, but in a state of exhaustion, Teddy was knocked out.

I reached my arm over Teddy's dresser and pulled my phone out the charger. Too much notifications to know which one to hit up first. I didn't realize how little I looked at my phone when I was around Teddy. Most times she had my undivided attention. I noticed a few texts from Reggie, and I clicked the message board to view what they said.

At least his grandmother was ok. Apparently her car accident hadn't been anything serious, but you never know with how little hospitals share with you over the phone. I texted back my condolences, and placed my phone back on the dresser, only for it to go off again.

It wasn't until I had it back in my hand that I realized it was Teddy's, and that Reggie'd been texting her too. Nothing sappy or anything, but it was enough to cause a guilt trip. Especially considering we were no close to telling him than before.

I didn't want to create more turmoil, but I hated feeling guilty when this was where I wanted—fuck it, needed to be. But nothing made me what to tell him more than the text that was prominent on Teddy's landing page.

Reggie: *Could use a friend...*

Which was ironic because at this point, the both of us could be furthest from that.

## CHAPTER NINE

**Teddy**

I hated sounding like a rich spoiled brat but...

This part-time position at a grocery store? Not my ideal first job. I should've *asked* Asher what to expect from my first week instead of flirting with him the whole time I was training. It was the department he worked in after all. But I figured how hard could it be? All I'd be doing is ringing up customers, bagging a few groceries. Simple enough, right?

My biggest mistake was never having been in the store on its busiest days at the beginning of the month. I knew that's when they usually did some of their best sales, but it was information I'd learned, stored and never used. I hadn't expected my first week to look like Best Buy on Black Friday.

I barely had two days of basic training before I was on a register, nursing sixteen-cart lines, getting yelled at like it was my fault it was so busy. Why did everyone buy groceries at the same damn time?

I regretted not taking my parents up on their offer to study in a new place, tuition- and rent-free. I'd be able to get my BA much quicker with help, but I'd never lived anywhere outside of Miami. It was the place I loved most. Sure, the universities here were no Howard, but I wasn't my parents and I wasn't trying to be.

I'd rather save and go on my own account, even if it was just an okay school. Hopefully my first check would tell me how many classes I could afford to take when the fall semester hit. Even if I didn't have enough, maybe I'd qualify for some grants or financial aid. I wouldn't know until next Friday, since you didn't get paid the first week you were there. Just great.

What sucked most about a store like this? When you had your light off, even if you managed to get your line down, customers hopped right back in yours. It was stressful enough explaining to people you were closed and had been for several minutes. People were just so impatient. Being a quick ringer=more customers. Noted.

When Asher approached my register, I figured he'd come to save me. Instead he reached in and turned my light on, after I'd just managed to get it down.

"Wanna do returns?"

Did he not see my growing line? Especially since he'd just thrown a wrench in my progress.

"When I magically have no customers?" I snarked back. He laughed, but then again, everything was funny to him.

"I'll send someone over to relieve you. When they come, cash out your till." He walked off in the direction of the cash office. I was lane nineteen, which meant I was the first one people saw (and hopped into), but I was close enough to get a load of the ten+ overflowing carts of items customers didn't want or couldn't afford when they hit the register. Wasn't sure which was worse. At least I got off an hour from now. It meant I wouldn't have to struggle to get off a register.

When a girl came to replace me, I signed off and brought my till to the door of the cashier side of the office (if you wanted to call it that—more like an interrogation box). When Asher buzzed me in, he waited for me to stick my till through the glass window that separated his side from mine.

"My feet are killing me," I said as I sat down on one of the random crates holding up a box of flyers. I hoped Asher's end looked nicer than this end. Between the work aprons scattered everywhere, the laundry basket that we were supposed to throw them in, empty cash tills, and ripped coin wrapping paper, it could use a good sweep.

"But you're doing good," Asher said. "I thought you'd crack under pressure, but you're proving me wrong. I like that."

"I love how you have so little faith in me," I said in a pout. I knew he couldn't see it, but I did it anyway.

"What I mean is—and I'm trying to use my words carefully here…" He held up his hands defensively. "Most people don't last in retail. You don't *have* to like it to do it, but I'm glad you're pushing through. Most people quit after a month."

There was a short bout of silence save for the sound of coin wrappers hitting the edge of a surface.

"You are, like, seriously on everyone's holla list. It's not even funny," Asher joked, as if it were something that mattered to me. That ass who felt it was his gentleman-y duty to walk me to the kiosk when I applied was the only one I knew. But if I was being honest, I might've purposely ignored the vibe of everyone who spoke to me.

"I don't really care about that crap."

But it didn't stop Asher from talking about it. "Edwin? That dude in porting? He goes, '*Who's the girl upfront with the cornrows?*' So now I'm everyone's best friend because I know you, so they think I have all the answers."

I stood, trying to figure out why it was taking longer than usual. Through the window, I saw a hint of red on the portal screen. That never meant anything good.

"You're short a dollar."

"What?"

Asher leaned on the counter and peered at me with sympathetic eyes. "I counted it twice. I can do it again, but it'll probably come up the same."

It was too early for this, and I hadn't even been here more than two weeks. "Am I going to get a write-up?"

Asher leaned back and slid the empty till through the window, and I put it back in its rightful place. "Only five bucks or more. Just be careful around this time. It's easier to make mistakes." He pointed to the laundry basket. "You probably won't need that apron. I doubt you'll even get far with it if you keep it on," he said as he walked out his side of the cash office.

I was tired of wearing this damn thing anyway. If they washed them, it wasn't often enough to prevent picking up a dirty one. I untied it from my waist and threw it with the rest.

A knock at the side of my door surprised me, but it could've been a cashier clocking in. I was always a little happy when I had to wait ten minutes for a till, especially when all the supervisors were busy, so if they didn't catch Asher before he disappeared, it'd at least cut a few minutes from their shift. I reached over to turn the knob to let the person in.

I should've expected Asher on the other end, but he caught me off-guard when he slammed the door behind him. This must've been another place without cameras. Asher knelt down to take my lips between his. He tasted sweet, like peppermint or candy. It made me really wish we weren't at work. My mouth stacked up against his, and I ran my fingers along his scruffy stubble. He took two short drags against my lips again, gently taking my bottom lip between his teeth, nibbling on it before leaning back. Asher didn't say anything. He just looked me up and down, bit his lip, and walked back out of the room.

If he was trying to have me thinking about him, it worked. I'd be looking forward to a lot more than that when I saw him next.

The weightless feeling of euphoria didn't last long, though.

Somehow in the course of ten minutes, three new unorganized carts were suddenly in the vicinity where the returns were.

"What the fuck, Ash?" I mumbled to myself. I wasn't sure if I should organize the new ones or just go and put back the carts available to me. I didn't know the store as well as a veteran employee, so I did the latter. I'd be guessing more than anything else, so I took my chances with carts already organized. This place was bananas.

This was going to take more than the last forty-five minutes left on my shift. The aisles were jam-packed with customers, and they were more interested in shopping than making room to let people through. I guess it beat ringing.

"Having fun yet?"

I glanced over my shoulder. Reggie was pulling a huge crate full of pomegranates to his department floor. He had it easier compared to the rest of us in the front end. I know every customer's journey began in produce, but it ended at the register. Once they left produce, they were gone for good. Wish it were that easy when they were paying.

I rolled my eyes at him. "Heh, yeah right."

"But you wanted this job, though," he laughed back, trying and succeeding to get on my nerves.

"Funny." I followed with a lip curl. "How's your gramma?" Even though we both knew she didn't like me, it seemed like the polite thing to ask. She was all he had.

"She's fine. Thanks for asking." He smiled, but most likely because she *was* all right, not because I asked. "What time you get off?"

My eyes darted to the ceiling. "Two forty-five. Ugh, I can't wait."

"I get off at three. You busy?"

I studied Reggie's face to figure out how friendly he'd meant that "you busy." Outside of the texts he'd sent before I worked here, he didn't seem *that* hung up. Or, at least, not in the way

Asher always claimed. Not that I wanted him to be. We made better friends. This wasn't news. But my history with Reg made it difficult to know whether he'd ever look past the things we'd done, the stuff we'd gone through.

He was never as comfortable talking about my health, but that was okay. I didn't expect him to be, and it was why I preferred him as a friend. "Why? Do you need a ride?"

"Nah. Just figured we could hang out or something. It's cool if you don't want to, though."

"I'm cool with chilling if it's *just* chilling." Asher wasn't the jealous type. If he were, he wouldn't be kicking it to me. It never bothered him that I hung out with Reggie alone because I didn't give him a reason to be bothered by it. But we were exclusive, even if that just meant we were exclusively single, so I made it clear anytime Reggie and I did chill, boundaries needed to be set in place.

"Netflix and chill?" Reggie joked.

I laughed, leaning in to punch him in the shoulder. "You think you're cute."

But he knew my weakness. "Starbucks at three? Figure rest out later?"

It sounded good. I agreed to the plans, especially since Asher'd be working doubles until this was over, so I wouldn't see as much of him as I wanted. After that kiss? All I could think about were those lips.

* * *

Why the hell did I hang with this dude? Clearly he didn't understand logic. After some heavy, long-winded convincing, I'd been forced into watching the new *Star Wars* flick (trust me, I'd been avoiding it—just never been a fan) for the first time. This kid raved about it all last year and the beginning of this one, like that hadn't been enough.

Anyone who'd seen it five times was bound to have bias, right? God forbid I have an opinion that steers far from his about the movie. As entertaining as it was, I only *kind of* liked it. Only because I *kind of* hated it. Confusing, right? I'm not a film critic, but it was pretty damn close to the original. But try telling Reggie that.

"You're always talking about Black people in sci-fi. Now that there's Black folk in sci-fi, onscreen for your eyes to see, it's not good enough."

"I didn't say it didn't entertain. Clearly I have to tell you that, since you're putting so many words in my mouth. It's a popular movie. I just didn't think it was Boyega's best."

It was no secret the most handsome man alive was none other than John Boyega. British accent, gorgeous smile, chocolate skin. Nearly everyone I knew could go somewhere when it came to him. I'd been a fan of his since *Attack the Block*, a cult classic.

Sure, my boo was moving on to bigger and better, but I didn't think I'd wait in the rain for movie tickets for the next one. Cop that shit on Amazon Prime on something.

"It was better than *Attack the Block*, though," Reggie murmured under his breath, like it wasn't meant for me to hear.

"What'd you say?"

"It was better than *Attack the Block*, though," he said boldly this time, not even trying to hide it. We went on for another fifteen minutes on which movie was better, but there didn't seem to be an end to this. Neither of us could win.

"So why did you apply at PriceSlash anyway?"

Was he really going to make me repeat myself? "I'm saving up for school." Reggie's voice cracked into a laugh, and I leaned into nudge him. "What's so funny?"

"I thought your parents had good jobs. You're really trying to pay for school working at PriceSlash?"

"Shut up. My parents want me to go out of state, but I don't want to uproot my life. Is that so wrong?" I could say it until I was tired of saying it. They meant well, but it was my life. I wanted to live it the way I wanted to.

"What's so good about Miami?"

"Aside from most my family? If I move out of state, outside of aunts and cousins in New Jersey, I'd be around no one I know. My oncologists are here, and let me tell you. Getting to know new ones is not my idea of cool. Even if I didn't switch doctors, it'd mean I'd be going back and forth every six weeks, as if chemotherapy isn't stressful enough. Every single person I know is here. How many reasons do you need?"

Did I think Miami was the best city in the world? No. Did I see it as the city of endless opportunity and dreams? Hell no. But even being away for four months had been hard. There were, like, no Latins in Minnesota. I'd even been to New York once, a place that was supposed to be diverse. All I ever got asked was *"What are you?"* and *"Why do you speak Spanish?"*

And that was from fellow Latinos. If you wanted to find a Cuban, it'd take looking under every rock, and they were almost never Black. I think I'd stick to Miami, where being a Black person who spoke Spanish made sense to people.

"You know you'd miss me if I left," I said as I pressed a finger in the space between Reggie's eyebrows.

"Would you miss *me*?"

I shrugged. It was an open question, but I didn't see why I couldn't answer it honestly. "Yeah."

"That's cool. I keep thinking you don't like me anymore or something."

"Reggie, you know I love you," I said as my eyes searched the space around him. "But as a friend."

He stretched out on the couch cushion, his expression souring in a grimace. "Don't tell me you're about to hit me with that 'like my brother shit.'"

I scowled at Reggie through squinted eyes, shoulders up to my ears. "Why do I have to measure how I see you? Why can't you just take that I love you as a friend?"

"Because my feelings haven't changed. Just because I'm cool with being friends doesn't mean I don't wish we were more sometimes."

I placed my hand on his and lightly squeezed, leaning in close so he'd see the genuineness in my words. "Reggie. You're my boy. We had, and have, a lot of good times. And I think you'd make a great guy…for someone else. What I needed—you weren't always that dude."

"You're really gonna judge me on some old shit? Before I knew you had cancer?"

"See, this is why we're just friends. I was looking for you to be there when you didn't know. Not just because you do *now*. I don't want you to get it twisted like I'm not attracted to you or that I didn't enjoy everything we did. I did. Even now, I'm glad we can still hang out. But I'm not the girl for you. I'm too needy. Shit, right now, I need a Gatorade from my fridge, and I know asking you is just going to give me a fight."

Reggie laughed, which in turn made me smile. I was glad. It was meant to lighten the mood. "I don't want to change you, and I don't want to be changed. I just want you as a friend. It's okay if you're not okay with that, but…I really want one of them to be you because I love you so much."

Reggie nodded with pursed lips, processing my response, but ultimately okay with my answer. A part of me prepared myself for a different outcome, but I was happy he was okay with it.

I didn't want him to answer any other way.

# CHAPTER TEN

**Teddy**

Urgh, was it Friday already? I'd worked four days scheduled and a call-in last week and had to wait until today to see the fruits of my labor.

"Damn, it's not even ten o'clock yet," a supervisor named Deana joked. She was annoying as hell but hilarious. It probably wasn't her goal, but she reminded me of Adepero Oduye's character in that movie *Pariah*. Short, butch, skinny. Out of all the people Asher claimed were checking for me, she'd been the only one bold enough to approach me.

She was cute. I guess if I hadn't been trying this monogamous thing, I would've considered it. But she was more assertive than I liked. I was used to having my way most times, and I had a feeling she did, too. Two alphas did not mix.

"But you have them, right?" I batted my eyelashes, playfully flirting back.

"I'm probably the only person who'd do this, so you better not brag to anyone I hooked you up." Deana flipped through the check stubs, slid mine through when she found the Ks, and had me sign out for it. I'd worked nearly thirty hours, but a few cashiers let me in on the fact that wasn't common most weeks.

Two weeks of the month were steady or slow, the other two weeks fast or busy. I didn't care—anything would bring me closer to my goal, so I wasn't complaining. Even though the schedule wasn't up, I headed for the break room. It wouldn't be up until a manager got off their butt to do it, but I didn't want to make two drives to find out when I'd work next week.

"You got your check?" Reggie asked, walking into the break room. I shushed him, considering how anal the supervisors were about giving out checks too early.

I ripped open both sides of the security envelope to reveal my big takeaway. Was this right? After twenty-nine and a half hours, had I really only made one hundred and seventy-eight dollars? I dropped the check on the table, rubbing the side of my forehead. If this was a check on a good week, it'd take me a year to save up for a semester as a full-time student. At best, I could take two classes each session. I'd probably be a student until I was in my thirties.

I took a ripped napkin from the break room table and wrote out the expense it'd cost to attend full-time versus part-time. Then I calculated what a month might look like if I cut this week's check in half. So I couldn't get as many credits as I wanted as soon as I wanted. My plan hadn't changed.

There was still work to do. I just had to pace myself and be patient. I'd been so wrapped up in these damn numbers floating around in my head, I hadn't noticed Reggie left the room. By now, I wasn't the only one in here, but it was clique-y. Most people stuck to themselves or people they predicted would last more than their first week. That was fine by me. There seemed to be a lot of drama here, and I had enough in my life to deal with.

When Reggie returned, he had his own check stub in hand as he sat down across from me. Cashiers didn't make as much as other people, so I was guessing his check looked better than mine.

"So…how was that big fat PriceSlash check?"

I wanted to slap him. Instead, I made an unintelligible noise and shooed him away for reminding me. "For the record? Retail sucks." I rested an elbow on the table, cupping my chin in my hand. My eyes wandered around the room and what little it had to offer. A mid-sized fold-up table for starters. Made you kind of feel you were in a third grade lunch room. There was a glass bulletin that held the printout of the schedule whenever it was *actually* ready. Teamwork and company posters too cheesy for words. Basic amenities like a fridge and a microwave. All topped off by red, white, and blue, two-week-old, Independence Day-themed wall decals.

They were all around the front end, so I guess it was supposed to make the store look festive. Back here, not so much. A list of names and dates in bold print caught my attention. I'd walked by it a few times, but I was just noticing the name:

```
Asher Rose  July 18th
```

"Reggie, what is that?" I pointed behind him, and he turned to see what I referred to. His eyebrows met in the middle of his face, as he pointed to the pickle poster next to it.

"From the training video?"

"No! The one with the names and dates."

Reggie's posture relaxed as he leaned on the table. "Oh. That's just employee birthdays. Not like they give you shit. The least they can do is give you a day off, but they only do that if you request it."

I squinted just to make sure I saw it right. "So Asher's birthday is, like, Monday?"

"I guess." Reggie shrugged, unimpressed.

"We should do something. Kidnap him. Hold him hostage. Put him up for ransom. I don't know, something fun we can all do together." I didn't know Asher's birthday, but I'd never asked. To be honest, I wasn't even sure how old he was. I didn't care if he was younger, but I was curious. He wore the right amount of facial hair that aged him, but there could've been a nineteen-year-old hiding underneath there. His height really threw you off. He was taller than most, so I only assumed he was my age or older.

I doubt Reggie was nosy enough to know, but it couldn't hurt to ask. "How old is Asher?"

He clucked his tongue. "I don't know."

"Why do you want to know how old I am?" Asher walked into the room, using his key to open the glass door to replace last week's schedule. Awesome. It meant I wouldn't have to wait all day to deposit my check. Even so, I was caught red-handed. I laughed into my hand, hiding all signs of curiosity.

"I don't know. Your birthday is in three days. We wanted to do something with you."

"We did?" Reggie coughed, a hint of confusion in his voice. I hit him from across the table, then stood to swoop underneath Ash to write down my schedule. When I got back to my seat, Asher'd taken it, the only one left at the table. I couldn't squeeze in, so I sat on his lap instead.

"Yeah, we did! But just in case we want to get you a cake with candles, what number should it say?" I put my arms around him, but in a way that didn't suggest anything explicit. I never changed the way I acted in front of Reggie. If I did, that'd look more suspicious than pretending nothing went on between us. Reggie never saw anything by it, and I was comfortable here anyway.

"You guys don't have to. I work here, so I don't plan on doing much but get wasted or smoke," Asher joked. "But I'm turning twenty-three."

A small laugh burst from my throat, as I said "wow" a little too loud.

"What?"

"For some reason, I thought you were older."

His eyes widened, something he did unintentionally when he asked a question. "Why? How old are you?"

"Not twenty-three." My birthday wasn't until November, but until then I was twenty-five. It wasn't a huge age difference, but considering guys aged much slower in comparison, Ash was actually more mature than I was two and a half years ago. I guess it was so cultural to be less than a guy—weigh less, be shorter, be younger. It didn't matter, but I would've cringed at anything younger than twenty-one.

"You can't be, like, over twenty-two, right?" Reggie added, his nosy ass. I knew Reggie was about my age, but only because he'd mentioned being old enough to rent a car.

"I'm not telling you now. I feel old." I didn't mean it, but I felt shy all of a sudden. Asher didn't push hard, but after asking one more time, I whispered it in his ear to piss Reggie off.

"You made it seem like you were twice my age. That's not that serious," Asher snapped back.

"So...I have Monday and Thursday off. I saw that neither of you are scheduled then. What do you guys say?"

Asher pointed to Reggie, looking for confirmation. He muttered an "I guess" as Asher rubbed his palms together.

"It's not that serious, but I'll chill if you guys want. It's just a day to me," he said.

He'd probably expect it anyway, so I didn't bother mentioning birthday sex, even if I just said it as a joke.

"I'm gonna go deposit this dinosaur arm of a check. I'll catch you guys later, though. Who's working Sunday around close?" Reggie raised his hand, and I reached in for a high-five. Yes, I was that corny.

* * *

Waiting for Reggie took the longest. I should've picked him up first, but Asher was already at my place. I didn't want Ash to feel like he *had* to spend his birthday with just me, and we always had way more fun when we all hung out.

"You sure he's coming?" Asher stared out the window toward Reggie's house. I didn't dare beep. All I'd probably hear next time I ran into his grams was how rude I was for not knocking. It was better to text.

When he finally made his appearance, shotgun was already claimed, and he didn't argue. He hopped into the backseat. It *was* Asher's birthday after all.

"So where to first?" Reggie asked from the back.

Asher leaned over from the front seat as I drove to our first destination. "It was supposed to be a day filled with things *I* wanted to do. But she's the ride, so we're going to hit up Seaquarium. She refuses to go elsewhere until we get to do that." With his lying ass. Asher knew the minute we got in this car, the first thing he'd said to me was, "*I want to do whatever you want to do.*" I didn't see why we shouldn't, though. We'd left early enough, and we'd finally get to see it and put it through our rearview.

It took twenty minutes to get from Reggie's house to the packed-as-hell parking lot for the Miami Seaquarium. I was forced to pay the ten-dollar parking fee just to go further, but I dropped them as close to the park entrance as possible before looking to find a decent enough spot. The parking lot was ridiculous, so I hadn't found anything close. By the time I walked toward the entrance, the lines weren't too bad.

Much better than Busch Gardens or Universal Studios. Asher and Reg were off to the side, so I assumed they'd bought their tickets.

"You guys already got yours?" Both of them hid behind smiles and stilted postures. "Uh, what's going on?"

Asher held out his hands defensively. "Teddy, don't be mad. Please don't be mad. But we didn't know the tickets were forty-eight bucks. Between the both of us, we've only got sixty-eight. We are *not* getting in."

Messing with these fools. "I wish y'all broke asses would've told me that before I paid ten dollars for parking."

"Last time I went to an aquarium was when I was nine," Reggie butted in, like it'd matter who the excuses were coming from. "And it was a school trip. How were we supposed to know it cost half a buck?"

Google much? "It didn't dawn on either of you to check the website while I was driving?"

"You wanted to go! Why can't you just spot us thirty-two, and we'll pay you back?"

I shook my head, contemplating what to say next. "I'm not about to lend anybody money after paying ten bucks for a parking lot when we might not even get in. I'm tempted to buy a ticket and leave you guys out here."

Asher pouted his lower lip. "Sorry." He was so lucky that *kind of* worked on me.

"Well, where do you want to go that you can actually afford?" I hadn't been against spotting them the difference, but I was usually the ride. I hadn't known the tickets were forty-eight either, but I didn't ask for gas or reimbursement. I think that was a fair trade. Plus, if we went out to eat, I wanted enough to do so without having to dip into my savings or trust.

Asher took out his phone. "There's paintball. But I think you need a reservation for that. Hmmm...I'd hit up Trampoline High."

"What is Trampoline High?"

Asher filled us in on the indoor trampoline park on the walk from the aquarium's long lines to my car. It was cheaper, despite requiring thirty-minute time slots. We had to sign waivers on the website and book a time to go. It was a good thing it was a

Monday. That allowed us to pick the earliest spot available to book ninety minutes of bouncing time.

I'd never been to a trampoline park before, so I didn't know what we'd deal with. It was literally an entire room filled with boxed-together trampoline floors. You had to buy their special socks to have more grip on the surface, but they seemed like a way to milk you out of two bucks. Me and Reggie didn't have the hang of it right away, but Asher seemed like he went here a lot.

I wouldn't call him acrobatic, but he was much better at maneuvering his weight with back flips one after the other. He was so tall that he looked like a long pendulum moving back and forth. I was just getting the hang of jumping in a straight line. Don't get me started on my landings.

Definitely a workout. After just forty-five minutes of jumping, I needed a short break. I was drenched in my sweat's sweat. Birthday sex? Not happening until this girl had a shower. I watched the two of them dual each other over whose jump game was better, but it was hard to compete with someone a head taller than you.

I wasn't about to spend my short break bored, so I checked my phone's messages and noticed a missed call from the job. Out of curiosity, I called the number back. Deana picked up and cut right to the chase.

"Is this Theodora?" Extra emphasis on the *dora*. I had no idea why she put so much stress on it, but she did that *all* the time.

"Yeah, what's up?"

"Can you work?"

"Can I work?" I repeated, like I hadn't understood the first time. Someone called out. At least I knew why their turnover was high. It was a short shift close to closing, but *not* closing. I scratched my head, considering it but not that hard. I hated the idea of ending things so sudden. "I kinda made plans—"

"Plans for what?"

I was getting tired of him walking in on conversation, and just by the smile on Asher's face, he could tell. He bounced to the trampoline edge, sitting on its corner. I put my hand over the receiver and mumbled. "They're asking me to work."

I thought he'd object to the idea, but he didn't. "It's cool if you want to. I know you're saving up for school. Definitely more important than doing dumb shit on my birthday. I had fun anyway. I don't mind a raincheck."

"Really?"

"Unless you just don't want to," he said with a shrug.

I thought about it. I was having fun, but sometimes you sacrificed to make time for fun. Fun could come later. I needed to save everything I could from this job, and if he was okay with it...

"As long as it doesn't bother you."

"Teddy, seriously, I'm fine."

The shift didn't start until four, so we still had a few hours to get settled and paint the town red before I went in. In my own way, I'd just have to make it up to him.

* * *

*Asher*

It'd been such a long day, I was glad to see it over with. I was still up to my neck in double shifts, but I wasn't mad at that over-time. Whenever I saw a regular forty-hour check after two straight weeks of overtime, I cringed. I was in the cash office most the time Teddy worked today, so I barely got to see her. And since she didn't close, she was gone by the time I was on the floor. She was saving up to finish her degree, so I didn't want to stand in the way of that. Especially since she was trying to do it here and any other option meant she might leave.

It was just a little after ten when I got home, and even though I wasn't tired, my back was killing me. I couldn't wait to collapse face-first on my mattress. I passed one of my roommates on the way in, but he'd been too busy watching TV to exchange more than a "hey" in my direction. I made one stop to the kitchen, taking care of the last cup of unmarked orange juice, and then stalked to my room in a drunken state and turned on the light.

I don't know what I was expecting to see, but it definitely hadn't been Teddy stretched out on my bed in nothing more than a red lace bra and panties. Right now I was a lot of things, but tired wasn't one of them.

"Oh, hell yeah." I slammed and locked the door behind me, pulling my hoodie over my head. In less than two seconds, I was on the bed on top of Teddy, with lips as drawn to her neck as my hands were to the rest of her body.

I kissed up to her ear and murmured, "I didn't see your car."

"I wanted to surprise you."

My hands caressed every beautiful inch of her dark brown skin. I leaned up to face her before leaning back in to nibble her neck.

"Surprised."

Horny or hysterical. I wasn't sure which I was more at this point. Teddy looked hot, but she kind of always did to me. Lingerie wasn't her thing. Half the time her underwear only matched when she knew she was about to get it. I laughed at the effort this probably took. I sat up to admire her body and how much it looked like wrapping paper ready to tear off. I bit my lip. "Damn, girl, red is your color."

I slid the top of her bra down. Seeing her tits through the bra wasn't enough.

She giggled, pulling the bra back up. "Stop."

"This shit again." The one thing I missed from when she was heavier was her confidence level. It wasn't gone, but she was insecure a lot less before she lost weight. I had to use pliers to get her to have sex without her bra on, but I figured she'd at least ease up since she was trying to surprise me.

"Damn, aren't I the birthday boy? I want to see all of you. This bra needs to come off."

"My boobs look better in the bra—"

"No, they look better between my lips, but they're not getting there stuck in this thing." I flicked one of her straps with my finger. If she was going to fight me on this, I'd take matters into my own hands. I pinned her down on the mattress as my lips connected to the area above her chest.

"Boy, stop." Which I assumed she didn't mean. The smile on her face looked too suspect. When I managed to get one of her tits out, her tune changed once her nipple was between my lips. "Mmm…"

"Yeah, mmm…" I imitated back. She bit her lip, easing up on the struggle, so there wasn't a need to keep her pinned. She smelled so good. Something about her body wash or lotion, mixed in with her natural scent, just drove me wild. "I am going to fuck the shit out of you."

A knock came at my door, but I chose to ignore it. Whatever it was, it wasn't more important than this.

"Yo, Ash. Why is your door locked?"

Reggie's voice caught us both off-guard. Teddy pushed me back and mouthed, *What is he doing here?*

The hell if I knew. I shrugged and answered him back. "Uh… what are you doing here?"

He turned the knob, and Teddy hid underneath the sheet on my bed. "Damn, can you open the door so I'm not yelling through a wall here?" He ended it with a laugh.

*Get rid of him,* Teddy mouthed before hiding completely underneath the sheet.

Shit. Talk about messed-up timing. I thought about who the hell might have let him in at this hour, but it had to have been the same genius who'd let Teddy in. In a flash, I was out the door and met Reggie on the other side. His posture didn't betray anything about him. Was it coincidence? He couldn't have known Teddy was at my place, especially since her car hadn't been in plain view. It could've been fate's way of saying, *Just tell him now.*

Before I revealed anything, it was best to know what he was even over here for.

"Kinda late for this, Reg."

He held out his arms defensively. "It's not even eleven o'clock."

"Were you just in the neighborhood?"

"I was looking to buy. You know how it goes. I usually ride with you to hook me up, and I figured since I ain't get you shit yesterday…session?"

I rubbed the back of my neck, and leaned my back against my room door. "You know you could've asked me when I got off, before I got home and comfortable."

Reggie pointed to my door as a smirk collected on his face. "Don't…don't tell me you got someone in there." I faked a smile that added to my confirmation. "Damn, my bad."

"Yeah. *Your* bad."

"I guess I should've hit you up first. Figured after an uneventful b-day, you'd be down for a surprise session, but okay."

I gestured back and forth to my room door, with a sense of urgency of things to attend to. "I'm gonna need you to wrap it up. I really appreciate you coming down here for weed, but this is a really bad time. Any other time I would've been down. Right now, I'm not down. In fact, every minute I stand out here and talk to you, I'm not getting down. You feel me?"

"My bad. Happy belated fam." He held out his hand for me to shake, which transitioned into a semi-embrace that lasted no more than a few seconds. I faked another smile and waited a bit until I was convinced he was a reasonable distance down the hallway before I crept back inside my room. Teddy was still stretched underneath the sheets, only this time it was up to her chest as she peered at her cell phone.

I got hornier trying to remember what she looked like underneath that, and I took my rightful spot on the bed again. I was taken aback at her pushing me away as I leaned in to kiss her neck. She was more concerned with her phone than me.

"Teddy, what the hell?"

She reached for her clothes and slipped into them. "I'm just not feeling it anymore."

"He's gone if that's what you're worried about. For the record, I had no idea he was going to show up. In the whole time I've known him, he's only done that, like, once." I watched as every scintillating inch hid from view the more clothes she put on.

"That's okay. It was just…too close, I guess. Imagine if you hadn't locked your door. That would've been how he found out about us."

"And then he would've known you were here, and we wouldn't have to hide it anymore."

She laughed to herself and slipped on her sandals. "I'm just gonna go." She leaned back down and left a kiss on my forehead, before grabbing her car keys and leaving for good.

* * *

The days that followed were full of awkward hi's and goodbyes. She never avoided me at work—how could she?—but then again, she didn't go out of her way to seek me either. I got it. We were at work, so *that* I didn't mind. But the two days of no texts, no calls. Hell, even a reply would've been nice. Nothing.

I found out quick that you shouldn't wish for something unless you really wanted it. When you got it, it might not be the outcome you wanted.

Teddy: *I think we need to take a step back.*

* * *

**Teddy**

I considered all day how to send that text. *We should take a break. Maybe we should end things for a while.* All texts I considered until ultimately deciding that *I think we need to take a step back* sounded the most emotionally detached. I would've called, but I knew he'd be working and I didn't want him thinking about it all day. His phone in his locker meant he didn't have to.

He must've been on a lunch when he got it because the back-and-forth was well beyond fifteen minutes.

Asher: *You are not about to do this through a text message*

Teddy: *I would've called but...idk*

Asher: *Is this about the other day?*

Teddy: *Maybe...*

Asher: *You make me just want to tell him right now*

Teddy: *Please don't*

Asher: *Then I'm coming over there*

Teddy: *y*

Asher: *Because if you're gonna dump me, you're gonna do it to my face. Not through some fucking text message*

I should've known doing it through text was tacky. It was too hard to consider doing so in person, though. We've been doing the back-and-forth since we'd met. I didn't want to keep doing it unless I was sure I was okay what I'd lose should the worst happen. I was selfish, but I didn't want to lose anything. I was too conflicted. On the one hand, I loved Asher. I wanted to be with him. In public, and not just as friends.

But Reggie was my friend, too. It felt like I'd lose him, even though I wasn't leading him on to think something might ever happen between us. I just didn't want to lose people. And I didn't want to feel I had to choose to have one or the other. I never thought about this stuff in the beginning, but things never made sense until something happened.

When a knock came at my door, I peered through the peep-hole, but I knew it'd be Asher. He didn't waste any time when I opened the door for him either. He pulled me in by the waist, leaned down, and kissed me. It was a tug of war of lips, and his trembled against mine, soft and sweet, one last time before leaning out.

"Do you still want to take a step back?" he asked, peering those big blue eyes into mine.

Seeing him. Touching him. Kissing him. This was why I'd avoided telling him what I needed to say in person. I almost wanted to yell "Kidding!" and spend the next half-hour boinking each other's brains out. But the other day brought out a ton of feelings, more than just Reggie. It felt like we'd never be normal.

"This is why I didn't want to tell you in person. Because you'd try to talk me out of it. I was serious."

Asher let go of me, pacing in the opposite direction as he pulled at his hair. "Sometimes I'm convinced you only want something when you can't actually have it."

I didn't understand what he meant. Nothing ever stood in the way where I couldn't have him, so I didn't know where that came from. Asher laughed and leaned on the counter where my living room and kitchen met. He must've been waiting for me to say something, or defend myself, because he wasn't done.

"Well, it's true, isn't it? When we're convenient, you're not happy. When we're inconvenient, you're not happy. If you don't want me, be straight up. Stop wasting my time—"

"Asher, I never said I wanted to take a step back forever. I just need to figure some things out."

"When will that be? I mean, Reggie is my boy, but stop using him as an excuse. I'm not saying his friendship isn't important to me, but I haven't been with him for fucking four weeks. I've been with you."

Asher didn't get it sometimes. But it wasn't his fault. Or, at least, not all the time. "Well, the difference between me and you is that I don't want to lose friends over..." I didn't want to say the wrong thing, but I couldn't predict I'd say the right thing either. I was stuck no matter what.

"Fine, Teddy. Just don't call me for the shit you usually call me for then. Just treat me how you do Reggie. You do anyway."

It was a low blow. Maybe he hadn't meant it to come out the

way it had, but the damage was done. I wasn't prepared for Asher's douchebag side, nor was I in the mood for it. But I wasn't about to show him that I cared so much.

"Fine. Just go then." I hoped he couldn't hear the weight in my voice as I excused myself from the room.

My bedroom was the place I felt most comfortable to get away from everything. The first thing I did was wipe at my wet eyes before it turned into something bigger.

"I know you're not crying," Asher said, standing outside the threshold.

"You're just such an asshole sometimes."

"What did I do? You're the one breaking up with me!"

Here went nothing. I was having trouble explaining the real reason I'd booked it the other day. One text could change your entire mood. And I hadn't been looking for a pity party.

"A kid in my support group isn't doing well, if you must know. I would've told you, but we had enough going on. Plus, I didn't think you'd get it anyway."

"Is that why you were mad the other day?" Asher stalked over toward my side of the bed and knelt down to study my face. "You could've just told me."

"It's not like you ever met him. I have it hard enough talking about my own shit."

Asher rubbed his hand across my leg. "Are you guys close?"

"I wouldn't say close. But he's still cool. Not even sixteen. I guess I just feel bad for his mom. She was the one who told me about him."

I thought it'd been him the other day, in the mood for an unofficial meeting. But I wasn't surprised to hear from his mother, asking if I wanted to visit just in case, to say my respects. He wasn't dying, but...we knew he had a difficult time with leukemia. He seemed so much stronger than us, but the body could only fight back so much. I hadn't seen him since I'd left

Miami in March, and I'd made so little effort in the time I'd been back.

I figured I'd always have time. I hoped he'd make it through, but if not, I wished I could've exchanged more than a few words beforehand.

"Teddy, I care about you. Even about the stuff you think I don't get. I hate it, but I fucking love you. It sucks sometimes but…I just don't think you need a boyfriend. I think you need a friend, which I'm more than prepared to be. I'm trying to be your best friend *and* more than that, but most times I don't think I can do both. You want everything, but you don't want to lose anything."

He was finally getting it, even if I wasn't sure I wanted him to. Maybe I *was* attracted to the situation more when it was confusing.

"But I don't want you to be mad at me if I can't wait on you. I don't mind being there. I don't think there's anything you can ever say that wouldn't have me running if you needed me." He laughed, tossing my hands between his. "But this? Us? Either you want us, like this, or you don't. Don't make me do this back-and-forth with you again."

I nodded. I wasn't being fair, and there was never a time something wasn't going on with me. Right now was too soon to say we'd ever just…be.

I leaned in to kiss him, but he pushed me back, wearing a flirtatious smirk on his face. "Don't get me started, Teddy. You still owe me birthday sex."

Even in the heat of the moment, I'd lost my drive that night in his room. I'd gone through the motions for a few days, but masturbation wasn't going to cut it while I had the real thing in front of me right now. If we were taking a break or walking away for good, I wasn't going to do it without at least having something to remember him by.

"Mmm…you know I'm weak. Don't do this to me." The hum of his mouth vibrated against my lips.

"Stop me then."

"You already know I'm not gonna," he said, pinning me on the mattress. I thought I could kiss him for hours until he lowered his lips to my neck to send me into a giggling frenzy. He paused for a second. Was he having second thoughts?

He knelt back onto the floor, reaching for my shorts. I could almost see the hunger in the naughty way his eyes appraised me, each time he laid a kiss or lick on my upper or inner thighs. Let's hope he was too horny to notice the paisley print on my panties didn't match the polka dots on my bra.

I was getting wet just thinking about how his mouth would feel when his tongue finally made contact with my body. I already wanted him—this one last time. It'd be what I'd regret most doing and not doing at the same time.

* * *

It was hard to feel anything afterward. Outside of what you were supposed to feel anyway. We knew each other's bodies well enough that it did what it was meant to do, but we didn't exchange words or excuses. No goodbyes. What'd be the point? We'd see each other tomorrow at work. We knew we'd go back to being…just.

He lit a cigarette and shared it with me as we sat in silence. He reached over the side of the bed to gather his clothes. When he slipped into them, I figured he'd turn back, but he didn't. He just walked out of the room and left.

# CHAPTER ELEVEN

**Asher**

Could this day be over yet? It was my first shift in four days where I didn't close. I'd get to experience daylight for once, and I didn't even know what to do with it. I was babysitting my niece tomorrow, so I hadn't planned much, considering it was a day off. My sister was in between jobs, but looking for a better one. I couldn't stand her, but I rarely said no when she asked me to watch Mimi, especially since we got along so well.

I'd probably just watch cartoons all day and take her out to eat. What I'd do with the rest of today was the bigger question.

I texted a few people. I got a few replies. I wasn't up to it as much as I thought, so I probably wouldn't reply when they were ready to get up. Was I over Teddy? Hell no. Was I ready to move on? Sometimes it was yes, sometimes no.

It'd only been a few days since I was last over her place, making amazing love to her, knowing it could be the last time for a while—maybe forever. I wasn't bothered by her dumping me. It didn't mean I was out her life. Just that I couldn't be with her in the way that made the most sense to me. But I'd always told her that I'd be the same friend without any of it. What kind of friend would I be if I went back on my word now?

There were still things I didn't understand, that I was trying to, but I had needs, too. The dance between us either had to end or change, and she wasn't ready for it to change. I wasn't ready for it to end. So I'd have to just ignore how her laugh at my bad jokes (or good, I wasn't that corny) made me smile. Or how every time a comment that annoyed her at work resulted in an "oh my god," I remembered making her say that in a much. Sexier. Way.

I still loved her. But I loved myself, too, so I couldn't look back. Because I knew if I did…it'd prove I loved her more.

* * *

*Teddy*

There was a countdown whenever I sat down and had lunch with my mother. How long would it take for her to make a comment about my clothes? How soon before she made a fuss about my food choice? And my personal favorite, commenting on and correcting my Spanish.

My mom was born in Cienfuegos, a city between Havana and Trinidad, but spent most of her youth in San Juan until moving to the United States. She'd spent my entire life trying to prove how "proper" she could sound. She spoke with an accent, but there was a clarity to her voice that rarely raised certain questions about her heritage. But she was never asked to repeat herself due to a misunderstanding.

My father didn't care, but she hated the way I spoke Spanish. Claimed it was too "Americanized." If my Spanish was such a problem, raising me in Miami was to blame. What did they really expect? I'm not even going to go into the fact both my parents often used Puerto Rican slang.

Papi was always more critical of my choices, while mami was naturally critical of my looks and eating habits, whether she knew it or not. She always used to tell me, *Too bad you didn't get your father's hair. You'd be so much prettier with your father's hair,* but I'd fully accepted that there wasn't anything wrong with hers. The only thing I'd inherited from my father was his stubbornness and his love for reading. My papi loved to read.

"Nena, you should order something healthier. You don't know how they prepare their waffles. Here, mira." She pointed to a "lean and fit" choice off the menu that was a poor excuse for scrambled eggs and bell peppers on the side. I bet they didn't even season it. *Strike one.*

"Mom, I'm getting what I want. I actually feel like I can eat today. Stop being so fussy. I just want to eat. Déjame."

Her lips pressed into a hard line as she relayed what she wanted to the waiter and handed him the menu. "I'm just trying to help…"

"Ma, you're not helping by starving me."

"Well, you look better. You know you got a little chubby recently. Even though whatever it is you have on adds weight to the top. Why are you wearing that ugly flannel shirt and those boots? You look like eh…este…Paul Bunyan." She snapped her fingers as the name came to her. "I swear, I don't understand fashion amongst young people. You'll wear anything if a person on TV says it's cool."

*Strike two.* She let out a long, drawn-out sigh, interlocking her fingers with her elbows rested on the table. "So you register for classes next week, no?"

I nodded. I had no plans on elaborating. With the money I'd made from work, all I'd been able to swing was two classes, and that wasn't even including all the other fees this place was charging me. Sure, I was registering, but I wasn't going all out like I'd initially planned.

The way my trust fund was set up, I couldn't get my hands on enough cash to pay for a full-time semester in one shot. It was only enough to handle living expenses that didn't have a set price, like food, toiletries, and gas.

The upside was the monthly limits kept the balance intact and made it hard to overspend. The bad news was that, in order to make a large purchase, I had to go directly to my parents. That didn't happen often.

"So you're father and I have been talking, and we're proud that you got a job to pay for your education. If you can do it without loans, that is the right way to do it. Not everyone is fortunate to do it that way." My mom had a habit of overstressing the last word of certain sentences. She hated it when I pointed it out, but it always made me laugh.

The waiter brought out my waffles, hash browns, and links of sausage and my mom's oatmeal and black coffee. He asked if we needed anything else, but because we didn't, we sent him on his way. My mom's face pinched at the first sip of coffee like the java snob she was. She preferred her coffee the Cuban way.

"Anyways. Papi and I discussed it, and while we'd rather you go to an out-of-state university, we still want to help. Whatever you have saved up for school, we'll match it come registration day. If matching it still isn't enough, we'll pay the difference. As long as you maintain the job part-time and put more effort into your studies. No need to offer our help if you're going to perform poorly."

At that moment, I pranced over to my mom and engulfed her in my arms. I was sure I looked like a complete nut job since my mom was never big on hugs, but I didn't care. I was so happy.

"Gracias, mami. Vas a estar *proud* de mi," I said, forgetting the Spanish word for proud in my good spirits. I think it was orgullosa. I didn't care. With the extra money, I'd get to register as a full-time student. As I sat down, my mom tore into me with her soft black eyes.

"Odio cuando hace eso. Speak it right or don't speak it at all.

This making up words…this is why I don't want you studying in Miami."

In my defense, proud wasn't made up. It was the actual English equivalent. But what'd I tell you? *Strike three.*

"Let one of us know how much it all is a few days before so we can write you the check. And por favor, nena. Don't use it as an excuse to go on a shopping spree. Unless it's to get some prettier clothes."

* * *

Whoever made the rule that new registers had to apply for their classes in person probably didn't work those first days of registration. I'd spent all morning in a meeting with an advisor, then another hour and a half waiting in line at the registration office.

If I'd known I'd be standing up for so long, I would've worn sneakers instead of sandals. Looks like I'd be canceling that hair appointment I'd made a few days ago for a blowout. I thought I'd spend this day ecstatic that, come next week, I'd be a proud attendee of the University of Miami. Instead I was tired and spent the remainder of the morning in line at the bookstore.

When I finally made it off the campus, it was half past one, making my total time there five hours. Thank the heavens that next semester I'd be able to register online and far ahead of new registers; I looked forward to starting the fall with three introductory anthropology classes. Neither medicine nor engineering interested me like it did my parents, but the study of humanity, culturally and socially, did.

I could do this. I could totally do this.

Was it sad that I was hoping for the job to call me? With no plans, working would've made me feel better about wasting this day, but when I called to see if they needed any help, I was met with a no.

Me: *Hey, Reg, busy? Wanna grab a coffee?*

Within minutes, I heard back from him.

Reggie: *At work. Don't get off until six. Sorry.*

Just great. The only other person in my phone who I'd actually tolerate was Asher, but for days we'd had minimal contact outside of work. We were still figuring out how to be friends without being lovers, and until we sorted that out, it was just easier to cut the small talk. We both risked saying the wrong things, but even with all the extra stuff going on, I still considered him one of my closest friends. I was ready to get rid of the act. The first step to being friends was to *actually* be friends. That meant not being afraid to call or text, even if it was just to say hi.

Me: *Hey*

Asher was usually one of those fast texters, but this time it took him a few minutes as I wasted away in my car.

Asher: *Hey*

Me: *You're probably busy, but if not, wanna take a ride or something?*

This time his response was instant.

Asher: *You're right I am busy.*

Me: *Okay...*

Why did I even try?

Asher: *Busy babysitting.*

Me: *Okay...*

It seemed like a lie, but who was I to decipher truth from fabrications by way of a text? Although would the lie really be necessary if we were only friends? An incoming video message revealed Asher and a little girl as they waved to the camera.

"Say, 'hi, Teddy,'" Asher said off-screen.

"Hi, Teddy," the girl said with a mouth full of more gums than teeth so it sounded more like *Theddy*.

Asher: *Niece*

Me: *She's cute.*

Asher: *That she is. If you're bored, drop by. I don't know if you like kids or not though...*

Me: *What's the address?*

* * *

Allahpattah was just past Wynwood, where Asher lived, give or take a mile. The apartment building was painted a bright red and contrasting yellow that made me think of the McDonald's logo. *You'll know it when you see it,* he'd texted me. He was right about that. There was no missing this place.

A sense of relief ran through me as I pulled into the parking of this so-called building. I, for one, was not a fan of parking my car in neighborhoods I wasn't familiar with, so a garage gave me a sense of security. I pulled into a space and didn't realize it was assigned until the person who it belonged to damn near cussed me out. Back and forth we went in Spanish before she got around to telling me that the visitor parking was just a few rows away. Why couldn't she have done that in the first place?

Me: *Thanks for telling me I couldn't just park anywhere. Got cussed out by some old Dominican lady.*

Asher: *My bad, figured you'd see.*

Next time enlighten me.

Asher: *On the third floor. Apartment 308.*

I was just about to ask if there were anything I should look out for, but he beat me to it.

Asher: *Follow the metal mailboxes, they lead to the elevator. Take it up and go right. Meet you in the hall.*

Just as he mentioned, the elevator was near the mailboxes, and I entered and pressed the button for the third floor twice when it didn't light up the first time. Everything about this place was reminiscent of a three-star-hotel-meets-housing-project, but I still thought it was nice despite of it.

I took a right out of the elevator, and there he was, leaning against the balcony that overlooked the ground-level car lot. Asher had a sense of style that I ragged on any chance I got but secretly always loved. I'd never had the confidence to wear Doc Martens, but Asher had them in every wearable color. Today he wore red ones with acid-washed jeans and a tight, lightweight sweater that hugged his upper body sinfully, making me forget we were on break until further notice. The sort of get-up he'd wear to a rave. He'd taken me a few times, but I couldn't get into the music or the light shows. The dancing wasn't like anything I'd ever grown up doing, so needless to say I've never had as much fun as he did.

The sound of my shuffling sandals caused him to look in my direction, a look in his eye that straddled disappointment and fascination. He was almost good at hiding it, and I already missed the way his corner lip piercing sent a chill down my spine when he kissed me. Our first day together as friends. Let's see how this panned out.

"Hey." He stuck his hands deep inside his pockets.

"Hey."

"Sorry about the lady downstairs. I thought you'd notice the numbers on the parking spots. Come inside." He gestured. "I don't want to leave my niece alone for too long."

He signaled for me to follow him as I closed the door behind me. The apartment was small, maybe half the size of mine, but surprisingly clean with simple furniture and lots of empty space on the walls. Maybe his sister just moved here or maybe she wasn't big on decorating, but all this place needed were a few photos hanging up or even a change of paint to look like more than just a base apartment.

Walking to the only bedroom, Asher whistled for the attention of his niece, who jumped up from the bed and into his arms. He kissed her on the forehead and mumbled something I couldn't hear from out here, but the way they interacted gave me a newfound appreciation for how caring he was. He was so sweet with her.

He put her down, and they walked hand in hand into the

living room. At the sight of me, she disappeared behind his legs, making me feel like she already hated me. Little kids had a way of being honest about things we adults didn't have the courage to.

"C'mon, Mimi. Stop being rude, okay? I told you my friend Teddy was coming. She just wants to say hi to you." Asher's tone didn't change when he spoke to her, a culture shock when all your family members talked to anyone under nine as if they were babies. Even at twenty-five, my abuelita insisted on conversing with me in baby talk, something my mom couldn't even escape. Phone calls from my grams were either passed to me or answered once a week when my mom was in a good mood.

Mimi was light brown, with wild, undefined curls that hung down her shoulders that could only be explained if her father wasn't white. I thought it was cute how her glasses made her eyes looked turned in a little, and her smile was all the more adorable in person.

"Your girlfriend's so pretty."

We both smiled, his face turning red at the sound of *your* and *girlfriend* leaving the lips of his innocent, assuming three-year-old niece. The moment could have been potentially awkward, but lucky for us, we laughed it off.

"She's not my girlfriend, Mimi. But she is pretty, though," he added with a wink. "Stop being so shy. Tell her your name." She stepped out in front of him, introducing herself as Mariah. Was I this cute when I was three?

"But tell her what you like to be called, Mariah," he added, patting her unruly hair with his palm.

"Mimi," she giggled before retreating back to Asher's wall of protection.

"If she didn't like you, she wouldn't hide. She's just shy, that's all."

While I was completely prepared to hang out here and chill, I took it as an opportunity to suggest taking his niece someplace fun. Like him, his sister didn't have a car, and for a working mom, the closest parks were a little ways from here. My guess was she spent most of her free time in this apartment. Five more minutes here and even the most grounded person could go mad.

"I have to ask her mom first. I like for her to know where I am just in case something happens."

I nodded in agreement as Asher went into the kitchen to make a phone call, leaving me and Mimi alone together in the living room.

"C'mon, sweetheart, let's sit down."

Building up her courage, she took my hand and led me to the couch. She sat next to me, taking a braid in her hand with extreme curiosity.

"I like your hair," she gushed.

"You do?" I asked in a high-pitched voice. As much as I hated baby talk, I knew no other way. "Guess what? I do my own hair. Want me to do yours?"

She nodded enthusiastically and turned her back to me as I contemplated what style to put it in. I loved braiding hair. I think it was the only useful thing I'd ever learned from my mom that didn't make my head hurt.

My mother was a huge science geek, and while I found escapism in science fiction, the topics in real life didn't hold my attention enough to stay interested. Literature and cultural studies were always what I liked the most about school. In short, my mom and I only bonded when she was braiding my hair.

I settled on two French braids, as it was both age-appropriate and easy to do on any hair type. Hers wasn't as coarse as mine but was far from easy to deal with. Reasons why I embraced my kinks without dreaming for someone else's hair type.

Asher returned to the room, his eyebrow cocked to one side. "I like your hair, Mimi."

She ran up to him as he ran his hand along the protrusions of her braid. "My sister says it's okay. What did you have in mind?"

                                  * * *

By now, the line we were standing in was almost thirty people deep. I was thrilled when some guy went around selling ice cream by the scoop, otherwise this wait would've felt longer than it was. We'd hit up a local fair with more to do than there was time to do it, but the moment we set foot in the place, there was no argument. Mimi wanted to ride the ponies.

What was it about ponies anyway? There must have been some memo I missed as a kid that riding animals were fun. We were next in line, and I already couldn't wait to get into something else around here.

A twenty-minute wait for a two-minute circle around a stable was only something a child could do without complaining, but the look on her face when the trainer helped her on the pony's back made me feel like I could wait another ten minutes. She was so full of energy. What I wouldn't give to be that carefree again.

"You have such a beautiful child," a person said in passing as we scooted over to the stable's exit. We laughed it off, but it was beginning to feel like everyone around us was going to assume we were together at a time in our lives we were trying so hard *not* to be together. Could two people just be friends without passersbyers thinking we were a couple?

"I've never gotten mistaken for her father. Then you come along and folks start piecing things together. That's hilarious."

"To be honest, I don't even know if I can have kids," I said without thinking. "I always get the '*Oh, well, you're young. You never know*' speech. I froze my eggs like a million years ago, but I know most people don't want to deal with all that. I've had people flat out tell me to have kids early. The first time I was in remission, I really thought about it, but I was barely eighteen."

He leaned against the railing, most likely confused on how to follow that. "Shit, Teddy," was all he managed to say. "Do you want kids?"

Did I want kids? The short answer was yes, but maybe my twenties wasn't the best time to be thinking about it. While money wasn't something I worried about, there were a list of things I wanted to accomplish before I entered that stage of my life. My mom'd already graduated with her master's degree and was working for an international company by the time she was a few years older than me. I had a lot of catching up to do.

"Yeah, but who the hell is going to deal with all the shit I'm going through? People say they're not out here trying to make babies, but when they get with a girl who possibly can't have their children, all of a sudden it's like they have baby fever."

None of this was based on my own experiences, but a few other girls I'd known with some serious cases had heard it all.

"Everything's about what you can give a person. Just really sucks." I scooped up the last bit of caramel ribbon-infused ice cream, and the near-melted liquid still packed enough chill to numb the inside of my mouth.

His niece came running to the side exit, begging and pleading to wait in line again, but dios bendiga, I was so glad when he said no.

"Let's do some other stuff, Mimi. We don't have a lot of time here. You might have fun doing some other things."

Mimi broke free of our clasped hands, skipping and squeeing to the nearby game booths. She stopped at one with oversized stuffed animals and blown-up crayon balloons.

Asher wrapped his arms around me, overwhelming me with his rich, masculine scent as his perfect lips pressed up against the side of my neck. I took a deep breath to center myself and was quickly snapped out of it when he took off after his niece. He didn't touch me like that for the rest of the day, but maybe it was better that way.

* * *

When I pulled into the garage parking lot, his sister was already waiting for us by the elevator that led to her place. They were definitely siblings; both shared the same light brown hair and blue eyes. She was almost as tall as him, or tall for a girl, but had a body like mine before my weight loss. I was still getting used to being a size four, considering I liked myself better when I was a size ten, but I supposed I should be grateful. Since my time back, I felt healthy, and it never crossed anyone's mind that there was something wrong with me. That's how I liked it. For things not to change.

It was funny seeing Asher and his sister exchange cheap shots every so often as they talked to each other. My older sister died years before I was born, so I always felt like I was an only child. I envied people who had siblings, especially when they looked as close as they did.

His sister waved to me, and I, in turn, waved back. He waited until they were both on the elevator to walk toward my car. I rolled down the window, and he kneeled down to rest his elbows in the car door.

"My sister told me to tell you thank you."

"It's cool. I had fun."

"Yea, me too." His eyes wandered with no particular target until he attempted to cut the moment short by telling me goodbye.

"I can give you a lift. It's not that far, Ash." I rolled my eyes. In reality, I just didn't want the day to end.

"It's cool. I don't really mind cabbing it. Didn't know if you had plans tonight."

"Oh, just shut up and get in."

He shrugged. "Okay." He got in and strapped on his seatbelt as I put the car in drive and pulled out of the parking lot.

"Hey, how was registration today? I remember you saying something the other day about registering for classes."

I let out a yawn, a clear sign of this long day. "Good, I guess. I was there all morning, though, which was why I wanted to end the day doing something."

He laughed and rested his head against the window, wordless for the rest of the ride. I pulled up to his apartment building's driveway, and he slipped off his seatbelt and finally broke the awkward silence.

"Thanks for the ride, Teddy." He edged over to my side, my heart skittering in my chest as he pressed his forehead against mine. He was so close that the warm trickle of his breath tickled my lips. I wanted him to kiss me. Why didn't he kiss me?

"You know some people aren't so hung up with what you *can't* give them, but with what you can. Anyone who can't see what I see…well, then they don't deserve you."

Without saying another word, he got out and started for his front door.

# CHAPTER TWELVE

**Teddy**

There wasn't a thing I could do to beat the cold. An electric blanket was *supposed* to help, but cold caps still managed to send frost from my highest to my lowest points, so no amount of cover ever masked it. I guess I got some relief. There was always a thirty- to sixty-second window for me to replace the next one, but I was a popsicle by then.

The audiobook I listened to bored me. It wasn't even trying to keep my attention. Maybe it was the narrator. Maybe the story sucked. Or maybe I had too much on my mind to concentrate.

This was my first maintenance therapy session. They were scheduled about four to six weeks apart from one another, but I still didn't feel better about it. I was ashamed to admit how big a part of me just wished my body would respond the way it was supposed to, considering all the damage chemo did in its wake.

It felt like my body wasn't even mine anymore.

I still couldn't believe I'd admitted to someone that, at twenty-five, my eggs were nearly shot. It was hard to admit that, if and when I wanted kids, it'd be a major struggle fertility-wise. People always told you your options, but never validated your feelings about it because it just wasn't happening to *them.*

Not to mention, I was already a huge contender for early menopause. Add that to the list of potentially difficult subjects I'd have to unload on someone or avoid talking about until the time for it came.

I was *really* trying to stay positive, but it was getting harder to do. I was supposedly doing fine by an oncologist's standards. My check-in periods never resulted in anything new forming, so I should've been grateful for no news. It was always better than bad news. It was just difficult trying to convince myself that this life wouldn't be the only one I'd know.

My success story was tied to me living with cancer, but never really beating it. I was alive, but everything else was just…complicated.

* * *

You'd think I'd be done with hospitals by now.

But I wanted to see him. I felt like I should, since I'd waited so long to since I'd been back. I hadn't heard from his mother or him, but some folks at the unofficial support group mentioned him being at Mercy Hospital. Racer was a cool kid. I didn't know why I'd been so afraid until now, but I wanted to make sure he was at least okay. Even if that didn't mean the same thing in the real world as it did in here.

I was surprised at how few people were around. Outside of nurses bustling through the hallways, the pediatric cancer wing usually had rooms filled with worried parents, kids getting other kids to play video games in the lounge, or at least people crying. Today was quiet.

Racer's family didn't have a ton of money, so it had to be a fortune him even being here. He sat on the bed, fragile and tired, not looking as well as I'd seen him the last time we smoked. But then again, I didn't know much about his health beyond what he told folks. For all I knew, he could've been doing better.

"Do I smell weed brownies?" he asked, slowly opening his eyes for the first time since I'd sat down across from him. The smell of lemon cleaner and linen lingered all around, so of course he'd be able to pick up on something foreign. His motions were slower, like he had less control. Either he was in a lot of pain or doped up on painkillers—either option wasn't much to hope for.

"Teddy?" he said in a dragged-out, exhausted voice.

"Hey," was the only response I managed without sounding corny or filled with a ton of other emotions.

"Didn't think I'd see you here. Marta…" he started, but slowly dragged out, like he was holding onto the sentence. "…sometimes she comes. But you know? Everyone's got lives. You didn't have to."

"I wanted to." I reached for his hand to squeeze, but was only met with a small pull one wouldn't expect from a teenage boy. "How ya doing?"

He sighed. "My best, I guess. Which from your point might not seem that great, but I'm really trying."

I opened the bag that sat on my lap, revealing a small sandwich bag with two brownies in it, and laid it on the table next to him. His eyes wandered to it, but he didn't move.

"I'd probably get in trouble if they found those here," he pointed out, and I suggested he just eat them now. "You should take them." His face washed away the disappointment all over his medium brown features. "By the time I have the energy to sit up, they'll probably be bad anyway."

I knew the feeling when your body didn't respond as fast as your brain did. It wasn't a dick-measuring contest, but leukemia seemed so much harder than Hodgkin's, and I was proof that the statement was not an easy one to make. He was in constant pain all the time.

Sometimes I felt all right. Other times not so much. He probably wouldn't want me to, but I broke a brownie into a few pieces and reached one toward his mouth. He chewed each bite, piece by piece, as tears streamed down his face. "Thank you, Teddy."

Once we got over the awkwardness, Racer went into a short conversation about how much help he needed at this point. Not all the time, but he was in pain when he wasn't on meds. When he was on meds, he had less control, so tasks he used to perform normally were more challenging than a few months ago. He didn't like telling his folks how much pain he was really in, but I didn't see why.

Maybe it could be viewed as complaining to other people, but voicing pain shouldn't be seen as weakness. I know why I didn't always tell people when I was in pain. No one wanted to feel bad about themselves that they weren't going through it. Which was why I never did well with therapists. People didn't want to hear you complain, but they'd pay good money for you to do so with someone else. Most times, I didn't even think talking about it got through to anyone who wasn't a survivor.

"I don't tell my friends either. They're, like, the pillars of health. They kinda don't get it either," I told him.

"Only one friend comes to visit me now. I think all my friends get bored that I don't have the energy to do much these days."

"I'm sorry."

"You're sorry? Don't take this the wrong way, Ted, but it feels condescending you feeling sorry for me. I don't feel sorry for you. Please do me the same."

Ouch. But he had a point. No pity parties. I didn't even bother apologizing.

"I'm honestly not sure I'm happy with the way things are going for me either. I'm trying my damnedest, but I just don't know anymore."

"Teddy, from where I'm sitting, you're up and out. So pretty. If I were just, like, three years older..." He couldn't finish before we both laughed. He was so silly. "Seriously. I know you're not skating through stuff easy either, but you're right there. And I'm right here. Shit seems a lot greener from where I'm sitting."

"I respectfully disagree, Race, but you're entitled your opinion." I went on to explain my own issues, even though at the time when I'd shared them with Ash, I'd been so embarrassed. Racer admitted he didn't get it. That a lot of what I worried about were "girl" problems. But he saw a different perspective I wasn't looking for.

"Society-wise, you're supposed to be able to have kids, or at least that's what we learn. I think you were only embarrassed because you like the guy. You seem really good at pushing people away, though. I don't think someone would care if they liked you back. Maybe they would at first, but they'd get over it. But what do I know…I've never even kissed a girl."

I laughed, even though it wasn't very funny. "Well, I know there isn't anyone stronger out there than you. There'll be a time when you're sitting in this chair, and you'll see. But until then…" I leaned up and kissed him on the forehead. "At least a girl has kissed you."

# CHAPTER THIRTEEN

**Teddy**

If another person jumped into my line again, I swear I was going to call out tomorrow. I hated being an express lane. More than I hated being toward the further lanes. I was as impatient as the next person, but even I was considerate enough not to hop in a fifteen-items-or-less lane, if I was twenty items over. I didn't ring *that* damn fast, and it always worked its way into getting yelled at by the customer behind them, like it was my fault they didn't want to wait.

I'd felt dizzy and nauseous a few minutes ago, but by the time my line went down, I didn't have time to ask for a bathroom break. Today was just one of those days for me.

I was two seconds from a vein popping out of my forehead, when two hands rested on my shoulders and gently squeezed. The slight scent of vanilla, wood, and citrus told me who it was without me turning around.

"Lucille's coming to relieve you. When she comes, you can do returns until seven."

"Dag, you know I get off at 8:45, right?"

Asher walked around me, swiping his key over the register when an item rang up twice. "You can take your break right after. Bruna can't, she's too slow."

Of course she was. So busy flirting and taking unofficial breaks in the bathroom, doing anything but work. They should've fired her behind.

Maybe I was bugging because she had a big crush on Asher. Half the people who worked on the front end seemed to. I didn't know how he didn't see it, but he was like every female cashier's work crush. They must've all thought he only talked to White girls, because he was singularly known as that "one White boy I would fuck with" by everyone.

I couldn't imagine him capitalizing on it, so it must've only been chatter amongst cashiers. Listening to them fawn over him kind of sucked, especially because I *had* been kind of dating him. He'd never been invasively hands-on at work for obvious reasons, but it was a stupid as hell reason why people never shipped us.

Because of Reggie, people'd seen me before, but the minute I started working here, everyone was convinced I was really a lesbian because I always wore goddess braids or cornrows to work. Top it off that I was best friends with two guys, and people couldn't keep their mouths shut. I wasn't offended—I just wasn't one, and I wasn't going to argue about it every damn shift. Can you be friends with guys, and not be mislabeled?

When Lucille finally came, eight minutes later than Asher claimed she would, I couldn't wait to be off that register. I was about to take my sweet-ass time with these returns, just like all the other lazy people who worked here. In two days, I wouldn't be worried about this place for almost a week.

After two unsuccessful attempts to hit up Seaquarium, the three of us finally decided to put our heads together and plan bigger, plan better. If we were going to hit up any aquarium, the real trip was in SeaWorld, a three-and-a-half-hour drive away, all the way in Orlando.

It wouldn't be like Seaquarium, where one could go and see everything in one visit, and it didn't seem worth it to take off for the day without making a road trip of it. The thing was, it required planning based off Asher's schedule. He was a cash office manager, so we didn't even know until two weeks ago his request for time off had been approved.

We split the trip three ways. Reggie made sure to get the car rental, as well as spot for gas, Asher'd been in charge of finding a decent hotel, and I opted for the park tickets, but only because I wanted to *maybe* hit up Busch Gardens. If we planned well, we'd have time, but I knew they didn't want to pay for it, so I stuck it in for myself.

Murking through the aisles with a cart, I shook my head at essentials like baking soda and salt getting left behind. Bet cookies and fruit roll-ups made it to people's grocery bags though.

Vicki solidified herself out of nowhere. "You're really going on vacation with Reggie and Asher?"

She was nosy as hell and a bit annoying for my taste, but she was nice and never talked crap about anyone, so I felt bad giving her attitude. "Yeah. So?" Maybe I was too used to keeping secrets. Working around people who constantly wanted to know my business never sat well, even with the employees I got along with.

Vicki clucked her tongue, shaking her head in a half-smile. She was officially on my nerves.

"What?" Wasn't homegirl off? What was she bothering me for?

"Nothing. I just never heard of a girl road tripping with two guys."

"Girl, I have to do these returns. Did you want something?"

Vicki giggled, assuring me she was messing with me before she skipped off. People were so nosy. I couldn't just like who I hung around? It wasn't like I was a girl hater/man lover. But I wasn't a girl's girl either. Maybe my bias made it hard to see it like other people, but our trip to SeaWorld wasn't an illicit one. Right? I mean, it wasn't like me and Ash were figuring out stuff anymore. We were just done. Were we not allowed to have fun with each other anymore?

* * *

*Asher*

Don't you hate when people who live nowhere nearby show up at your job just to see what you're doing? There was no other reason to see Serena and Ariana at PriceSlash, unless Ari was messing with Reggie. Which, after a long session full of weed and beer two months ago, I knew they weren't.

I wasn't phony, so I couldn't pretend not to see them. I just didn't want Serena to ask about…you know.

"Hey, playboy. Where you been at?" Ari asked, with her nosy ass.

I played it off, flirting and smiling, aware she was trying to be slick. "Y'all know where I stay at. Clearly, you know where I work." I might've mentioned it, but even though I wouldn't call us friends, we still gave each other heat if we all didn't cross paths every once in a while.

"I hear you're going out of town?" Serena wasn't as bold as Ari, but she wasn't afraid to be nosy either.

"Yeah. Get away from this hell hole."

"Is your girlfriend going?" Now she was getting to Ari's status.

"When have I ever said I had a girlfriend? I'm just going with two friends."

Teddy stomped up, pointing at the new cart of perishables customers left behind for folks to put back. "Asher, it's like 7:10. I keep doing returns, and every time I'm almost done, you keep giving me more."

"Just go on break, girl. Little whiner."

She stuck her middle finger up at me, running toward the time clock. I wasn't sure what Serena was staring at, but she had this confused look on her face, watching Teddy from a distance.

"Well, I'm gonna let you girls go."

Both of them reached in for a hug before walking toward the exit, exchanging words to one another as they peered back at me. What was their problem?

There was a supervisor upfront, and since we weren't busy, I let her know I was taking my lunch before the time clock did it for me. I ran into Reggie on my way back there. He, too, had been subjected to Ari and Serena's probing, but it made sense to know she'd just been returning a lost IPod.

"On some real shit, now that the day's coming, I don't even know whether I want to go to Orlando."

That was a lie. I wanted to go, but my roots were longer than the rest of my hair. Who the hell took off looking like a train wreck?

"Over some dark roots, homie? Why don't you just dye that shit back?"

I was getting vain over that bleached hair look. It caught too many people's eye to risk going back now. "I don't know, man. We're going somewhere where no one know us, where there'll probably be women in bikinis single as fuck, just waiting for us. Don't tell me I'm not allowed to look fresh."

"Damn, why don't you just ask Teddy to do it?"

We were walking into the breakroom, and she looked up when she heard her name. "Ask me to do what?"

Of course she'd be back here. I'd sent her on break almost fifteen minutes ago. She was probably due to go back soon, but Reggie took the empty seat next to her. I opted to sit across them.

"This diva over here acting like he can't go because his hair's grown out. Help homeboy out and hook him up with a touch up."

Teddy's spoon hit the bottom of her empty yogurt cup. "You

guys must think I'm a hair salon or something," she said as she stood, stalking over the trashcan to throw her cup away.

"See? I told you she wouldn't want to."

"I didn't say I wouldn't. But you guys get on my nerves asking for stuff last minute. You better have hair bleach by the time you get off, because I only feel like it tonight."

She walked out of the breakroom. Reggie and I shot each other shared looks of satisfied smugness. Teddy wasn't the same since we'd quit each other, but I wasn't sure if it was a good or bad different. At least she treated us both the same in front of Reggie. But I did kind of miss the way she was when we were still sweet on each other. Not that I wasn't anymore. But…it was complicated. We were just *less* complicated this way.

* * *

A pained tingle etched into my nervous system every time a dot of peroxide hit a soft spot of my already irritated scalp. It was the third time Teddy applied the bleach to my hair, and she wasn't exactly sympathetic every time it burned. I sat on the floor in front of her while she greased my ears and forehead down with Vaseline, even though she'd already done it twice since the last wash.

"Ah. Dammit!" I twitched underneath her, and she pressed her thighs down on my shoulders, leaving me little chance for wiggle room.

"I wish you would stop moving."

I tried to distract myself from the discomfort, but the only thing worth drawing my attention were her glittery green toes propped up against the top of my thighs. Had it not been for Reggie sitting across from us, I would've been tempted to tickle her just for fun. It beat just sitting there letting her torture me.

"Seriously, I'm shaving my head when this shit grows out. It looks hot, but I'm not down with the upkeep."

"Oh, hush, you big baby. Can't be that bad compared to a relaxer."

The comment seemed to spark a reaction out of Reggie, who up until now had been too busy sifting through the magazines on her coffee table. He'd already read the copy of *Niobe*, some comic Teddy put both of us onto twice. But in his defense, it was entertaining. It mirrored Teddy's taste in books, and at least that shit had pictures to help visualize everything.

"Yo, when homegirl coming out with another one? This shit was fire."

"*I don't know*. You have a phone—why don't you google it? You see I'm doing something." She rubbed a spot that seemed to activate every pain nerve in my upper body, and I couldn't help but groan in discomfort.

"Teddy, it seem like you keep nursing the *same* damn spot. I have a *whole* head. You know that, right?"

"Oh, shut up. I'm done. Go to the sink."

I let my long legs carry me faster than they ever had to wash the bleach out my hair for good. She'd been more careful the last time, but since my hair wasn't exactly pale, to get the look I was going for, it took dyeing it three times. I must've been high the first time because I didn't remember it burning that much.

"What the hell is that?" Reggie yelled over the sink's running water. The cool wet relief of the tap had my mind somewhere else, but I heard Teddy mumble, "My suitcase."

I didn't understand why Reggie was laughing until I saw it for myself. Teddy's suitcase went beyond the domestic carry-on size both of us would've expected her to bring. We were only going to be gone a few days. It seemed like she packed enough for a friggin' month.

"Seriously, Teddy?"

She shrugged defensively. "What? I didn't want to forget anything."

The suitcase sat on the outskirts of her kitchen. All it took was a kick to the front to feel it was probably just *stuff*. What I'd packed fit into a book bag. I couldn't imagine a few outfit changes required all this.

"Well, there's a pool at the hotel, right? And what if I want to read or something?"

Reggie snorted. "Teddy, only you would want to read while we're supposed to be having fun. You can read anytime."

It must've hurt her feelings because her face soured, like she was embarrassed.

"Chill, Reg. If that's what she's trying to bring, let her. Just don't ask either of us to carry it for you," I teased, hoping to change the mood. She hit me, before adding a comment about there'd be no need to, considering there'd be no *real* men to ask anyway. Just for that, I tossed the mail on her counter to the floor. When she threatened me to pick it up, I hid away in the bathroom and snatched her blow dryer to complete my look. When I was done, I searched her cabinets for anything to put in my dry hair. I opted for the only thing that looked appropriate—a leave-in conditioner.

Teddy and Reggie were having a friendly debate, one I walked right into before I got the chance to figure out what it was about.

"I already told you. I'm not driving!"

"I feel like I'm paying for the rental, so I shouldn't have to drive there and back too—"

"Do you want a cookie? I drive you bozos around all the time. If anything, that should exempt me."

Reggie and Teddy's gazes swerved toward me, making me the new target.

"You hear that, Ash? Looks like you're driving." Reggie said, before I could defend it.

I wasn't about to go down without a fight. Three hours wasn't a long time when you were a passenger, but when I couldn't move around, my back and legs got stiff as hell. I didn't know how Teddy'd done it, but her sixth sense put her in the clear.

Reggie and I were left to a mean game of Rock-Paper-Scissors before it was decided Reg would drive there and I'd be in charge on the way back.

* * *

"Tough luck, bruh," Teddy teased from the backseat. She was laughing now, but she couldn't play DJ from all the way back there. I didn't hate her musical choices, but I was hearing so much bachata and reggaeton, I was salsa-ing in my sleep. At least Reggie played that dumb shit we went nuts over. Teddy didn't seem too concerned. An hour into the ride, she stretched out in the backseat and went to sleep.

She looked car sick for some reason, but when we probed, all she'd admit to was the lack of sleep she'd gotten last night. Between traffic and two rest stops, the three-and-a-half-hour trip took nearly five hours. There was one advantage to running late. By the time we got to the hotel's parking lot, we were a few minutes away from an early check-in time.

Since I'd been in charge of looking up the hotels, I'd tried to find the best deal closest to everything we'd want to drive to. The pictures online gave me mixed signals about the place. Some reviews hated it, some liked it, but just from the lobby, the Monumental already exceeded its expectations.

"Damn, this is *a lot* nicer than I thought you'd pick out." Reggie said.

We had fifteen minutes until two o'clock, but even as we waited, the sights kept getting better and better. Some of the most beautiful women we'd ever seen walked into the lobby, heading toward what seemed to be the pool.

"Aye, Ash, you see that?"

My mouth was too busy catching flies. "Girls of all complexions. I like cinnamon."

Teddy swiped a page on her e-reader and rolled her eyes. "You guys are so corny. And you call *me* corny."

Her pursed lips suggested I'd gone too far, but that's really how I was around Reg. I was just trying to treat her like one of the guys. Maybe I should tone it down. I wasn't that insensitive.

"Excuse me, Mr. Rose?" the guest service rep at the front desk called out over the busy chatter from the lobby. We were just a few minutes past two, and she needed my photo ID and card information.

"We're just waiting on confirmation that your room is ready."

I sat back down, waiting patiently to hear back. As soon as she called my name again, we were three keys away from heading to the third floor.

* * *

*Teddy*

*Oh my god.* How are we friends? These two were getting on my last nerves. If they brought up *NBA 2K* one more time, I was considering headphones the remainder of the trip. I guess I didn't blame them. All they ever talked about were the only three things they had in common. Video games, weed, and girls. Sometimes sports, but it was only to argue because they preferred different teams. If *I* wasn't here, they'd never talk about anything new. They needed me to liven things up. But they got on my duck-plucking nerves.

By the time we got off the elevator, it dawned on me that no one'd ever discussed sleeping arrangements for the room. I didn't know any affordable hotels that offered three beds a room, so most likely we'd be forced to figure out what to do with two doubles.

There were a lot of reasons why I wanted my own bed. For one, I didn't want to share one with someone I used to sleep with… Maybe Asher wouldn't fight me on it, but I was expecting to get a ton of pushback from Reggie.

The room was nice, decently sized, with two cream-covered doubles, a flat screen in the middle of the room, and three dressers of all different sizes dressers on opposite sides. The bathroom was small. You almost missed it since it was so close to the room door, but for the price, convenience, and location, it was a pretty good deal.

Asher threw his travel bag toward the door to the bathroom, hopping onto the bed closest to the door to claim as his territory. "Two beds. Three people. What we doing?"

It wasn't open for discussion. I was the only woman. I wasn't sharing a bed. "Why don't you guys take that one, and I'll just take the one furthest from the door," I said as I sat on the mattress, hoping to not get a fight. Why did I have that much expectation?

Reggie's upper body and facial features flared at the fact I'd even suggest it. "Seriously? Teddy, this dude takes up, like, three-quarters of a bed. You're the smallest. If anything *you*, should have to share."

Unless we were switching to a room with a couch, I wasn't going to give up on my stance. Reggie and me continued to go back and forth about what was and wasn't fair. Even when he suggested, I be the one to bed with Ash, I had to lie about how I wasn't feeling the idea.

"No offense, Ash. I love you, but I don't know you like that."

Asher's shoulders dropped and he hid behind a hunched posture and tightly pressed lips. Other than that, he wasn't slighted by the comment. He slid off the bed, reaching into his bag for something.

"How about we do this? We're not gonna do Rock-Paper-Scissors because Teddy stay cheating." He revealed a quarter he twirled between two fingers. "Heads or tails?"

My intuition told me to pick tails, but something about the

way Asher kept playing with the damn thing made me pick heads.

It only took two rounds to make me sole proprietor of the bed I'd already made claim to. We could've saved five minutes if they'd just listened to me from the jump. Reggie slumped down in defeat, reaching down for the room's only remote control. In our attempt to beat traffic, not one of us took a shower before the drive. Before anyone else could, I thought it best to claim the bathroom.

I'd brought my own amenities. I wasn't picky, but I had a hunch Ash and Reg wouldn't remember to bring any. I wasn't about to split hotel toothpaste and soap with them, so it was best to be prepared. And I took my time, too. Or, at least, they must've thought so since they kept knocking on the door. They actually had the audacity to say I was taking so long on purpose.

"You guys are so impatient."

Reggie zoomed past the open door the minute I walked out. We didn't even know what we were going to do our first hours here, but since I'd have to wait for the two of them anyway, I took it as a time to devour books on my Nook. Or so I thought.

Have you ever been forced to listen to a Fetty Wap song and wondered…why? Multiply that times one hundred when you're forced to listen to someone with even fewer vocal skills sing his songs. Reggie's wailing and the TV aside, it was quiet between the rest of the hotel room. Asher and I never forced conversation, even when we were *like* that. And it was hard to talk about pre-Reggie stuff, or post-Reggie stuff, so it limited what we actually brought up when he was in earshot.

Reggie didn't take as long as I had, but when he came out in swim trunks and a bag of his former clothes, Asher shot up on the bed. "Where are *you* about to go?"

"I know you ain't forget those girls we saw in the lobby."

Asher hopped off the bed, kneeling to grab a pair of trunks

and a towel as he was next in line for the bathroom. "Say no fucking more. Give me a minute, I'll meet you down there."

This crap again. I wasn't about to sit in a hotel room while the two of them had fun, but I'd have to wait until Asher showered before I'd have access to the mirror in the bathroom again.

I had over a dozen or two swimsuits, but like most my clothes, they didn't fit the same after the weight loss. My hips weren't as wide, my boobs not as perky, and even gaining a few pounds didn't fill them out the way I used to. I'd been able to get two in my current size during a Forever 21 trip with Asher on his search for a new belt. How he survived with just one in the first place was beyond me.

While he'd been figuring out himself out in the men's section of the store, I'd managed to sneak a tankini and decently wired two-piece, crediting it to a cute dress I'd seen online. Asher didn't ask questions when he wasn't curious, so there hadn't been a need to explain. I didn't know why I'd waited until the trip to try them on. They still had the tags on them. But before I went out there, I just wanted to make sure I looked all right in them.

It was easier for them. All they'd have to do was throw on some water-safe shorts and they were ready to hit the pool. Asher was on it, because he took even less time than Reggie before he hightailed out the door.

Now that I had the room to myself, I tried on each swimsuit, studying the effect of each one. The navy blue two-piece popped against my skin and made the tattoo on my shoulder more prom-inent. The underwire worked miracles and made my boobs look better than they did in my regular bras. But thinking back to those girls in the lobby—plethoras of toned stomachs, small waists, and bigger butts than mine that were too nice to not have been paid for—brought my confidence level down.

When I was chubby, my stomach hadn't been flat, but…I'd just taken the things that had made my body unique for granted. I didn't lose it overnight, so the confidence wouldn't come back that soon either. Maybe I should start exercising. Girls got nice bodies that way all the time. When we got back, I had to look into joining a gym or hiring a personal trainer. Right now? I just wanted to know why this tankini made me look shapeless.

Maybe shapeless was the wrong word, but it did make me look way more angular than I actually was. I was starting to think that, no matter which one I chose, I'd find something wrong with it. Since we still had a few days upon us, if we did make the amusement park trip, I'd need heavy-duty underwire for rides. Guess the tankini won by default.

I didn't plan on doing much swimming in it anyway. A slick of lip-gloss, a fully synced Kindle-to-Nook app, and my trusty chanclas, and I was on my way to the lobby.

Even if the hotel looked average up until now, the pool was definitely a standout, with bright blue water and a spacious patio and lounge area. The statue lions spitting water back into the pool was overkill, but I was content not having to fight for pool-side space as I made myself comfortable under a tent.

It didn't take long to spot Ash and Reggie. Right where they wanted to be—surrounded by girls that were probably going to play them. Just from a distance, not all of them seemed impressed, but the boys had their ways. Maybe I didn't have as much experience with girls as they did, but my approach would've been more dead-on. Less flirting, more talking. But I'm sure whatever they were doing worked for them. It worked on me.

I needed to get back to my book and stop worrying about them. All I was doing was getting myself riled up for nothing. I was two books into the *Her Instruments* trilogy, and the main character wasn't working me. The books were good, but she needed a heavy dose of common sense.

My vision was acting up again, but I wasn't sure if it was from lack of sleep or the sun beaming down through the mesh. I was having trouble keeping my attention on my e-reader, and to top off the dizzy vision, my nose started to run. I didn't have any tissues, but I'd managed to remember to bring a towel from the room. Just in case.

A fresh bright-red line stained the towel.

How long had my nose been bleeding? I couldn't let anyone see me like this. I was more prone to the occasional nosebleed during chemotherapy, but it didn't mean I never got them when I wasn't. Not wanting to disturb the atmosphere of the trip over nothing, I chose to omit this small detail. If they asked questions, they'd think something was wrong. It was best to just leave the poolside and figure everything out until the bleeding stopped. I'd been fine during a follow-up three weeks ago. It was best to just be careful.

I hadn't pictured my first few hours here to be stuck locked in a bathroom nursing a nosebleed. I sure as hell didn't want my whole time here to be like that. By the time the bleeding stopped, the sound of the boys' rowdy exchanges filled the main area of the room. I wasn't going to leave the towel here. The best I could do was wrap it into another one and get them replaced. Or I could blame my period. Guys never fought you on that.

I tried zooming past them, but Reggie wouldn't let me without drilling me. "What happened to you? One second we saw you, the next we—"

I interrupted him before he could finish, hoping neither would probe further than that.

"These towels are friggin' gross. All this money, you'd think they'd replace them with clean ones. I'm about to complain to the front desk for some *actual* clean ones."

Neither questioned me, which was good. I wouldn't have had a follow-up if they had. I was a little embarrassed. Asher saw me during chemo, but I didn't think Reggie was prepared to know things like that. In his defense, I didn't think either of them could handle it. The only difference? In the past, Asher chose not to ignore when he noticed things were off with me. But he'd been *way* more into me then. Now that he didn't have to notice, he probably wouldn't.

When I got back to the room from the front desk, the first thing Asher did was throw my Nook on my mattress. "You were in such a rush, you forgot it. I would've left it, but I figured you had to be the only person at the hotel *that I knew* with an 'I got that good hair' sticker on the back of her e-reader."

My bad. When I thought back, I wasn't even worried about it, but I was grateful someone thought to pick it up for me.

Reggie stretched out on their shared bed and turned on the TV again. He'd managed to change into sweats and a T-shirt, even though I hadn't seen him change.

"Damn, what did we do? Seem like we only been here a few minutes and it's already eight o'clock," he said as he channel-surfed for nothing in particular.

Right? Like they assumed flirting would be an in-and-out process…

"I'm friggin' straving," Asher mumbled, rubbing his face. "I haven't eaten since this morning."

"Bet if y'all woulda listened to me we wouldn't be hungry." Remind me to thank the two geniuses who'd suggested Dunkin' Donuts while on the highway. I'd told them to wait, but they said they couldn't. A Starbucks popped up fifteen minutes after we hopped back on the highway. Not a single person in the car could appreciate DD once you've been nursed on Starbucks, so all we'd had were donuts and a few half-drunken lattes. At least some real espresso would've suppressed the appetite.

They moaned and groaned as if it'd been the fifth time I mentioned it today. Guess a big fat "I told you so" was hard to hear every other minute.

"We could get bar food? Take out? Head out?" I suggested.

But every single one of us was hell-bent on riding, not driving. If I didn't feel so off, I would've, but being behind the wheel when you were looking for something to pass wasn't smart.

"Well?" I offered again.

Asher stretched on their bed, opposite of Reggie. "You driving?"

"You know what? You guys can do whatever. I'm hitting up GrubHub. Since you want to be stupid."

You would've thought all that flirting brought some off-set energy or something. Asher kicked the side of Reggie's arm, mumbling something between "you trying to eat?" or "you hungry?" I wasn't sure; my brain was too wired on the sound of the television on in the background.

I didn't use the app enough to keep it on my phone all the time, but I figured I might need it for the trip, so I downloaded it to get a better look at menus. Orlando wasn't too different from Miami, but we definitely had a lot more Latin restaurants willing to deliver. We could almost always agree on something Colombian, Peruvian, or Brazilian. Everything here was burger spots, wing joints, and bar food.

Ash and Reg both rolled off their bed, joining on opposite sides on mine, debating what to order. "What about Bobby G's?" Reggie asked.

Asher was quick to dismiss, and I didn't blame him. "That place don't even have reviews. And it looks like thet just serve wings."

"I was basing it on the wait times. Almost every place up here predicts a 90-100 minute wait time," Reggie said, shutting Asher's initial comment down. None of us were willing to wait over an hour just for takeout, but it looked like in the end we'd have little choice. If we had to wait, it'd better be worth it.

Asher reached over, tapping the "next page" cursor on the bottom of the page. All it revealed was a new set of places none of us were sure about. "What about Lam's Garden?"

"Dude, what is it with White folk and Chinese food?"

Asher's middle finger shot up at Reggie. "Fuck you. It's a fifteen-dollar minimum with a two-dollar delivery fee. Most these places are charging, like, seven dollars."

I scrunched my nose up at the idea. "I'm not in the mood for Chinese." All it'd do was tear up our stomachs, and I wasn't about to experience a bathroom with two guys after Chinese food.

"You better not suggest sushi. Three rolls and my ass is still hungry," Asher countered.

They weren't suggesting anything we could all eat comfortably. I was hungry, but nausea could get the best of me if I ate the wrong thing. We all universally agreed pizza was out, but it seemed that was all we agreed on.

"Well, I'm not ordering from a burger spot. Out of the twelve they have, none of them deviate far from the options they serve."

Asher shook his head, smiling. "You are getting on my nerves with that picky-eater mess."

Said the person who didn't want sushi. Between Thai, Cuban, and Vietnamese, we all knew we could find better Cuban spots in Miami. For *much* cheaper. Plus we could have that anytime. I wanted to try something new.

"What about Vietnamese?" Reggie finally suggested.

"What *about* Vietnamese?" Asher asked dismissively.

I was curious to explore the menu myself, as there were more Japanese and Chinese places than anything in Miami. Tapping on the extended menu revealed a ton of diverse options. There was even vegetarian, not that I was one.

"I've never had it before. But I like their menu so far. Beats burgers," I said.

Asher picked the phone out of my hand and stretched out on my mattress. "I'm going to need serious convincing."

"They serve, like, a million things. There'll be something you'd eat," Reggie said.

"Y'all decided amongst each other that's what *you* wanted. Can I at least see if there's anything I'd eat up here?"

Of course he was about to be difficult. Asher's stare danced along the scrolled screen as he studied and tapped on every single item that called out to him. It wasn't until he dropped the phone on the bed that we figured it'd be the best place to order from.

"I mean, I'll fuck with it. Just don't get mad if I order mad shit. I don't know if I trust those dinner orders, but I'd get a sub because you can't eff those up. Worse comes to worse, I'll just smoke and be too hungry to care what it tastes like."

"You got weed?" Reggie asked, too anxious in his demeanor to hide it.

"Like I'd leave for three days without weed," Asher snapped back with a sly smirk. Reggie didn't require any special instructions for his pork stew, but Asher basically picked the whole menu. Ash wanted dessert, a sub, a dinner order, and none of this included a drink.

I debated whether to get tofu, chicken, or veggies as my main source of protein for the night. I didn't love tofu, but I ate it when my appetite for chicken wasn't strong.

"You're really about to spend fourteen bucks on soup?" Asher asked, with his annoying ass. "We coulda just got Chinese food at half this price!" He complained. He did always like Chinese food.

We didn't get drinks, but there was a beverage machine not far from the elevator. For once, Reggie volunteered to grab a bucket of ice, as well as any soft drink requests. As long as we gave him the money upfront. "Just making sure y'all ain't trying to play me."

The minutes-long gap between Reggie grabbing ice and coming back? Felt like hours since Ash and I didn't exchange much while we waited for Reggie's return. Maybe we were just nervous Reggie would walk in on the *wrong* conversation, so we chose not to converse at all.

"They only had Coke and Dasani. I got you a Coke," Reggie said as he threw the soda to Ash. Keeping the other Coke to himself, he tossed the remaining water to me.

"What's good with that kush?" Reggie asked as I walked toward the bathroom, rolling my suitcase closer to my side of the room. Asher pointed to his bag, and since I was already up, I took it upon myself to do the honors.

"Which pocket?" I knelt close to the bag. They'd been serious about not bringing more than a bag's worth of stuff. Made me feel bad I'd lugged a small suitcase around with too many options I couldn't possibly wear in three days.

"Front zip."

The front zip didn't have much, save for socks and condoms. If he'd tried to cram everything in here to prevent bringing a second book bag, it showed. The citrus-y scent of whatever blend he and Reg liked so much was tucked in the corner of the pocket, in a sandwich bag with roll paper. My hand grazed over a quarter that didn't really look like a quarter. They didn't normally have two faces, did they?

"You find it?"

I ignored it, grabbed the contents he asked for and threw it his way. I laid my suitcase at the head of the right side of me. I wasn't about to beg, but that shit looked too sweet not to blaze up right now.

Ash preceded to roll the weed in blunt paper, asking either of us for a lighter. I only had a book of two matches, and I was saving them for cigarettes, but thankfully Reggie supplied the lighter. As soon as Ash lit, the smoke scented the room.

"I'm only going to ask this once. What are we doing tomorrow, and when are we starting?"

"You got tickets to Busch Gardens, right?" Reggie, with his nosy ass. How the hell did he know?

"How'd you know I got Busch Garden passes?"

"The receipt, stupid."

I tossed a pillow Reggie's way just for the hell of it. Looking ass.

"Okay, so…we starting early? Because we have to get up to eat and shower, and I don't know how long either of you take in the morning."

"How early is *early*?" Asher chimed in.

I shrugged. "How about eight?"

Asher's eyes widened, like he couldn't believe I was suggesting it. "In the morning? Damn, I was thinking, like, eleven."

"Do you know how packed Busch Gardens is this time of year?" Clearly they didn't. The arguing ceased once I reminded how little time we'd have here.

"So we're getting up at eight? Or we're getting ready *by* eight? Because those two are totally different." He took one puff and passed it to me, which by now, was needed. These kids acted like this trip was supposed to be watching bikinis and hitting on girls the entire trip.

"Getting up by eight. But the earlier we're ready, the better."

"A'ight. I won't stay up mad late. Since I got you nagging me," Asher joked.

Dude was testing me. It was a good thing the effects of inhaling were already working its magic. I was getting too damn aggravated today for little to no reason. I reached between the open space separating our beds to hand it to Reggie. By now I was hungry.

"Y'all better act like this was worth taking off for," I said to no one in particular.

The room was full of contact-high giggles and pointing out all the ways I nagged them. I hit both of them with pillows, until my phone rung, the go-ahead that our food was finally here.

# CHAPTER FOURTEEN

**Asher**

How did I expect to wake up? Definitely not with a pillow thrashed across my face.

"What the frack?" My eyes adjusted to the low-lit darkness of the room. Teddy stood a few feet away from me, edging toward Reggie's side to give him the same wake-up call.

"Gosh. Are you guys ever going to get up? I've been up for hours. I'm tired of waiting on your beauty sleep."

I pointed to the alarm clock close to my side before I gave it a second look. "It's not even..." Hmph. Word to wise. Never start that sentence unless you can actually make an argument. It already read 12:16 in the afternoon. Not even close to the time we'd planned. "Damn. Never mind. My bad." Two in the morning was not a decent bedtime to start a day off early, I'd done it before, but the pressure not to get up didn't motivate me. Now we got Teddy all pissed. It did *not* look good for us.

"Seriously, Ted. It's dark as hell in here. I was so sure it was seven o'clock." Reggie stretched out, and Teddy ripped both the sheets we wore and threw them to the floor.

"Damn, homie. You don't even know if I was dressed under that," I joked, sitting up in my underwear. It was a good thing I didn't have morning wood.

Teddy stalked around the room to turn on the light. Reggie and I groaned as our eyes adjusted to the change. "All this stalling. Could you two get up and dressed, please? We're already running late."

I couldn't speak for Reg, but getting rushed just made me slower. "Who got the shower first, me or you?" I said, directing my comment toward Reggie.

"I'm not even ready. If you're straight, by all means."

Guess there was no time to waste. Teddy waited long enough, and nothing would wake me better than a cold shower. Before I knew it, I was showered, dressed, and bored waiting on Reggie to finish up in the bathroom.

I tried to let my phone preoccupy me as I *pretended* not to watch Teddy slick lotion all over her bare legs. It'd been so long since I'd run my hands all over them, I was afraid I'd forget what they felt like. Would I ever get the chance to again? Ever since she'd gotten on this whole "let's be actual just-friends" thing, I'd respected the boundaries that came with it. I hated it, but I had to live my life, too.

"So…" Teddy started, but paused between words as she steadied her hand to put mascara on. "Two-headed coin. Clever."

The room filled with silence before she finally turned to me, expecting a response or reaction. I dropped my phone onto my stomach, slumping forward into a shrug. "Did you want to share a bed or not?"

Everything was so complicated between us, even when it wasn't trying to be. The situation. Us. Even our friendship was still complicated. Everything we did around each other tested comfort zones. The line between weird and normal was always going to be thin. But Teddy never got to answer. Reggie emerged from the bathroom fully dressed and ready to go. After a mean game of Rock-Paper-Scissors (which convinced me Teddy was a mind reader), I was driving. No one had eaten, so with control of the wheel, I drove to the closest Waffle House I could find.

Maybe it was because I was too used to Miami, but Orlando natives didn't seem as friendly. If Disney World, Epcot, and Universal Studios wasn't enough to put you in a good mood, I didn't know shit that would. Maybe with all it had going on, they were sick of tourists. By the time we were assigned a booth, we'd mutually agreed not to piss off the waiter. Wouldn't want anything extra with our food.

"So we tried the early thing. That might work for Reg, but I'm in bum mode when I know I don't have to get up for work," I said before Reggie interrupted me.

"Like the rest of us aren't?"

"Dude, they got me working twelve- to fourteen-hour shifts most times with no days off to recharge. This is my vacation."

It was probably insensitive to bring up, especially since half the time, they were begging for hours. They were never forced on them based in the high volume of callouts, like me.

"Well, how about we switch places for a week, and I'll take your check, and you can have mine?" Reggie said as the waitress came around to take our orders.

"Let me get an All-Star, with an extra side of eggs and sausage?" I was hungry. If I could've ordered the whole menu, I would've.

"I'll take a Texas Bacon. Can I get grits as my side?" Reggie requested. Damn, I should've gotten grits. Oh, well, I'd just help myself when he wasn't looking. Though, doing so in the past always got me in trouble.

When it came Teddy's turn to order, she looked a little out of it. She kept rubbing her eyebrow, like she couldn't concentrate on the menu. "I'll just have an orange juice and an egg-and-cheese melt."

"That's it?" Reggie beat me to it.

"I'm not that hungry right now." She handed her menu to the waitress, who disappeared into the back of the restaurant. I leaned over the table, reaching my fingers to interlock with Teddy's.

"You okay?" Something seemed off, but I definitely wasn't expecting her to snatch her hand away and end with "weirdo." Even if she was joking, it still felt…I don't know. Maybe she was just in a bad mood. If she was going to be that way the whole trip, I'd keep to myself or stay out of her way.

We ate while discussing plans. It was a ninety-minute drive to Busch Gardens, so it was best to fill up now and figure out what to do from there.

"Well, between driving there, rides, chilling, I'm going to be hungry afterwards. Or we could always eat there," Reggie said. I wasn't against it, but the food was more expensive at a theme park than the outskirts. We probably wouldn't know what we'd do until we get there.

SeaWorld was only a few minutes from the hotel, but we all weighed in. If we wanted our last day here memorable, it'd have to wait. Plus, there was no way we'd take an hour-and-a-half drive to Busch Gardens after exploring SeaWorld. I ordered a coffee, which didn't suck considering it wasn't Starbucks, while Teddy excused herself to use the restroom.

"Yo, what's her problem?" Reggie whispered.

Like I'd know? I shrugged. "Probably just pissed we woke up late."

We didn't have time to reach an open dialogue before Teddy got back. By then, the waitress already left the check on the table. I left a twenty, even though my stuff came up to a little under sixteen. Teddy hadn't ordered much, so she left a ten.

"What's good, Reggie? Chip-ins?"

"Dag, it looks like y'all covered it," Reggie said, a smile plastered on his face. The bill almost came up to thirty, but that wasn't even including tip.

"If you're not gonna pay your third, at least leave a tip!"

Reggie gestured to the waitress at the end of the busy room. "That chick didn't even do anything."

"If you're about to be like that…" I waved over our waitress when she had a free minute. "Yeah, can we get this ticket itemized? We're actually not paying together."

Reggie shot me a face like he'd been trying to pull a fast one and was mad he got caught out. "Oh, so you 'bout to be petty now, too?"

"See it as payback for Rock-Paper-Scissors."

* * *

*Teddy*

Nausea didn't begin to describe the way my insides felt. I hadn't eaten much, but even a small breakfast put me through the ringer. I'd been so hungry last night. Clearly it was something that'd pass, but I couldn't stand the back-and-forth. I didn't want to say anything about it, especially since we spent all this money getting here. Asher and Reggie wouldn't know how to handle *nothing* anyway. If I said I didn't feel well, they'd just want to go home.

I could tough it out for now. I just wouldn't eat when I wasn't hungry. If I couldn't handle a ride, I might even sit out. But I wasn't going to let it ruin the fun. We were only here another day.

* * *

Damn, we were dumb. It only took a ninety-minute drive to Tampa to realize everyone forgot their swimsuit. We traveled around the park, trying to read the map to figure out which way to go. None of us had been here for years.

"I wasn't trying to walk around in wet clothes. Guess all the water rides are out," Reggie said.

We debated which rides would accommodate all three of us at the same time. Most rides didn't, so we took turns being third wheels to someone else's party or that lone weirdo who comes to the park by themselves.

We should've anticipated a busy park, even for a weekday. Any day in the summertime was bound to be full of people, so most of the thrill rides had sixty-plus minute waits. We'd be lucky to sweep the park's best rides if the lines moved along fast enough. Bet they wouldn't be against waking up early tomorrow.

"It's Armageddon out here," Asher said, referring to the heat. We couldn't help where we were standing. The line only moved every five minutes, so the sun was beaming down like the world was about to end. Reggie needed to hurry up. When he left to go to the bathroom eight minutes ago, the line was already long.

But as we waited for the newest addition to Busch Gardens, the Cobra's Curse, the line kept getting ridiculously longer, even for an amusement park. I was afraid by the time he got back, people wouldn't let him through to find us. You weren't supposed to cut, but everybody did, so…

"I wish this dude would hurry up. There's already a shit load of people past the sixty-minute point," I said as we approached the thirty-minute point.

Asher stretched his arms over his head, clasping his hands behind him, and laughed. "He didn't seem to care the first time he did it."

If it'd been me, I would've just held it. Reggie had to be a big baby about it.

A muffled ringtone went off in Asher's pocket, which he didn't hesitate to answer. "Yo." He mouthed to me that it was Reggie as a surge of people lurched forward, bringing us closer to the fifteen-minute point. "Where are you?" Asher tapped my shoulder, and we both looked around for Reggie in the crowd behind us. Reggie propped himself on a line separator, gesturing for us to come his way. Asher waved him off and covered the bottom of his phone. "They're not letting him through."

Figures. He should've gone *before* we went to wait in line. "Dude, you wait until we're almost on the ride. Why don't you wait back there, and when we're done, we can just go on it again?" We ascended some new stairs, and now that we were standing on them, I couldn't believe it had taken more than an hour to get to.

"I don't know what to tell you. I'm not getting out of line. Teddy told you not to get out of line. Yeah, I thought she was being annoying, too, but that's why you're back there and we're up here." Asher put the phone away. "Heh, he hung up on me."

"You know? I'm standing right here."

Asher laughed, beside himself as usual. "My bad. I didn't mean it in a bad way. Just…you know how you get."

I had to refrain myself from showing any emotional tells that might unintentionally prove whatever point he was trying to make. "How do I *get?*"

"Oh, come on. You know you get mad for no reason. Don't shoot the messenger. I'm only repeating what we both noticed."

Both noticed? What the hell was that supposed to mean? "Sorry I can't be Little Miss Sunshine all the time."

"See, there you go." The line advanced once more, and we were two waits away from riding the rollercoaster. It didn't seem as cool as the ride it replaced, but at least I'd get to try it. Might be years before I felt like coming again.

"Whatever, I guess. Didn't know I always had to be a cheerleader with my friends."

"Ted, you know I didn't mean it like that. But we're just trying to have fun. You nagging or scowling at us 24/7 just brings the mood down. We're supposed to be having fun, right?"

Didn't know keeping track of time was considered nagging. Noted.

"What, no comeback? Snarky remark? Not even a nasty look?" Asher shot back, like he was trying to get a reaction.

"You already said how you felt. Do things your way. I don't care."

"You seem like you're mad at me, and I don't even know what I did. It's not just the trip. But I'm telling you now. I notice."

"Believe it or not, Ash, I can have problems that don't have shit to do with you." Maybe that was a little harsh. His expression change said he took it harder than I meant it.

"I wasn't suggesting…you know what? Never mind."

* * *

Well, that was a situation I never wanted to relive. Why were things so awkward between me and Ash now? We weren't the same as we were when I first got back, but I could still take him up on an offer to hit up the movies. Or the mall. What made this trip so different? We'd started out so normal in the beginning. I kept second-guessing things. It wasn't what I thought it would or thought they'd be. I kept imagining a trip full of adventures, like we were the hood Harry Potter and squad.

Maybe I was just bitter I wasn't really over him, but he looked hella-over me. And that was just the thought I allowed myself to admit.

By the time we got back to the hotel room, we were moments away from championing where to eat. I was the only person who hadn't driven since we started the trip, so I volunteered, since I'd never hear the end of it. I was a little less queasy. Strong emphasis on little. But I was up for it, even if I wasn't that hungry.

My clothes were too sweaty to feel comfortable in, so after a quick change, I washed my face and debated whether I should redo my makeup to match what I wore. Reggie had to make a quick run to the car, anyway, so I wasn't rushing. In all the excitement, he'd left his phone in the car and wanted to charge it before we left. I was in the bathroom when I heard our hotel room door open.

"Aye yo, Ash. I gotta tell you something," Reggie whispered, though not quiet enough where I couldn't hear him. Asher seemed to follow suit, and by the way his voice lowered, I could imagine a great big grin on his face as he replied with a, "What?"

"Pool party. We're invited. Homegirl from the other day was asking for you."

"Who? That chick with the big ass?"

I didn't know why, but I felt compelled to look at my own behind in the mirror. I was still skinny, but I'd gained *some* weight. I didn't know why I was insecure all of a sudden. I looked hot. Or at least, I think I did. I didn't have much time with myself before someone knocked on the threshold of the bathroom door. "You dressed?"

"What?"

The two of them popped their heads inside. Was it possible to look as pathetic as they sounded just a minute ago?

"Rain check on dinner?" Both of them grinned.

"You guys are really about to ditch me for some girls?"

"Not ditch. More like postpone." Reggie talked with his hands. "You don't mind, right? What's another twenty, forty-five minutes tops?"

Wow. This was really about to happen. "So I'm supposed to wait until the two of you are ready?"

"You could come with," Asher offered.

"No thanks." I slipped on some flats, grabbed the only set of car keys, and made my way through to the door.

"Damn, what's your problem?"

"Does it matter? I'll just be back. Hope you guys have fun."

I wasn't that hungry, but my foot hit the gas in search of a place to go. There were plenty of clubs, bars, or tapa spots I could set my sights on, but I wasn't up for a long drive. I pulled into the first wings joint I saw and planted myself at the almost-empty bar.

"Are you waiting for someone?" the bartender asked, wiping off the end of the bar I wasn't sitting at.

"No…it's just me."

* * *

*Asher*

There was nothing on but Spike TV, Adult Swim, or softcore porn, and with no more weed, it was no longer as entertaining. I didn't know about Reggie, but my attention wouldn't last long, especially since it was already past one in the morning. We were both tired as hell, especially after tonight.

"Seriously, fuck those chicks. They weren't even that cute anyway."

I wasn't as slighted as Reggie was. Sure, the pool party had turned out to be a bust the minute we found out the girls we'd clung to all night weren't interested as soon as some ballers came around. But a part of me hadn't really wanted to. I wouldn't have stopped it if anything had, but I was relieved it hadn't.

The girls had been definitely pretty enough, and I was drunk and horny enough. But it didn't feel right, especially after Teddy left to do her own thing. I was surprised I hadn't heard from her since we got back.

"Yeah, whatever. Someone's just gonna fuck them and leave them. Then they'll be looking for dudes like us, and by then, we'd probably fuck them and leave them, too," I said, sticking my tongue out, dapping my joining fist to his.

I mostly felt for Reggie. I knew he looked forward to it more than I did. But now that we were back, Teddy's absence haunted me more and more, and I was letting it worry me. "You heard from Teddy yet?" I asked nonchalantly.

"Nah."

Neither of us heard from her since six, and then we were so lit and pissed, it didn't dawn on either of us to call and check up on her.

"I'll text her to see if she's out. You should, too. Just in case." I wasn't sure she'd want to hear from me after that salty exchange before we'd left for the party. It was confusing, especially since she'd made it clear other liaisons outside of each other would be forgiven.

Two separate vibrations went off on her side of the room. Of course no one'd heard from her. Her phone was right where she'd left it. I wasn't sure if it was my protective instinct, especially since she was a girl in a foreign place, but neither one of us were doing anything more important than watching reruns of *Animal Hospital.*

"We need a fucking better buddy system. We should've at least checked up on Teddy, just to make sure she wasn't by herself."

Reggie didn't seem as concerned at first, but he eventually caught on once he realized the seriousness of the situation. "You know Teddy gonna do what she wanna do. But I do wanna know if she's okay, so give me a sec. We'll go check the obvious."

As soon as Reggie slipped on his shoes, the hotel door opened, and in poured Teddy. She held her own shoes in her hand and had since tied her braids in a bun.

Reggie clucked his tongue. "Man, see? She's okay. Getting me worried for nothing." He kicked off his shoes, diving face-first onto the mattress. "We were about to go look for you."

Teddy crawled over her bed, grabbing flip-flops and a box of cigarettes from the front flap of the suitcase on her side of the room. "Hope you weren't about to go through all that trouble just for me."

There was just enough bite to her tone to make me regret even going to that damn party, but with Reggie inches away, I chose to ignore it. She made her way to the door and disappeared again.

Drown out Reggie's snoring? Check out what Teddy's deal is? I would've needed to be dead-tired to fall asleep next to that dude again, and since I was feeling some kind of way with how Teddy and I left things, I choose to follow up on her. She had a good head start, but she'd most likely be in the parking lot with the rental. Checking there first meant I didn't have to go far.

The backseat door was open, and she was just putting out a half-smoked cigarette when I approached her. Since we were alone, she didn't ignore me like I thought she would. She angled her eyes toward me as I leaned against the hood of the car but didn't object when I asked her to scoot over to make room for me in the back.

I sat with just enough room to have a comfortable distance, but for a long time no one said anything, like she was waiting for me to start things off. Her impatience won. "What, Ash?"

The Teddy I knew would be waiting for me to say the wrong thing. There was no right way a conversation about us would go. "I thought we weren't getting mad at each other for stuff like this."

Teddy just laughed. "Guess I was just giving you privacy. It isn't on my wish list to walk in on you and Reggie hooking up."

I rubbed my hand over my face. "I didn't do anything if that's what you're asking."

"I wouldn't care if you did." Her eyes rolled over to me, her expression as glassed over as she could manage.

I smiled. "We're not good at this."

"Good at what?"

"Staying away from each other."

She might not admit it, but she knew I was right. Because it was just as hard for me. Teddy pursed her lips to one side, picking at the scratched-up polish on her fingernails. "I know we're supposed to be doing our own thing. I haven't forgotten that. I just...I haven't yet. So I guess I'm a little jealous, that's all. It's not a big deal. I'll get over it—" Even though I did my best to hide it, the involuntary laugh I let out betrayed me. "I know you're not laughing at me."

I wasn't. But I might as well come clean since I was caught. "I'm not laughing at you, just… I haven't either. I've had opportunities. But it's hard." At least I wasn't the only one. She had to have had dozens of people, any one of them waiting by the phone for that "let's get up" text. Shit, six months ago, that was me. She wouldn't have any issue scratching an itch. It caught me off-guard we were on the same boat.

"Well, if you had your way, you would've—"

"Teddy, if I had my way, I'd be between those thighs making you speak Spanish right now."

"Ash, you're so full of shit." It was easier for Teddy to dismiss me than take me seriously. I didn't want to go back to any point where we were. I wanted to go further. I wanted to be new. Even with all the risks.

"I told you how I felt when we ended things. But we don't give Reggie enough credit. He's a big boy."

Teddy shuffled, crossing one leg over the other on the other side of the backseat. "We're out here road-tripping with each other. I'm going to be real—I don't have a whole ton of people in my life willing to spend more than a twenty-minute car ride to my house to hang out with me. I want both of your friendships. I have both of your friendships. I just didn't think everything else would be this hard for someone who wasn't my boyfriend."

"I want to be your boyfriend. I want to be that person you can talk to about anything. I want to be that person who gets on your nerves." I laced her fingers in mine, and she shot me one of those where-are-you-going-with-this looks. "But I want to be that person who makes you weak without touching you, too. For me, everything about us is worth it. But I can't help it that sometimes you need more than me—"

Teddy rolled her eyes, like she was going to say something harsh, but the words coming out actually sounded nice. "Asher, don't even play me like that. I care about you. I hate that you think you're not enough for me. I want all those things, too, but I'm my own person. Sometimes I just want a person who's *not* you who I can talk to. Maybe even so I can talk *about* you," she joked. It was cute. Everything up to this point was so severe, there hadn't been an earnest way to lighten the mood.

My right eyebrow shot up, sizing Teddy up as her eyes burned with desire in my direction. Mere seconds gave us plenty of time to close any distance between us, urging our lips to come to a place they'd both missed for too long. Her lips were still soft and full like I remembered them. She angled her mouth under mine, and it only took a few quick adjustments for her to straddle my lap so we were face-to-face.

If she hadn't already been driving me into complete overdrive when she slid her tongue between my lips, she knew exactly what she was doing when her exploring tongue hit the side of my mouth. All it'd take is a flick or two there and I wouldn't want to stop. I gently pushed her away from me, urging her to stop.

"Look, it's all fun and games until someone's dick is hard. We said what we had to say. Don't start nothing you can't finish."

She bit her lower lip, rubbing her body against me. "Who says I can't finish you?" she moaned, dragging her lips against mine again. The small of her naked back called to me, and my hands ran against the smooth skin, making me want to do other things to it. All I'd have to do was pull her dress up, and we'd get to the point where neither of us would know where I started or she ended.

But it'd also only take a curious Reggie checking up on us to ruin everything, and that wasn't how either of us would've wanted him to find out. I peeled her mouth from mine, suggesting we get another room.

"For just one time?"

I reached in for a peck, pulling her by the hips closer toward me, as if that was even possible at this point. "If you just wanted privacy, I'd rent it for however long you'd want." Or however long we were here, whichever came first. The things I wanted to do wouldn't hack it in the backseat of a car.

"Do you have any condoms?"

I huffed under my breath, reaching into every jean pocket I had to pull out two condoms. It was a good thing Reg hadn't bankrupted my stash because I didn't want to sneak back in and risk getting caught out.

Teddy leaned in and kissed me on the nose before snatching the condoms out my hand. "Get the room. I'll get my phone. Just tell me where to meet you." A seductive smile danced on her lips that could make me say yes to anything.

I made my way to the hotel lobby, insisting I needed a second room for the trip, which seemed to confuse the hell out of the clerk at the desk. Maybe they thought I intended to trash it or something. But one swipe of the card resulted in two room keys, especially should we decide to do more beyond the middle of the night.

I texted Teddy to meet me at room 213, a floor and a few doors down from our shared room with Reggie. He wouldn't hear a thing, but I couldn't promise the same thing for our neighbors. Minutes after I reached the room, I didn't have time to turn the light on before a knock came at the door. As soon as I opened it, Teddy poured in, wrapping her arms around me and inching us backward until we were on the bed.

She pulled off my shirt in one swipe, drawing shapes with her lips everywhere her fingers touched. She must've wanted it bad because I wasn't even half way on the bed before she'd worked my pants halfway down my legs. She leaned back up, grabbing my face and kissing me like she couldn't get enough. She was moving so fast; my body was still trying to catch up. It still didn't stop her from whipping me out my boxers to tease me with her tongue.

"Slow down, Teddy," was all I managed to groan back at her.

She peered up at me. Even in low light, those dark eyes mesmerized me. She crawled closer to me, and I kicked the rest of my jeans off, slipped out of my shorts, and pulled her on my lap.

Grabbing the waist of her skirt, I managed to slip it down until there was nothing but her bare beautiful legs wrapped around my hips. I slipped her top over her head, leaving nothing but a strapless bra and pair of panties between us. They matched. Hmm…

I didn't know how either of us managed to get our underwear off, but she started rubbing her wet pussy against my dick. My body didn't need time catching up at that point, I'll tell you that.

"Mmm…where are those condoms?" I asked, my voice cracking under a laugh. She reached in the front of her bra, handing them to me, crawling just low enough for me to put it on. She slid her wet folds over my cock again, until she positioned herself right over me and I disappeared inside of her.

There was a sigh of relief on both our parts. The warmth of her body made the rest of my body tingle, like I'd never been here before. Had it been a little more than a month? It felt like years. I couldn't even fight the curl in my toes every time she lifted her body from my waist. I leaned up to reach my lips to hers because, let's face it, I couldn't resist a hot sex-kiss. It left her slightly off, and she placed her hands on my shoulders to keep herself balanced.

I let go a breath I'd been holding on to too long, as well as a combination of tongue-biting swears and groans. She knew the right speed to torture me with, not quite slow or fast, with just enough pressure to keep me from getting there before her. My hands moved from her waist to the back of her bra, with just enough unbuckling to loosen her out of it.

I loved her breasts. In the past, her insecurity with them kind of annoyed me because they didn't look that much different. But I loved the taste of them, the different texture of her nipples when they were erect compared to when they were soft, the contrast of them versus the rest of her skin. But most of all, I loved how it made her feel when I touched them.

She couldn't deny or fight it when I played with her tits. I'd never been with a chick who straight went into overdrive anytime I did. Her body just got super wet and made her feel that much more inviting. She slowed her hips down, focusing way too much on her tits between my lips to keep her rhythm. I didn't see a better time than now to take control and make her cry for more of me.

Driving my hips up to meet hers, she swore, gritting her teeth against each thrust. It didn't hurt having access to both her nipples, and she filled the room with sounds that only got higher the deeper I was inside her. It felt instinctive to go as deep as she'd allow me to, and she bit her lip, accepting every inch, urging me with "mas rapido, papi." The crack in her voice was weak beyond control.

"Just keep doing that. I think I'm gonna come," she managed in a strained voice. Her tense posture relaxed against me, worn down from all the fun. I tried to catch my breath, too, but I still had a way's to go in my attempt to wait her out.

"I'm guessing you're burnt out?" I asked between gasps.

She grabbed my face, pressing her mouth to mine. "Mmm… you didn't come?"

"I was trying to make you come first. I'm notoriously bad at that when I'm horny."

She laughed before whispering into my ear. "I like it when you come first. Then I get all your attention trying to get you back up there."

She kissed me and held on while I flipped her over onto her back. Our lips never left each other's as I finally did away with that bra completely. Her beautiful breasts, now covered in sweat, glided against my chest, echoing the way it felt to be inside her.

"You feel so fucking good, Teddy."

She hooked her ankles around my waist, whispering things I didn't understand completely, but from the gist of what Spanish words I knew, went along the lines of, "Just shut up and fuck me."

Which was exactly what I planned to do. I helped prop her head up with the pillows on the bed. We were too spoiled over that damn pillow wedge. It didn't seem functional not to be able to kiss her, attached at the waist like this.

I whispered back, "Speak that Spanish shit," and she wasted no time obliging to the request. I allowed my driving hips to buck forward, losing all control listening to her creamy voice egg me on. It only took a few minutes of short, hard strokes to do me in as my dick exploded uncontrollably, grinding up against her.

"Fuck. That was intense as shit." I wiped the sweat that gathered on my forehead, finally feeling the aftermath of how late it was. Sex was like physical caffeine. As long as you had it, you were wide awake.

Teddy kissed me once, and then I sat up to get rid of the condom. She waited for me, inviting me back into her embrace. She breathed into me, and we wound up tangled in each other across the mattress.

"That was fun." Her dancing eyes studied my face looking for any tells to figure out what I was thinking.

"That amongst other things."

Her smile faded, replaced by pursed lips, as she ran her fingers through my sweaty coif. "Guess we just needed an itch scratched."

"No, I just needed you."

Her smile returned, big enough to paint her entire face, as she put her hand over my face, pushing me inches away. "You're so corny, Ash."

"I'll be corny if it keeps us ending up like this."

She laughed again, this time not so dismissive. "Having sex with you just puts my mind in the gutter sometimes."

I wasn't sure that was an ideal response to get after such a wild session, but she had me curious. "I'm gonna need you to elaborate on that."

Teddy hid her eyes from mine, choosing to speak into a pillow. "I don't know. I just know you probably do stuff I don't do. I never know if I do everything you like."

"Trust me, Teddy. Everything you do, me likes." You probably only got, like, three people in your lifetime your body was made for. I might've just been high off of Teddy, but after tonight, she definitely ranked high as hell on that list.

Teddy took the pillow from her face, rolling her eyes to nothing in particular. "I guess sometimes I fantasize about you with another guy…"

"Okay?"

"I'm not, like, trying to fetishize you. I've just never been with someone who was bisexual like me. And you're so cute, and your phone is full of numbers," She paused between the last three words, playing with the ends of my hair that weren't soaked in sweat.

"I hope this conversation isn't going where I think it's going."

"Where do you think it's going?" She giggled with too much enthusiasm to be tired.

"It sounds like you're trying to suggest a threesome?" I didn't hate the idea of one, but it seemed awkwardly placed after tonight. Especially since I wasn't good at sharing at this point. Her eyes widened with shock, and she mouthed a silent *wow* before she said anything.

"That was reaching. I was kinda just talking about anal."

"Oh. Well, I'll give you a little heads up. You wouldn't like it." It wasn't hard to shoot her down. I'd been there, done that, and by now I could tell the type who didn't do it or did, who'd like it versus who wouldn't. I wasn't sure whether I should be offended to assume just because I didn't just sleep with women, that it was something I was into, but I knew she didn't mean any harm, so I entertained her when she kept going.

"What? You'd just shoot it down like that?"

"Take it from me—it's not, like, a standard. Even some guys don't like it. It's not as spontaneous as going down on you or anything like that. Porn warps it to look a certain way with editing, muscle relaxants, and numbing cream. But it's, like, no less than thirty minutes minimum prep time just to ease someone's nerves about it."

"So you don't like it?"

"I never said that." Sometimes it was great, sometimes it sucked, like all sex. I liked being the receiver more than the giver, but it was still an acquired taste that wasn't always for everyone. "You're not just asking me because you know I have, are you?"

"No! It just seems like an only-live-once trip. Sometimes you just want to do things you wouldn't normally do when you're home. Plus, if I hated it, I'd know. I definitely wouldn't want to bring anything I didn't like home with me. Just the fact that you're concerned whether I'd like it is reason enough to want to."

Fair enough. I gave her a small rundown on what to expect if she was actually serious about it. Lots of lube, way more condoms, and more than just a few minutes to kill, should her mind not change. Meaning, it was not happening right now.

We decided it was best to gather our scattered clothes before we got too comfortable to fall asleep. I didn't want anything more than to lie there and be next to her, but we hadn't figured out a damn thing and the last thing we needed was Reggie to get wise.

# CHAPTER FIFTEEN

**Teddy**

The morning was full of disagreement. I wasn't feeling yesterday's Waffle House, but no one was in the mood for Starbucks a few miles out. I'd need a ride if I didn't have the rental. We all eventually rode together, but as soon as I had my breakfast, I was ready to get dropped back off. Since Ash was the chauffeur, he had no issue sending me on my way.

I wasn't sure how we planned to do this, but I knew neither of us planned to hit up SeaWorld until we were all fed and compliant with one another. I'm sure they'd split up eventually, but being by myself gave me plenty of time to hit up that empty hotel room without anyone seeing me.

I was nervous. There were things I was better at and things Asher excelled with, but everything that was about to happen was last minute, so the only prep I'd have was foreplay. The worst thing you could have was time on your hands. Googling anal sex on your phone brought up all the worst scenarios. I felt the need to shower twice due to every insecurity that resurfaced.

He told me he didn't like it all the time. Sometimes the feeling was too tight or he could tell the other person wasn't that into it. He'd even admitted, in his experience, women were naturally more curious and it'd surprise me how many dudes preferred intimacy over it. I trusted him not to go full throttle or anything, so I let the thought of his occasional gentle nature calm my jitters.

It was way too early for it, but with the accessibility of soft-core porn, I figured I might as well rev myself up with an added bonus. It couldn't hurt, right? The only thing that sucked was the selection. Nothing but white het couples. It'd have to do for now, but I normally got off better with f/f or at least with a girl who actually *looked* like me.

There was nearly a thirty-minute gap before any sign of Ash. I turned off the TV when a knock came at the door, but I made sure to check the peephole just in case it was housekeeping. He had his own key, so he didn't have a reason to knock. Upon opening the door, his hands were full with a drugstore bag in one hand and the remnants of his breakfast. He kicked the door closed with his foot, and even though he held a cheap cup of coffee between his teeth, I noticed an unmistakable smirk.

He threw the bag on the bed and used his free hand to put his coffee on a table in the middle of the room. "You okay?" He must've felt my discomfort if he was already asking questions.

"Yes, stupid," I joked. He put the rest of his leftovers on the table, excusing himself to brush his teeth. Which I appreciated, by the way, when he greeted me with a minty fresh sloppy kiss. He bit his lip and bent down, slipping my shorts down my legs.

"I want you to relax. I'm not going to do anything without telling you what I'm doing first, and it'll probably be a minute before I think you're ready."

I answered back with an emotionless *okay*. He stood back up, bending down to meet his lips to mine and pulling me over until he was sitting on the bed and I was standing over him.

"Turn around," he instructed, pushing the back of my shirt up, kissing my lower back and outside of my behind through my panties. I felt his lips and teeth lightly nibble on the cheek of my ass, kisses following not far behind them. "Your body is, like, so fuckin' sexy."

When Ash said things like that, I *actually* believed him. He didn't have a reason to lie, even though I know he loved the way my body used to look. I thought I still looked good, too, but it was just nice being told it sometimes.

"Can I take these off?" he asked, referring to the only thing separating his lips from my bare skin. I giggled, helping him pull my panties down from my hips to the floor. He continued to kiss my skin, stimulating all different kinds of sensory stimuli. He placed his hand on my back, guiding me to keep my body arched as his fingers traveled, lightly rubbing my clit.

"Damn, Teddy you're wet. Let me know you been masturbating." He laughed, laving his fingers in my wetness, using it as a weapon against me as my knees buckled. I felt his warm breath and wet tongue swipe between my cheeks, and I screamed by accident. I couldn't help but laugh.

"You all right over there?"

"Yeah. Just wasn't expecting that. It felt weird."

"A good weird or a bad weird?"

"I don't know. Just weird." I giggled.

"Sit on the bed." He laid back, waiting for me to crawl toward him, his legs dangling off the edge of the bed. He pulled me onto his lap and devoured my lips, temporarily setting my initial fears aside. His kisses were softer than normal. He usually liked things sloppy, which wasn't hard to do when your raging hormones got the best of you. But this time his lips gently tugged on mine as he whispered his future plans for me.

"Face the other way. I just want to get you comfortable first." He waited until we were in a 69 position, and by then I was grabbing for his pants zipper. He stopped me in my tracks before I could do anything. "Don't. Just…relax. You're just gonna tense up if you're doing two things at once. Just get used to the different sensations."

A part of me wanted to feel everything all at once just to get it over with, but Asher insisted on taking his time, so I didn't argue. He lightly tugged at my hips and urged me to scoot backward toward his face.

"I don't want you to not expect anything, so I'm about to eat you out and play with you a little."

"Okay," I said.

"Don't be nervous."

It was hard not to be, but I figured the least I could do was try. His lips lightly smacked against the folds of my pussy, as he took his time kissing and licking everything but the clit. He seemed to get off on my suffering, because I felt the hum of his laugh as I squirmed, just wanting to feel his tongue hit the right spot. When he finally separated my lips with his tongue, his mouth didn't linger in one spot like it normally did in this position. He swiped his tongue upward until it tickled between my cheeks. He stopped to laugh.

"I can tell you're more nervous than you say. You tensed up on me."

"I can't help it." I knew he was being patient. It's what I liked most about him. It was just hard because I couldn't see what he was doing, so it was difficult not to be startled by anything.

"I'm just gonna lick your clit for a while. When I think you're ready, I'm going to rub you and stick a finger inside you. Is that okay?" When I agreed, he paused for a second, and I heard the sound of something squirting out of a bottle.

When I turned to investigate, he held out his hand to show me it was just lube. When I was confident enough to adjust myself to the original position, he took his time nibbling and kissing my thighs. I bit my lip at the warmth of his tongue parting my lips again, as his slippery fingers massaged up and down the crack of my cheeks. I felt his lips come together in a kiss outside the folds of my pussy, and his tongue returned back to my center, causing a toe-curling sensation all over again.

I don't think it enhanced it when a lubricated finger slowly slid into the hollow between my cheeks, but his busy tongue went to work lapping my clit, making me weaker than I wanted to be in this position. I didn't know if I wanted to like it or not. I couldn't tell if I actually did. But his tongue concentrated on continuous feathery flicks as I felt the pressure of a second finger slide inside me.

Outside of the occasional mishap that'd never went past, "Hey, buddy, wrong hole," I'd never had someone spend so much time back here. There were so many nerves, and I wasn't sure they were all good. But even with that thought blowing my high, my body tensed and released against Asher's busy tongue in knee-weakening spasms. He pulled his fingers out, leaning in to kiss the backs of my thighs and rim his tongue between the cheeks of my behind until I was too squeamish not to pull away.

"Mmm…did you like that?" he asked as I repositioned my body to face him.

"I didn't hate it."

"You seemed like you did," he said with hunger in his eyes.

"I liked you eating me out."

To that response, Asher wore a smirk on his face that wouldn't wipe off, even as he reached in to kiss the space above my chest. "I think you're just embarrassed to admit you liked it better than you thought you would."

Maybe I was. Maybe I wasn't brave enough to admit it right this second. It felt more weird than good, but I'd leave it at good-weird if it made him feel better.

I was still ready to go all the way. I helped him out of his shirt as he reached for the belt at his waist. He kicked his sneakers off and crept out of those skinny little jeans he liked wearing. I was *going* to ignore what he was working with, but he saw the look on my face at the size of his dick poking against his boxer briefs.

"My dick makes me look like I'm lying, but I swear I'm not normally this hard this soon in similar situations."

I reached in and rubbed him through the fabric anyway, as he helped me out of the rest of my clothes. When he asked me to lay on my side, it felt like no turning back. He slipped on a condom, laving it in lube, and proceeded to rub some on, around, and inside the ridge of my chasm. His finger slowly explored, lubricating the walls to prepare me for his width.

"It'll probably hurt the most when I stick the head in. Your muscles are going to do everything in their power to stop me from going further, but if it hurts too much, just tell me to stop. I'll probably notice, but just in case I don't, just tell me and I won't go further."

That made me more nervous than I should've been, but his fingers hadn't felt as bad as I'd anticipated. Asher thought I was ready, I felt ready, this was happening. He knelt down by my side, rubbing more lube over the condom before he attempted to make contact for the first time. The head of his cock gave its best gentle attempt to stretch the walls of my anus, and he pushed my thigh to my chest to keep me spread apart.

I groaned at the friction. Noticeably so. Even with tons of lube and the warm-up, the pain wasn't like anything I'd felt before.

Asher didn't pull out, but his hips stopped in their tracks. "You don't look like you're having fun. Want me to stop?"

I was already here, and at this point, it was awkward as fuck to switch it up now. "Just go slow please." Though, there wasn't a way for him to possibly go slower than he already was.

"We can stop if you want. That's just your reaction to the head, with no strokes."

He said it'd take work on both our parts to go further. He eased my bent knee over his shoulder and asked me to touch myself as he made slow, deliberate thrusts inside me, to get my body used to something being there. I literally felt every inch of him, something I couldn't say the other way around.

But even self-stimulation couldn't mask the pain, Ash didn't ignore my pitchy outbursts.

"Baby, what do you want me to do? Do you want me to stop?" he asked with real concern to his tone. It sucked that he might be enjoying it, but my body wasn't getting with the program. "Can you just kiss me baby?"

He lowered my leg down and laid behind me. His lips and tongue glided down the small of my upper back, until I turned my face to meet his. He kept the kisses sweet and light, a strong contrast to everything else going on. It wasn't enough to completely relax me, but I still felt safe being there with him.

His hand slipped underneath the side of my ribs, and he gently tugged one of my breasts out of the cup of my bra, lightly pinching it with his index finger and thumb. I reached my arm over his face, relaxing my upper body a bit. His body eased deeper into mine, and his teeth bit into my lower lip each attempt.

"Tell me if it hurts too much baby," he whispered, tangling his lips between mine again.

I still processed everything as pain, but Asher was too sweet. I relaxed more and more at each gritted moan he tried to hide. The feeling was different. It was ten times stronger than being inside my vagina, and it wasn't really in a good way. But he kept up with the lube, never going long without a refill. His grip grew tighter, and his husky voice continued on in breathless groans, so I knew he was close. All it took was a little dirty talk for him to tense up, taking longer, deeper breaths as he swore out loud and gently pulled out.

He leaned in to kiss me on the cheek. I was more sore than I wanted to be from the exchange, but I didn't object when Asher buried his face between my legs and went down on me again. I think with all the pressure from the anal, my body was just ready to feel anything but pain. Just a few minutes in and I was pushing Ash away from me, no longer able to take the sensitivity.

He crawled back behind me, pushing my braids to the side to have better access to my neck. "You did good for a first time," he said as he kissed my cheek.

"That was a little intense. I don't know how to feel about it. It might be a while before I'm willing to do that again."

Asher took turns kissing my back, chin and neck. "So there'll be a next time?"

That's right. We'd never discussed whether this would go past the trip. We'd needed last night, and today was about exploration and escapism. But I wasn't sure we could have sex again without our feelings getting in the way.

"I don't know."

Asher shot me a puppy-dog pout, reaching into kiss me again. "I want there to be."

I placed my hands around his neck, studying him closely. "Will we have this room for a little while longer?" He nodded as my fingers got lost in his colorless locks. "Then I guess we'll figure it out."

"You know, I don't even think Reggie would care anymore about us. The sex is great, Teddy, but the promise of something more is better. I'm not exactly going anywhere."

There was always a time and a place to talk about this sort of thing, but while it was the place, it wasn't the time. I got up, feeling dizzy and tired. Asher harbored a worried look in his eyes, so I sucked it up and pushed through. Right now, I didn't want to talk about anything. I just wanted to start the day.

"I really want to hop in the shower before we head out. I'll feel all dirty if I don't." I grabbed a towel and proceeded to the bathroom. He knocked on the frame of the door to get my attention, but I was already in the shower, washing away any sign of the hour I'd just spent with him.

"Hey, I'm gonna just head back to the other room. I forgot my trunks and don't want to leave without them. Meet me in the lobby." And then he was gone.

* * *

We waited in the hotel's lobby, knee-deep in an innocent game of *Words with Friends* when Reggie pulled up to the front with the car. Took him long enough. He beeped the horn for us to come outside, but we were too wrapped up in the game to get up right away.

The car made a round of annoying honks, over and over, until we finally answered Reggie's call. I hated that today would be our last day in Orlando. Come this time tomorrow, we'd be back in Miami and back at jobs every one of us hated. We told ourselves our weekly sessions were a way of us coping, but none of us really believed that.

Reggie got out of the car and tossed me the keys, which I almost didn't catch. I couldn't prolong that it was my turn to drive any longer than I had. For that, I was glad that SeaWorld wasn't far.

* * *

"Teddy, what the hell are you doing? There was a park right there," Asher yelled from the backseat when I passed a parking space that wasn't any different than the other three I'd dismissed. The parking lot was larger than I remembered, and I was not looking forward to walking an entire mile, only to have to wait in another line for fifteen-plus minutes.

The tingling sensation in my foot started up a few minutes ago, and it was already numb from just driving. It wasn't a big deal and happened sometimes as an inconvenient side effect of living with lymphoma. Most of the time it passed, but if I walked any more than I had to, I was not going to be a Pleasant Patty.

There was a family walking back to their car, a spot that was close enough to ease my worry about a long walk to the entrance. By the looks of things, they had a lot of shit to unpack, and by now the boys were getting aggravated that I was willing to wait on this one space.

"Really, Teddy? Chances are they're taking their time because they know you're waiting on them. Just park somewhere else," Reggie barked, despite no one asking for his damn opinion.

"You two are seriously getting on my nerves. Here—just take your damn tickets. I'll meet you two at the entrance." I handed him a ticket I'd put aside and watched him fly out of the car as if there was some prize waiting for him in that line. Asher was next, but he stopped and leaned into the front seat when Reggie was out of view.

"Everything okay?"

"Yeah, I just…" I sighed. "No, everything's okay."

"You want me to sit and wait with you?"

I put the car in park and circled my ankle in attempts to get some feeling back. "It's okay, Asher. Go on ahead with Reggie. I'll catch up."

With the tips of his fingers, he angled my head to face his and left me with a sweet kiss. "We'll be waiting for you, okay?"

And just as he approached the end of the parking lot, the family pulled out of the spot I so anxiously coveted.

* * *

I took refuge on a nearby bench just moments past the entrance, while Asher and Reggie headed on without me. I didn't want to be annoying, but it was already looking like I'd be a pain in the ass if I tried to keep up with them. It was always best to keep my feet elevated when I had a feeling like this coming on; I just hoped it'd pass since it wasn't on my agenda to spend all day on a bench when I'd just spent three hundred bucks to get in.

I dumped out the contents of my bag, silently kicking myself for not remembering to pack my Nook. My phone, a metal card case, mascara, and a Polaroid camera were all I'd had time to pack before Asher rushed me to the hotel lobby. The whole ride here, the boys teased me for my love for instant photos. In my defense, companies were still making instant cameras, so I couldn't have been the only proud owner of one in 2016.

Sure, I could take all the pictures I wanted on my phone, but something about Polaroid shots were always more interesting. I hardly ever looked at the photos in my phone's gallery, so the few I had hanging up at my house were all taken by my trusty Polaroid. Call me a lover of all things vintage.

"Hey, are you all right?" Asher snuck up behind me and sat down after scooting my things over on the bench.

Reggie wasn't far, but he looked aggravated and ready to argue. "Teddy, I know you're not just sitting here. We didn't come all the way out here so you can sit on this damn bench all day. Get up and walk the park with us. This is the last time we're taking off without you."

Great. Now I couldn't even let it pass in peace.

"I'm all right," I lied. "You two walk faster. Don't worry about me, I'll catch up. Just text me when you find something thrill-worthy."

Asher's eyes narrowed, not buying my "I'm all right" routine. "You don't have to be ashamed if you're not feeling up to it. At this point, that's the only excuse I'll accept after you just paid all this money to come here." I knew if I didn't tell them something, they were only going to ruin my day with their endless probing or I was going to ruin theirs with my dire need to camp out in this one spot. Ay, jodame!

"My feet hurt, damn. I don't feel like walking. Now will you two please just leave me alone? Text me when you get into something. How hard is that?"

Reggie and Asher exchanged glances, thinking what, I don't

know, but just when I was about to tell them both to beat it, Reggie lowered in front of me and encouraged me to hop on his back.

"You guys are so annoying."

"Teddy, I'm serious. I'm only trying to help you. I know we'll never hear the end of it if we leave you on this bench all day. Swallow your pride and take the ride. Besides you're like a fraction of what you used to weigh," he added, and I rewarded him with my fist to the back of his thigh. He cowered at the power in my punch as he reached back to massage his leg.

"If it makes you feel less uncomfortable, Reg and I can switch every once in a while. Beats sitting here people-watching."

Seeing Asher's point on the matter, I put my ego aside and took them up on their offer. "But I think I'll ride Asher first. You're walking like you might drop me after that sucker punch to the leg."

* * *

We weren't there long before we all mutually decided that the first thing on our agenda was to go and see the whale show. Going to SeaWorld and not attending a whale show was like not going at all. This was what most came to see, so it was best to get it out of the way early.

"It's hot as hell carrying you on my back. What's good with that Soak Zone?"

With my foot feeling better, I ordered Asher to put me down.

"If you want to do that, we'll have to get a locker or something. The Soak Zone is exactly how it sounds," I said as I made my way to the locker area just outside the stadium.

"Good thing we all remembered to dress smart," Reggie said, throwing the pants he had on over his swim trunks in the locker I paid a buck to rent. Asher didn't hesitate throwing all his things in next, but I was in no rush to strip down to my bathing suit.

Sure, I'd be wearing shorts and a tank top as a cover-up, but the closest bathroom was some ways from here so it looked like I'd be flashing a few bystanders in the process while I stripped out of my jeans and T-shirt.

"I'll go find us some seats before we can't snag any upfront. You two are taking forever." Reggie stalked off.

Now it was just me and Asher alone again. He whistled, wiggling his eyebrows in an attempt to make me laugh as I bit my lip, ashamed to admit it was working.

"You know I was joking when I said carrying you was making me hot. It was more like you sneaking in those sly neck kisses when Reggie wasn't looking."

I pretended not to know what he was talking about, which in turn made him more grab-happy and playful. At the risk of Reggie walking back, I pushed him off me, but not before letting him know what had been going through my mind all day. I wanted to be with Asher, and it was time I put my fear to the side and was honest about my feelings when it came us.

"When we get back home, I think there should be a next time. Maybe a more permanent next time."

He smiled wickedly and put his arm around me as we walked to meet Reggie to the stadium seating.

"Well, then, I can't wait to go home."

* * *

A trip to the gift shop watching Heckle and Jeckle orchestrate a plush orca fight proved how possible it was to make even the most mundane acts highly entertaining. After getting drenched from that whale show, it dawned on us that no one bothered to pack any towels, which meant we'd left the stadium freezing.

A thorough tour of the place brought us to a heartbreaking view of the tank that was home to the infamous orca by the name of Tilikum.

"That whale looks so fuckin' depressed, man." Asher said what all three of us were thinking as we peered into the pool. There was nothing to look at. With what I'd learned with a quick Google search, it was hard to believe that something so still and lifeless was responsible for three deaths in a thirty-year period. He just sat there, floating.

"I feel kinda bad for him. He's all by himself, like he's in solitary confinement. Can't he at least be around others like him?"

"Teddy, he brought one of his trainers down, along with two other orcas in San Diego. Company is the last thing this guy needs," Asher declared.

I touched the glass, as if somehow it could make me feel closer to the poor animal. No friends, minimal social interaction —it was like he was just dead inside, a feeling I knew all too well.

"Let's go, Teddy. Before we actually start needing one of those quick queue passes. Might as well hit up some rides before it gets too bad," Asher said as he led me to the park's main walkway, but what I really wanted was to trek through the shark exhibits via the glass tunnels. I got my way when I complained about my feet acting up and didn't want to waste time waiting in line, but really I was fine.

It was honestly one of the coolest things I'd ever seen. I didn't condone the capture of animals for the sole purpose of our entertainment, but that didn't take away from the fact that it was amazing to look at.

"You guys we should take a few pictures," I told them. "Just in case we don't come out here again."

The first few rounds of pictures came out great with Reggie's phone, but we couldn't get all three of us in the same one without someone getting cut out.

"No one thought to bring a selfie stick? You brought everything else with you," Asher addressed to me.

"I didn't see you guys bringing anything. I brought what I found to be the most necessary..."

"Only to find out that none of it was," Reggie said with a dumb-as-nails look on his face. "I think the best thing we could do is get someone to get one of us."

But we looked around at all the people going to and fro, only to all be stricken with fear at the thought of asking a stranger to take our photo.

"These days, you can't just be going up to random white people," Reggie confessed with a laugh. Asher rolled his eyes and approached the next person to walk past us, who was more than happy to capture all three of us in this man-made version of underwater paradise. I stood in the middle as Reggie and Asher flanked at my sides while this kind stranger took fifteen-odd photos of the three of us together. Maybe I was getting ahead of myself by admitting this, but for a trip that had the potential to be a disaster, it had turned out to be one of my favorite days all year. Maybe my whole life. I was grateful to have friends who were so willing to be there when I needed them, even when I didn't have the courage to ask.

# CHAPTER SIXTEEN

**Asher**

Did it ever annoy you to hear someone older than you hype up a decade you hadn't been born into? Too many times to count, right? I hated to say it, but I kind of had sympathy for them now. After today, I had a feeling it'd be on a mile-long list of stories I constantly lived through about the wild times I had in my twenties.

And to think, I wasn't even halfway through them.

I thought SeaWorld would be whack as hell, but I've never had so much fun. It might have just been the people. I was going on a limb here, but I didn't think I would've had half as much fun if I hadn't been doing it with Teddy and Reggie.

* * *

On the ride back to the hotel, the vote was unanimous—sleep in our own beds, or stay the night and get caught in traffic during rush hour the next day. Needless to say, two out of three of us were packed by the time we got to the room. I'd only brought a gym bag's worth of stuff so there wasn't much to it. Teddy? Alongside the oversized suitcase she'd brought, a revisit to the gift shop resulted in trying to repack a whole lot of nothing. Don't even get me started on Reggie insisting he required a shower before we hit the road.

All we had to do was be on the road by midnight to get home by three. Neither of them seemed to give a rat's ass how much time they wasted since neither of them were driving. It was okay, though. I had a playlist full of music to prevent them from getting a comfortable rest. It was petty, but I'd make sure no one had a pleasant sleep on me.

Teddy unpacked all her stuff to make the new stuff fit, but halfway through, she walked past me toward the hotel door. "Reggie's been in there a while. I need some fresh air. You mind?" she asked, leaning against the threshold.

"You done packing?" Why did I even ask; she clearly wasn't.

"I'll do it when I get back. It's just…really hot in here. It's hard to concentrate." I didn't argue and took her word for it. I noticed she left her room key on the table close to the door, so I grabbed it, stuffing it into my pocket. She wasn't even halfway down the hall before Reggie walked out of the bathroom, fully dressed.

"Where's Teddy?"

I shrugged. "I don't know. She claimed she needed fresh air or something."

Like me, he pointed to her suitcase with curiosity. "She know she ain't packed?"

"Said she'd be right back."

Reggie picked up his bag and headed for the door. "I'm going to go put my stuff in the car. Want me to bring yours down, too?" I threw him my bag, answering his question. I dug into my pocket, separating the loose dollar bills from the room keys I had stashed. "Turn those in too while you're down there."

Reggie snatched them up, but not without shooting me a

snarl. "Yeah, a'ight. Don't try and stick me with a bill. Let me find out you running a credit card scam," Reggie joked.

I laughed, unable to hold it all in. "I'm not even gonna dignify that with a response. Just go, so we can be out already. I'll wait on Teddy so she can get her stuff."

And with that, Reggie was gone. I sat on Teddy's bed, stretched out next to her suitcase full of mostly books and shoes. Against our advice, she'd made out like a bandit, leaving with a bag full of toys that'd make closing her suitcase that more difficult. I thought it was cute that she was too old for that shit, but she promised one was intended for my niece, which made it even cuter.

I got bored, so I took my phone out to pass the time. Had ten minutes gone by already? I wanted to manage our road time well. A Red Bull would only take me so far on the road. I decided, if she couldn't get it closed before, maybe she needed a stronger hand. I tried to close her suitcase, but like the times she'd tried. It…would…not…close.

*Jesus.* At least I knew to make sure she packed for a few days, not a damn month next time. I lowered the lid and sat on the top when Reggie stalked back in.

"Dude, the only way this is going down is if I put down all my weight and pray. Mind helping me zip this—"

But I didn't have any time to finish that sentence.

Should I have read Reggie's body language better? Would I have had time to? It felt like milliseconds from the time he swooped in too quick to close the door behind him. But even if I *had* noticed anything off, I would've never predicted Reggie's fist slamming into my face.

There wasn't time to think, no real time to react. When he brought his fist up again, he clocked me one more time in the space between my nose and cheek before I pushed him off me.

"What the hell is wrong with you, man?"

I wasn't sure if he was high, in another world, or on one. But as soon as I acknowledged him, he seemed to snap out of his enraged fit. "Fuck!" he yelled, putting a small distance between us.

That's all I was going to get? I fought that small urge to hit back because we were friends, but I was going to need a little more than a sorry.

"What the hell was that all about?"

Reggie put more distance between us as he paced behind the other bed. "I swear to god; I just came in here to talk. Then I saw you and…my emotions…"

"Yo, you better start talking, otherwise I'm about to make it a twin."

Reggie stopped pacing as he punched his palm into his fist, figuring out what he planned to say. "I just got one question, and I swear to god, you better not lie. Teddy and you? You and Teddy?"

He wasn't able to get the words out, but sadly I knew where this was going. I couldn't lie even if I wanted to. My lowering face told the truth before I could.

"Fuck! So it's true?" Reggie came at me but in the middle appeared to stop himself. "You know what? I'm good. I can keep my hands to myself. It's just that first time—" He put his hands on his waist with an angry grin. "That first time…"

Reggie paced around the room laughing, but I knew he didn't find the situation funny. I didn't even know what to say, what he'd ask, where the conversation would go, so I waited.

When I got tired of waiting, I broke the silence. "Reggie, I know what it looks like…"

"Pretty fucked up." Reggie went along, nodding his head.

"Okay, pretty fucked up. But we…tried. I tried to tell you. More than once I was going to, but every time it was never a good time."

"Oh, so a road trip seemed like the perfect time?" Reggie stepped closer to me. My reaction time was better, though. I knew his urge to hit me might come back at any time, but for now it'd be best to fight back with words.

"We weren't even together this whole trip, I swear. Haven't been for weeks." He started pacing again, and it made me nervous. "Could you stop pacing and listen?"

Reggie finally stopped and sat on the bed across from me. I pushed Teddy's suitcase to the middle of the bed where it wouldn't tumble and went on.

"Dude, I've been wanting to tell you. We both did. It's not like we just one day said, 'Let's fuck with Reggie and mess with each other.' Everything happened so fast, and once it happened, it was hard to stop." Not a lie. Either of us could have walked away anytime but couldn't. At least not now.

"I've been literally racking my brain. Beating myself up about if I should've just told you from the start. How you'd react if I had. Hell, we even took a break from each other because we just didn't know how. I was starting to think we were never gonna—"

"So if I hadn't confronted you, it'd just been your little secret?" Reggie interrupted.

"This is what I was trying to avoid. Being cornered and defensive. Now I'm trying to figure out how to say everything. I know it ain't easy considering you look like you want to punch me."

Reggie laughed, anxiously squirming around in place. "Not today, Satan. Not today," he said to himself, almost as a joke. If it hadn't been this conversation, I would've been cracking up. Reggie bent over, resting his hand in his chin, squinting his eyes in an inquisitive stare.

"It shouldn't matter, but I'm just curious. Where did we fuck up? Have you always known?" I asked.

He leaned back, wearing a look of astonishment. "On some real shit, you fucked up when you messed with Teddy. I hadn't even considered it until the start of the week, but now that I look back at the situation, there was always small shit. Like…" He snapped his fingers, as if trying to recall the moment. "Ari and

Serena stopping by the job to return that IPod. Girls was making jokes and comments. 'Why you going on a trip with them?' I kept thinking, 'Why would they say that?' But figured they were being petty since you never wanted Serena."

I was mad they blew up my spot. But then again, if I'd just said something before, there wouldn't have been a spot to blow.

"But I ignored it because it didn't make any sense. But then there was the pool party. Homegirl you was checking for? She was feeling you, even when her corny-ass friend played me. My brain didn't process it, but you were more worried about what Teddy was up to than her."

I hadn't really seen it that way. Technically, she never turned me down; she just did whatever her friend did. I thought by not following up with her, I was showing my solidarity, considering his unsuccessful attempt.

"I mean, because you're a good wingman, but you not *that* good. But that ain't even what did it for me," Reggie continued, laughing. The kind you only did when you were so mad, you didn't know what else to do. "No. Your mistake was just minutes ago when you asked me to return these damn room keys. Get this —I get down there to check out early. Dude at the desk asks *which room?* I play it off. Convince him to tell me the room numbers, plus get the keys back so I can make sure I didn't *leave* anything." Reggie's shoulders collapsed, and he rocked back and forth, unreadable.

"I didn't even know what I'd find. But Teddy's hair jewelry and a bottle of lube on the bed told me enough. I almost gave you the benefit of the doubt. But I knew you wouldn't rent another room to fool around with someone unless you had shit to hide. Guess my suspicion was right."

The room was suddenly more quiet than comfortable. I wiped the liquid streaming down my face that I knew was blood, and something told me we were about to have a long-ass car ride.

"Well? You got something to say?"

"You already said everything there was to say. Kind of hard to follow up on anything after that." Would anything I said even matter at this point? Would he believe it anyway?

"You know what you can tell me? Is when this all started." That was no bueno.

"I really don't think you want to know. I don't want to lie at this point, but once you open Pandora's box, you can't un-know anything."

"I just want to know. Was it two months? Three?" Reggie said, counting them off with his fingers. I bit my tongue, then let it go. The swelling from my face made it puff up, but not to the point where I couldn't see with both eyes.

"A week after I met her," I said in a low voice. Reggie's eyes widened, like they were seconds away from bursting out of their socket. He mouthed "wow" more than once before he got up and roamed around until he walked out of the room. I figured he left, but his silhouette stalked the hallway twice before returning back to the room.

"You do realize that was six months ago, right?" Reggie finally asked, louder than anything he'd said the whole night.

I just shrugged. "I guess."

He pointed a finger with a face so jovial, you'd never know betrayal was the main topic of our discussion. "So you Valentine's Day dude?" It wasn't really a question this time. His pacing made me nervous again, so I kept my guard up just in case he felt inclined to punch me. He didn't deserve retaliation, but that first one was a freebie.

He didn't stop pacing until he was just in front of the other bed again, with his hands at his waist, glancing toward the ceiling for god-knew-what. "Asher, you know what's fucked up about this situation?"

Did he mean outside of the obvious?

"I'd come to you for advice *about* Teddy. And it was good-ass advice. It was never 'fuck a few chicks, make that girl jealous.'

Nothing like that. 'Give her time. Give her space. If it's meant to be, it'll happen.'" He stomped his feet to match the tone of his words. "All while you're the dude she was bragging about this whole time. You're the clown she was kicking it to. You homeboy!"

"I know. I'm an asshole. A jerk. A clown. Whatever you want to call me. But I never did any of this on purpose. It just happened. Teddy and me just happened."

"All while y'all was laughing behind my back."

I leaned back up, giving him my attention even more now that he stood still. "That could not be furthest from the truth. My word's not shit right now, but…it's like one second we were chilling. Then all this touching, rubbing, and kissing led one thing to another—"

"I could do without the road map, buddy," Reggie interrupted.

"I'm just trying to say I wouldn't have risked making you look like an idiot if I didn't love that girl. I know we're not fucking lending each other kidneys and shit, but I always felt we were good enough friends where it still hurt to lie to you. Plus, Teddy loves you. You're like one of her best friends. She was so afraid you'd tell her to go to hell if you found out. She even dumped me. That's how much she didn't want to hurt you."

I didn't expect Reggie to want anything more from me than an explanation. I didn't think I could feel like more of a douchebag than I already did. But even if he wasn't interested in our friendship, I doubt Teddy would be as happy about him ending theirs. Reggie finally retired to the bed, defeated.

"Why couldn't you guys just be real? I'm, like…trying to see y'alls side of it. I know shit happens. In the same situation reversed, I don't think I would've been any different. But you want to know what has me so heated? That this was going on for six months, and I still wouldn't have known if I hadn't pieced it together myself."

"I know. And I haven't been sorrier about anything in my life before now."

"I don't know who to be madder at. All it would've taken was a 'Hey, Reg, I'm serious with someone. There's no chance,' or a 'Reg, I hooked up with Teddy by accident. We still cool?' But no. You went behind my back like I was a little-ass kid. I don't even think I'm surprised when it comes to you. But Teddy? That's beyond fucked up. I don't even know what I'm going to say to her when I see her next."

"If you want me to say it's my fault, it's my fault. But sometimes she needed a friend, and I was just always around."

"Oh, you were around all right."

"Fifty percent of the time before she came back was just me talking with her. She was undergoing chemotherapy and depression and I don't even know what else. I just know I got too close. But I think if you ever cared about your friendship with her, you'd at least hear her side. Because all my reasons for being with her are selfish as fuck. Her reasons for getting close to me? You'd have to ask her yourself."

It felt like a weight holding me down was somehow lighter. Maybe not gone, but less than before. Manageable. Easier to carry on. This wasn't the conversation I'd originally planned, but it was happening. That much wouldn't change. Reggie shook his head, rubbing his palms across his pants.

"I don't know, man. I don't know."

It was a lot to take in, sure. Hell, it was a lot to admit. Now that it was done, though? I wish it would've happened earlier. Who knows how this trip would've gone if we'd told him a lot sooner? Now all we had to look forward to were the next few hours. Whether they'd be spent in silence or constant bickering was too soon to tell.

We were still in the middle of conversation when Teddy returned to the room. She didn't look up from the floor as she came in, but she brought all the attention to her when her hand slid across the table near the door and then collapsed to the ground.

We both ran to her out of instinct. She was sweating so much it looked like she'd just come out of the rain or the shower. Even her temperature was far from normal.

"What the hell is wrong with her?" Reggie asked.

"I don't know. Just help me get her on the bed."

I called 911. I didn't know what was wrong, but I did my best explaining the little I did know. The operator over the phone suggested putting cold, damp towels all over her, rewetting them every time they got warm.

"Do you know what's wrong?" Reggie asked again.

"Do I look like I know what's wrong?" So many thoughts ran through my head. What if something was happening that neither of us could see? What if the last thing I said to her was why she hadn't packed her suitcase? What if the ambulance wouldn't make it before things went south? What if…?

# CHAPTER SEVENTEEN

**Asher**

I decided today was the day I officially hated movies. Movies left these hidden messages of finding light in the darkest situations, leaving you with the thought that waiting for someone to wake up was some romantic moment. For the record, it wasn't. It was nerve-wrecking and terrifying. Teddy was never one to mention the ins and outs of her lymphoma, but I hadn't known she was still being treated.

She hadn't said anything about it, but why would she? The way people treated her, the way I treated her—it was all different when we knew she wasn't doing so hot. I'd familiarized myself with certain symptoms, but she was so good at hiding it and pushing through as if nothing was wrong. Or maybe I was better at convincing myself she was fine. These past few months, I'd had no reason to think otherwise.

When it came to cancer, I'd admit, I only knew as much as the next guy. When things were good, they were good. When things were bad, they only got worse. Even with what I'd researched about Hodgkin's, I was still left with several types and stages I knew next to nothing about. Why did it never occur to me to ask? We were in the "good" phase, but now that she was in the worse phase, I hated not knowing.

Shit like this didn't happen. Not to anyone I knew and definitely not to me. Being in love with someone battling cancer was almost as bad as having it yourself. The times you didn't worry, you were angry, and the times you weren't angry, you didn't know what to feel that didn't read as privileged, abled, or just damn ignorant.

I kept thinking about how I could've done something, noticed sooner, reacted quicker. Anything to prevent sitting here waiting for her to wake up right now. I wanted to be the first person she saw, but it'd been hours and the air was being sucked out of the room. I needed to get out of here, even if only for a few minutes.

A seven-minute break from it all was just the time I needed to decide what I had to do. If I was going to do this—I mean, really do this—I had to be there for her. Even when she didn't want me meddling around, I was done with her pushing me away. She didn't have to carry the weight of the world on her shoulders alone. She had to know that.

Roaming the hallways, the things I wanted to say floated around in my head as I wondered if I'd ever get the chance to say them. I didn't know how bad it was, but it couldn't have been good. The only option was to wait and, hell, maybe even pray. I haven't done that in a while, but now seemed like a good enough reason to start.

Just as I was close enough to peer into her room, my heart stopped at the sight of her juggling an apple from hand to hand. She was awake. I knocked on the door's lining, waiting for her to acknowledge me.

"Can I come in?" I offered a smirk.

There was no yes, but I interpreted her low nod as an answer. I sat down to the left of her, the side where her IV wasn't in the way, and waited for the chance for her to explain to me what happened, what was going on, and to get in her ass for not telling me. Unfortunately, I got neither, but she wasn't getting off scot-free. I would make good on that promise to get in her ass.

"Teddy, I'm gonna give you three seconds to explain yourself without me jumping in and cutting you off. If you don't start talking, expect the worst." She didn't volunteer to start sharing information, so I took it as her way of saying ask away.

"Teddy, why didn't you tell me you were undergoing chemo again?"

She picked at her nails in a way that irritated me, like she couldn't find it in her to look in my direction.

"Asher, I don't know. I just wanted to be normal. Talk about normal shit. Take part in normal things. The way you look at me when you know, I swear I can't fucking stand it. Any time I've wanted to tell you, I lost the nerve. The fact that you never asked me about it, I assumed it always made you uncomfortable. Which I don't blame you for, I don't like talking about it either. Pretty much why I'm two seconds away from slamming my head against this tray. I try to avoid conversations like these."

Was this how it was always going to be with us? Only around each other for the good? How many times would we have this conversation about me being there for her? What had I ever done for her not to trust me with this sooner?

Turned out Teddy was fighting an infection she didn't even know she had. Her immune system was already weaker than someone who wasn't battling cancer and handling chemo, so she was lucky to have caught it when she did. Any longer and it may have been fatal.

I leaned back in my chair and scratched at my temples. "Your parents are here. Or were here. I think they went to get something to eat."

They hadn't looked thrilled when I'd introduced myself as Teddy's boyfriend. They'd said their hellos and shook my hand, but the rest of the time, they'd conversed only in Spanish and the word blanquito was pretty simple to translate. No doubt in my mind they were talking about me.

"God, I hate that they met you under these circumstances. Now I know I'm gonna hear it." She sighed. "Thanks for the warning." The stress of her situation wore heavy on her face, and if I hadn't known she'd only been here for hours, I would've guessed she'd been here for months. She looked that tired.

"Your folks were telling me you might be here a few days. They want to check some things out since they don't want your condition to worsen."

She banged her head back on her pillow, forking sections of her thick, messy hair in her fingers. Now wasn't the time to tell her hair looked a mess, but I decided to point it out anyways. I couldn't make her forget that she was sitting here in the hospital, but I could remind her that things between us would always be the same.

* * *

I wanted to be there every second I could. I'd already used up half of my sick days just to be by her side when she was able to have visitors, but she was understanding when I couldn't be there as often as I liked.

She never asked me about the bruise on my face. She didn't have to. If Teddy was anything, she was smart enough to figure shit out. I bet she already had an idea where it came from. I'd left out the lengthy details but let her know Reggie was hoping to come visit soon.

At first, he hadn't felt up to seeing her in the hospital. He, like me, built a false hope around her getting "better." He wasn't even mad anymore that Teddy and I had hooked up at some point and behind his back. He just hated that it'd taken so long for either of us to be honest about it. The way he'd found out wasn't the way either of us wanted, but I still thought he should hear Teddy's side of the story. If the roles were reversed, I'm sure I would've got him with a hook, too.

We all needed some time to be cool about it. Reggie's friendship always meant a lot to Teddy, something that always both frustrated and confused me. But a good week or two from now, it'd all blow over and we'd go back to being that dysfunctional bunch of friends we'd always been. I was happy with how things turned out. Feelings were hurt, but no one lost anyone in the process. As reluctant as I was to admit it, Reggie was a good friend to me, too. Our friendship ending over something petty would have harbored mixed feelings since, as of today, I didn't know which road Teddy and I were headed. It was probably best to hold onto the few relationships I had.

* * *

*Teddy*

I wasn't sure what to make of the next few weeks. I couldn't leave the hospital, so I couldn't work. I couldn't work, so I wasn't sure I could afford to attend school the semester coming up. Not to sound morbid, but this couldn't have happened at a worse time.

I was scheduled to have surgery to remove a dead tumor. Apparently, it was where the septicemia hosted itself, which is why I hadn't known until the infection presented itself. I wasn't worried that much about the surgery. I just wanted it gone. But I had a new problem to worry about. One that, no matter how much I avoided it, I couldn't escape it.

I was still scheduled for chemotherapy in the next coming weeks, but...

Zinc was as clear as day on this. He *would not* allow me to continue my maintenance therapy if I continued to wear a cold cap.

I knew the risks. Any type of lymphoma or blood cancer had

risks. But so did chemotherapy. Where was this dude's ethics, then? It *could* reach to my scalp, but it hadn't. I wasn't that far gone. But because of the infection, dude wasn't putting himself in the line of fire for malpractice, even if he was colleagues with my dad. I didn't know what to do. I was scared my cancer would come back. I hadn't fully completed my clinical trial after all.

It was just hair, everyone said. Yeah, ableist as fuck.

Of course it was just hair. *When* it was a choice. But my chemo regimen made me lose hair in a matter of weeks, with thinning so bad, I could see my entire scalp within days. In a month's time, I'd be the poster kid for cancer again, as people pointed and oohed and ahhed, grateful not to be me.

For the record, I didn't feel fucking sorry for myself.

But everyone was telling me what was good for me, and it seemed like my opinion was the only one that didn't matter. Even Asher wasn't on my side. He hit me with, "I never knew you went such great lengths to keep your hair. If I'd known, I wouldn't have encouraged it." This boyfriend mess was the pits. I missed that "just friends" Asher, where he told me what I wanted to hear.

He planned to shave his head in solidarity with me, to show he didn't care either way. Somehow, he'd even convinced me to do it, too, so I'd get used to how I looked before it started to shed. I'm not going to lie. I'd never cried so much in my life. I thought shaving my head would empower me. In any situation that *wasn't* this, it probably would have.

I just felt...like a cancer patient. But it was what I was. Why even fight it? My body was going through so much. I couldn't believe it was about to go through more. The road to recovery was never a short path. It probably never would be for me.

* * *

*18 months later...*

Red? Or pink?

Would it matter anyway?

It's not like anyone would see them. My lips. I'd be wearing a helmet half the time, so would it make a difference if I wore makeup? I contemplated between a row of lip stains and tubes, debating which would flatter me on a day like this.

I liked black. But it was definitely more for my carefree Black girl days. Plus, I could never wear it without thinking I'd end up with black lipstick on my teeth if I kissed someone. So it looked like it was between pink and red.

Pink made my lips look bigger. I liked that. But ever since I'd been rocking this teeny weeny, I hadn't been able to pry myself from red.

I missed my long hair. I should—it only took four years to grow. Ever since I'd stopped using cold caps, my hair'd fallen out. Big surprise there. I'd shaved it that former July, but since I was undergoing chemo, it didn't matter. It wouldn't grow back during the periods I had chemotherapy. It came to the point where I stopped asking Asher to shave his head. He insisted, but I felt silly. And it brought so much attention. I just wanted to look like it was normal for me. People who didn't know me didn't know I wasn't bald by choice. I figured if I had to rock it, might as well overcompensate with makeup and jewelry.

Earrings. Bangles. Necklaces. I even wore a fake septum ring sometimes. Folks really seemed to dig it on the beach.

I was getting used to my reflection. I didn't have a choice. My hair was so short; I couldn't hide behind it anymore. I guessed I was still pretty. Nothing else was different, save for a bit of my confidence. But I was working at that.

I'd have plenty of time to. As of last week, I was officially chemotherapy-free. Could my cancer come back? Maybe. But I was told my chances were good that it wouldn't. Was I still afraid it would? Of course. But I had to live my life. I was trying to, and nothing said "live life to the fullest" like red lipstick.

As I slipped into some comfy clothes, a few thoughts looming around my mind as I got dressed. A sense of relief for one. My boo Racer (who was not so little anymore) was a few months' shy of his eighteenth birthday. He was by no means fully recovered, but he was doing so much better than the time I'd visited him at the hospital so long ago. He was strong. And tall. It didn't make any sense for him to be that tall. Was everyone meant to tower over me by stories all of a sudden? We'd planned a small get-together for him soon. You know? Our *unofficial* support group. I was looking forward to him being out there. To finally get that real first kiss he'd been looking forward to.

I plopped on my bed and slipped into my boots as my phone notification went off.

*Knock knock.*

Another *"Where u at?"* text scrolled across my screen for the third time.

*On my way* 😬

Even though I hadn't even left my house yet. Only one of them was from Asher. The other two were from a frantic Reggie. Hold your horses, people, I'm on the way to my car.

I hopped on the freeway, and twenty minutes from Hollywood, my thought process lit up. Today wasn't a big deal. Only it was.

For the first time since our fallout, me and Asher were accompanying Reggie on a double date. We'd all stayed friends, but I knew it'd been a little weird. Ash and I never tried to throw it in Reggie's face, and out of respect, we kept the PDA to a minimum. But it'd taken a while to get back to old times.

My relationship with Ash never stopped me from keeping my friendship with Reggie. I could still hang out with him one-on-one without it ever being an issue. He'd even sat with me through a chemotherapy session once.

But he was honest. He admitted it hurt a little, how everything happened. Seeing me at my worst? That'd been hard for him, too. He'd never known anyone personally with cancer, so I'd had to walk him through the things that creeped him out a little. He claimed I made a lot more sense to him now. Whatever that meant, but I guess it didn't have to make sense to me.

I didn't need an apology, but he gave me one anyway. It didn't make sense to have any bad blood over stuff that happened years ago, but I appreciated it, even though I didn't know what he was sorry for. He just wanted to know one thing. Did Asher make me happy?

I tried not to sound too excited about it, but he did. As a friend, that was all Reggie wanted to know. And now? I was meeting his girlfriend. I had no idea what to expect.

* * *

"¿Que bola?"

"Mmm…bien, gracias."

"¡No mientas!"

She laughed and went on to tell me to step my game up come time to play. I took Marciela in. She was cute. Okay, I was hating. She was more than cute, but she was also nice. Playful or, at least, for a first impression. I was surprised Reggie was kicking it to someone Latina. He used to hate that I could switch to Spanish when I didn't want him to understand me. I wasn't saying home-girl couldn't speak English, but I could tell Spanish was her first language.

We mostly just small-talked while Reg and Asher talked shit to one another, making me want to forfeit all together.

"You know if it were gents against broads, it wouldn't even be a fair fight. So you know? Gotta help my girl, show her what it looks like to win and shit," Asher huffed, with a little bit *too* much confidence and stupidity. I pushed him, cutting him off before he could finish.

"Just for that, I'mma be speaking to Marciela in code through a walkie. Letting her know *all* our locations."

Marciela laughed, shooting me a high-five.

Asher pulled me toward him, a few steps out of earshot, and bent over, meeting his lips to mine in a light peck. It was sweet.

"You up for this?" he asked, seemingly concerned.

I wasn't the most active, even days after chemo, but today I just wanted to have fun. I nodded, hoping I looked convincing.

"You sure?" he asked again as his hands caressed both sides of my face.

"I'm sure," I said under my breath, just enough for him to hear me.

He smiled with his eyes, before it reached his mouth, and he reached in and kissed me on the nose.

"Happy anniversary, Teddy."

* * *

Thanks so much for making it all the way to the end of part two of Teddy and Asher's story! We so hope you devoured it! Before you go, we'd love if you could leave a few short words of what you thought of Friends That Still…!

Follow this link to review and tell others what you thought. Again, thank you for your purchase and be sure to flip through the end pages to discover more addictive reads from G.L. Tomas. Happy Reading!

# ABOUT THE AUTHOR

G.L. Tomas is a twin writing duo and lover of all things blerdy, fearless and fun. When they're not spending their time crafting swoon-worthy heroes, they're battling alien forces in other worlds but occasionally take days off in search mom and pop spots that make amazing pasteles and tostones fried to perfection.

They host salsa lessons and book boyfriend auditions in their secret headquarters located in Connecticut.
Head over to our Official website @ GLTomaswrites.com There we have a list of our upcoming titles and you can purchase our paperbacks directly, along with other swag!

Sign up for G.L. Tomas' newsletter.

You'll get exclusives, such as book release updates, chances to win or earn free swag, access to well thought-out book lists, and opportunities to save on books before anyone else!

Don't forget to connect with us on Bookbub and our exclusive Facebook Group! And be sure to send us an email to talk books and about your fave characters! Drop us a line at guinevere.libertad@gltomaswrites.com

If you liked reading *Friends That Still...* as much as we did writing it, please consider leaving a review!

Reviews are a huge part of how other readers discover and judge a book. It may seem like such a small gesture but it's a small gesture that goes a long way and makes the book you loved come up in more also bought searches and has the chance to be featured in consumer newsletters.

Just a quick "I loved this book" is praise enough and encourages your favorite writers to churn out that next favorite read. So don't be shy, if you enjoyed reading, a review would mean the world for a relatively new book! You can do that by clicking <u>here</u> to leave a review! Wink-wink.

*Evan Cattaneo was used to getting what he wanted.*

The successful career. **Check.**

The Penthouse apartment overlooking the city. **Check.**

Let's not forget the drop-dead gorgeous girlfriend. **Triple Check.**

Only now, being in the relationship of his dreams, he discovers one slight problem that puts a dent in his plans for the future. His girlfriend Luz doesn't see herself getting hitched.

Forcing Evan to confront their differences and understand their conflicting ideas.

**The Engagement Plan.**

A trip across the country, some much-needed therapy and their ability to work together as a couple fit into that neat little package. Only the closer he comes to uncovering the truth behind her reasons, he learns a devastating secret that will affect the state of their once happy union.

Pre-order now!

# AVAILABLE FOR PRE-ORDER: MELT FOR YOU

## BOOK TWO OF THE KINKY MATCHMAKER SERIES

L eomie Coutard was looking to create a fresh start. New place, new job prospects, the task she's yet to conquer? Her non-existent love life. Considering her unique taste, sadly, not just any guy would do.

SHE MET the man of her dreams presenting at a kink conference a year ago, but being oceans apart forced their two-week long connection to come to an end. Or did it?

DAMIEN KARAGIANNIS COULDN'T BELIEVE his luck. Settling into a different country and a new practice left him less time to meet people, let alone date. Through a wicked twist of fate, he not only gets the chance to reconnect to his budding Dominant stranger through matchmaker Mistress Alice she ends up being a part of his surgical team.

LEOMIE CAN'T GET the intimidatingly sexy surgeon out of her system. Damien craves that soft command he once explored. Their undeniable passion will have them breaking all their rules for each other.

MELT For You is a steamy May/December romance that features a gentle Domme with an appetite for masochism and an arrogant yet romantic male submissive who wants nothing but to make her wishes come true. It is BWWM with no cheating and a guaranteed HEA. If Dominance and submission aren't your style, sit this one out. If you like a little kink, let this Alpha submissive melt his way into your heart!

<u>Pre-order now!</u>

<u>Pre-order now!</u>

. . .

**BOOKISH FRIENDS TO LOVERS SERIES:**

*Book lovers find they have more than enough in common to take it there despite the circumstances.*

Same Page (Also available in audio)

Next Chapter

Pagebreak (sign up to learn when it drops)

Bookmark (sign up to learn when it drops)

www.ingramcontent.com/pod-product-compliance
Lightning Source LLC
Chambersburg PA
CBHW050348190726
48284CB00007BB/2198